EASY WAY DOWN

A NOVEL BY
IRVING WEINMAN

EASY
WAY
DOWN

FAWCETT COLUMBINE
NEW YORK

A Fawcett Columbine Book
Published by Ballantine Books
Copyright © 1990 by Irving Weinman

All rights reserved under International and
Pan-American Copyright Conventions. Published
in the United States by Ballantine Books, a division
of Random House, Inc., New York, and
simultaneously in Canada by Random House
of Canada Limited, Toronto.

LIBRARY OF CONGRESS CATALOGING-IN-PUBLICATION DATA
Weinman, Irving, 1937-
Easy way down: a novel / by Irving Weinman.
p.   cm.
ISBN: 0-449-90446-6
I. Title.
PS3573.E3963E17   1991
813'.54—dc20   90-82330
CIP

Designed by Beth Tondreau Design/Jane Treuhaft
Manufactured in the United States of America
First Edition: January 1991
10   9   8   7   6   5   4   3   2   1

To my dear sister
JEANNETTE

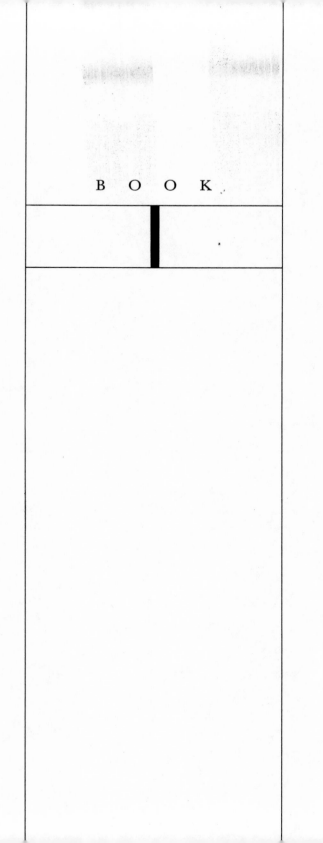

B O O K

CHAPTER 1

Schwartz blew his nose and looked out the car window. The place was like other derelict buildings on Avenue B: pocked brick, cement-blocked windows, and where the door had been, a space with two crossed four-by-eights filigreed in razor-blade barbed wire. But this building wasn't empty.

In minutes, Bob Malinowski would lead a team in to arrest two . . . what? Slime? Scum? No, Schwartz insisted the world only made sense if they were genuine, full-fledged men. Two men, then, who between them had murdered eleven people. People, he insisted, because though it was all crack-gang killing, if it wasn't *people* murdering *people*, no one should be arrested and mayhem should reign. All very well, but still he had no business being here.

"You know, Lenny, you have the authority, but you shouldn't be here," Gallagher said. "You're a detective inspector."

"My very thoughts, Tom. But if I shouldn't, you really shouldn't, Deputy Chief."

In the driver's seat, Gallagher looked straight ahead and shifted his weight. The car rocked. "Yeah, well, I'm here to keep an eye on you being here. How the hell you think Malinowski feels? He's a captain, for Christ's sake. You're treating him like a rookie."

Schwartz turned to look at Gallagher. His flak jacket pulled against his chest. "Malinowski is my best man. You know I trust him."

"So who don't you trust?"

Schwartz wondered if the killers holed up here belonged to Cruz. He looked into his right hand as if trying to read his palm.

The radio came on. "Malinowski, sir. We're in position, ready to go in."

"Okay," Schwartz said. "Go . . . No, wait. I'm coming."

Gallagher shook his head. "You going into that war zone with your dinky .38?"

Schwartz opened the door. "And my flak jacket *and* my rapid-fire wit."

Gallagher leaned over. "Lenny, take care." He put his head out the window. "Lenny, you're a jerk."

Schwartz ran to the side of the building where the bricks were down.

If Cruz *was* out to kill him, was it fair to let Malinowski lead the arrest team? A policeman dressed like a marine motioned with his automatic rifle and whispered, "Sir, the captain's waiting for you on the second floor. Remember the broken stairs."

Schwartz whispered, "Thanks. Remember Iwo Jima." He stepped out of the sunlight, ducked, and shut his eyes hard to the gloom. The place smelled of plaster and piss.

He opened his eyes. Maybe Malinowski wasn't up there. Maybe one of Cruz's gang was waiting there for him. Stupid. Nerves. The banister swayed under his hand. One stair, two stairs. The third sank down and the fourth . . . His foot swung through air. No fifth step, either. Maybe that was how they planned to kill him, like the kid in *Kidnapped*. But from a fall of three feet? He was out of his mind. With fear? Yes, more stairs now, a landing.

But it wasn't fear of *this* situation. It was . . . Jesus! Now he was hallucinating a gigantic thing, some monstrous apparition—

"Sir?"

"Bob!" Schwartz whispered back. "I thought you were Godzilla or John Galbraith. How many men are up there?"

"Three, waiting for me."

"Okay. Bob . . . Bob, I know how damned polite you are. Remember: you don't *have* to knock first when there's cause to believe it could endanger your life. Right?"

"Right. Are you—"

"No, I'll wait here. I'm interfering too much as it is. Just remember that getting in there fast and completely surprising them is your best chance of getting arrests rather than autopsies. Good luck."

"Thanks, sir."

Schwartz watched Malinowski cut across a shaft of light then disappear up the dark. He listened to a slight creaking overhead.

This was just a crack gang, probably nothing to do with Montanares's cocaine ring, Roberto Cruz's ring now that Montanares was dead. But if they *were* connected, Roberto would have good reason to kill him. No, he already had good reason: Montanares was dead. Schwartz hadn't killed him, had even

warned him away from the danger, but that needn't be Roberto's thug logic.

Schwartz listened. Nothing. Too quiet? Wasn't all this a
setup to get not only himself but the best part of his homicide
section?

How long, how long? Seconds, minutes? Too long and too
quiet. Malinowski didn't deserve this.

Cold drops of sweat rolled down his rib cage. Cruz would
need to kill him to show he was in full command of Montanares's
organization. So what better opportunity . . . ?

Damn it! Why wasn't anything happening? Maybe for
Bob's sake they should leave the building, make contact from
outside with bullhorns. . . .

Schwartz heard a click. He shouted, "Wait, Bob!"

There was a gunshot, a scream, and running feet. Then an
explosion, shouting, and plaster falling. Schwartz was running
up the stairs. He tripped, banged his chin, got up, pulled out
his gun running to the doorway, and jumped through, crouched
in firing position.

"It's all right, sir," Malinowski said from the floor beside
him. His hand was at his neck. He lifted it. His neck was slick
red.

"Bob, Jesus!"

"Just a nick, sir. Really."

Beyond Schwartz, two officers stood over two men
handcuffed from behind, facedown on the floor. A third
officer was admiring a smoking three-foot hole in the
wall.

Schwartz crouched to look at Malinowski's neck. It *was*
only grazed. "What happened?"

Malinowski shrugged.

The policeman by the wall said, "We were all set. The

damn door wasn't even locked. The captain had turned the handle and was about to throw it open for us when some asshole—"

"Morrissey!" said Malinowski.

Schwartz said, "Go on."

"Some asshole shouted, 'Wait!' and tipped these animals, who got off a round. An inch to the left and the captain would be dead. Christ! Anyhow, sir, we jumped in and I shot off a high-explosive round and these two slimes fell to the floor, saying, 'Don't shoot.' But if I find out—"

"That's all, Morrissey," said Malinowski.

Schwartz put his hand on Malinowski's. His fingers slid on the blood. "Officer Morrissey, I'm the asshole who shouted. I put everyone here in jeopardy, even your prisoners. I'm sorry."

Loud thumps came up the stairs and the room filled with police.

"Take care of the captain," Schwartz said, leaving. "He's had some good luck, considering the bad luck he's had."

Outside, Schwartz looked at his right hand. Bob's blood had streaked rust red across three fingers. He pulled up the waist of his windbreaker and unfastened the flak jacket. November air slapped his belly like an ice pack.

Two small crowds were gathering behind police barricades on both sides of the building. Schwartz didn't want to guess the odds on whether they'd cheer the good guys or the bad.

"Went okay, I heard," Gallagher said as Schwartz slid into the car.

"Like hell. It didn't go as badly as it could have."

They sat in silence for a few minutes. Gallagher held out a stick of spearmint gum to Schwartz, who he knew never chewed gum. Schwartz took it, unwrapped it, and folded it into his mouth. Then he took it out and dropped it into the ashtray.

"Tom, you know, before I went up there, you asked me who I don't trust?"

"Yeah."

"It's me. I'm so preoccupied with this Cruz thing that I don't trust myself anymore."

"Oh," said Gallagher, chewing gum. Then he said, "Well, if it's any consolation, I don't trust you, either."

CHAPTER 2

From the Bal Harbour Surf Club, the last of the storm appeared as a wall of gray, south, out over the Gulf Stream. It hadn't swung close enough to cool; the temperature was in the high eighties, up where it had hung for months.

The man with the thin mustache and streaked blond hair spooned ice into his beer and said, "There goes Lavinia."

"Where?" Roberto Cruz asked, looking from his folded hands back toward the swimming pool. "Who's this Lavinia, some piece of yours?"

"No, the storm, the one that missed us."

Cruz stared at the man. "You nuts, Jaime? You bothering me with some *clouds* out there and we're waiting to hear we been burned two million dollars! Why don't they call back?"

"I don't know. Maybe it's because it's Santo Domingo, an international call, and this is only a cordless phone. . . ." He picked the phone from the table, studying it.

"You're nuts, completely nuts. Why you think that's a bad

phone? You know what we pay for these each month?'' Cruz
flapped the lapels of his black silk jacket to fan a breeze.

"No, I don't know. That's Tony's job, accounts." Jaime
frowned at the phone. He put on sunglasses. "I'm sorry."

"You're sorry. And what's *your* job, besides being my
brother-in-law, besides *that* well-paid profession?"

Jaime glanced at a passing woman in a bikini and looked
back mournfully at the telephone's cordlessness.

Cruz pulled out his pocket handkerchief and wiped the
sweat pouring down his large, round face. "Your job is to be
on your toes. Get it? How long since I changed?"

Jaime looked at his watch. "Forty minutes."

"Well, I don't know. This shirt and jacket's drenched already. You bring the gray suit and shoes?"

"Sure, and the pink shirt and the tie we got yesterday at
the Shops. If you wore cooler clothes—"

"Don't start that again." Cruz flattened his hands on the
table. Sweat glistened on the ridges of blue veins. "I'm the
president of this organization now. I dress like it, with respect."

"But Montanares had that weird thing, always cold. He
never sweat a drop, let alone running like some hose—"

"Jaime, shut up. Just go and get the clothes from the car."

Cruz watched Jaime pick his way through the poolside section dense with sunbathing young women. Why could he handle
men twice as tough and ten times smarter but somehow be
brought down by his brother-in-law to this stupid rage? Jesus,
he thought, Jaime: his head's either in the clouds or some woman's tits. Hot; it was hot in the sun, but this was Montanares's
table and now, goddamn it, it was his and—

The phone buzzed.

Cruz reached across. The ice bucket tipped over.

"Hello, hello! *Sí?*" he said.

A waiter approached.

"Go away!" Cruz yelled, waving his free hand.

"No, nada, nada," he said into the mouthpiece. *"Sí, soy Roberto Cruz."* He curled his wide shoulders around the telephone. Cold water trickled onto his trousers.

"Porfirio? Qué passa?" he whispered.

"Nada?" he said.

"Nada?" he shouted.

"No, no, nada," he said.

"Comprendo. Luego, Porfirio," he whispered.

He shut the phone and looked down at his trousers.

Jaime came to the table with the clothes bag over his arm. "You get the call?"

"I got the call, yes. The phone works good. We been ripped off two million dollars, cash. That's some real money your pal Captain Bob has stole. You know?" Cruz looked out at the empty sand.

"Maybe—"

"Don't say maybe. Twenty-four hours' late delivery in this business is good-bye. Never, nothing, *nada.*"

"He's always delivered before, but . . . Hey, we have to get him."

Cruz looked up slowly. "Sure, right, Bob's gonna come back here to the Surf Club and say he's sorry!" Cruz put his hands on his thighs. His trousers were very cold. "Your buddy's in Rio or Hong Kong now, you great blond-streaked tithead!"

Jaime looked at the chrome bucket on it side, at the cordless telephone on ice. He wondered if he should do something. "You should do something, Roberto."

"I'm gonna."

Jaime said, "Maybe Bob's crew will turn up. I mean, I hear he uses crazies—*Marielitos* and rednecks. I could, you know, have some people watch out for crew throwing money around."

He was pleased to be on his toes again with good advice.

"What shit you talking now, Jaime? You think Bob's gonna give a good fock we got a couple of his fockin' rednecks? *Red fockin' necks,* Jaime?" Cruz's neck went red, his head seemed to swell. Then, in a lower voice, he said, "No, we're gonna give Captain Bob a warning he's gonna listen to *wherever* the fock he is: we're gonna find one of his big-wheel backers and we're gonna—we're gonna do something so Bob and every focking one else learns they can't rip me off. Everyone!"

Jaime was counting the rectangles on his crocodile shoe. He still felt it was a good idea to look for Bob's rednecks and—

"I got to change," Cruz said, standing.

Jaime said, "Holy shit, I seen you sweaty before but not like you pissed your pants!"

Cruz stared at Jaime. His face seemed to grow even bigger, rounder. Then he grabbed the clothes bag and, holding it close to his trousers, walked slowly through the lunchtime crowd.

CHAPTER 3

Once across Alton Road, Abe Zeigler let out a small sigh. How had he gotten into this? Not that the dog hadn't behaved; it came along just like Stanley said it would. But if something this size—like a small horse—decided to pull you along like a cart into the traffic . . .

"Come on, Maxi," Abe said.

The dog lifted its big block head, shook its dewlaps, and clomped on.

Leave it to Stanley, the four-flusher, the show-off, to have a Newfoundland, the biggest dog in the world. And in Miami Beach, with all this fur? Well, maybe it wasn't cruel, maybe it was like the ladies *schvitzing* in their minks at the Fontainebleau. Not Rose, of course. But Mary, he'd bet if he gave her a fur she wouldn't say no.

There, there was the cross street. Maxi knew the way.

Well, he wasn't giving Mary a fur. Leave that flashy stuff to the Stanley Zeiglers with their English cars and Chinese butlers. Meanwhile, why had he decided to take his cousin's dog for a walk? Because Stanley dared him: the two of them seventy-six years old and he'd fallen for a dare like he was fourteen!

He'd teased, "Why, Stanley? You have a dog could pull the Budweiser wagon, you couldn't be bothered to train it?"

And Stanley said, "Maxi's perfectly trained, the easiest dog in the world, Abe. But if you're a little scared, I understand. A great big dog, and there's Alton Road to cross, and let's face it, we're both *alter kockers*."

With that, Abe pushed the Scrabble bag away. "Speak for yourself, Stanley. Where's Maxi's lead?"

And now the dog was leading him. Okay, so let Maxi take him to this "secret" park of Stanley's here on North Bay Road. He wondered if anyone would mistake him for Stanley, with the dog. They were only second cousins, but they looked something alike, except that Stanley dressed like a Cuban bookie and was balder and fatter. Well, no one else was on the street, anyway. Just as well. Now the dog was tugging, walking faster. Abe could feel it in his shoulder. He scowled. "Maxi, take it easy! We'll get there!" He pulled back with both hands on the lead. Maxi slowed down.

All right, so Stanley was having some fun teasing him, thinking he was the poor-schlep cousin. That was okay. What was Stanley worth? A couple million? Five million? Good. And Stanley lived in that floodlit mansion and poor Abe lived in a little two-bedroom condo and poor Abe could buy and sell Stanley how many times, now? Well, let's say Stanley was worth five. That would be . . .

Maxi gave a short roar and lunged forward. Abe grunted and let go of the lead. The dog stopped, looked back, and then trotted off the sidewalk into the grass.

So this must be it, Stanley's "park," this open piece of land between two big houses where the bay washed in. Well, if the dog was happy here, good. If not, he wasn't going to break his neck being dragged around by it. "Perfectly trained." Typical Stanley bragging.

Abe looked at the high white walls curving down both sides of the lot to the water. Why wasn't the land owned? Maybe it was, maybe it belonged to one of these old places here and was kept just so nobody would build on it. Maybe so that the owners could walk their dogs here and let the city clean up . . .

Abe looked down at his feet. There was a gravel path he'd stick to. There, the dog was lifting his leg beside a palm. Stanley would know what kind of a palm. Rose too. But Rose was *interested*. Stanley was only interested to let you know he *knew*.

Abe walked to the water's edge and looked out. Maxi came up to him and sniffed off to the base of a ragged, multicolored bush. Biscayne Bay was smooth as glass, like a mirror where you could see the big clouds over Miami. And out there a boat and a water-skier.

Abe narrowed his eyes. The skier skimmed the water so lightly he seemed to be flying just over its surface. Rose had said something like that. Yes, it was very nice if you were young. But there was lots going for you at seventy-six if you were smart and quiet. So if Stanley was worth five—okay, give him the benefit, say five million—he could buy and sell him, what? How many times?

Maxi was growling behind him.

"What is it, Maxi, a rat? You find a palm rat to play with?" Abe asked, turning.

Two hours later, Harry Lee pressed the button in the Rolls and watched the garage door shut in the rearview mirror. He nudged Maxi through the garden door and hung up his lead. Then he went into the kitchen, poured a glass of ice water, and drank it fast. It left a narrow pain between his eyes. He set down the glass and ran up the backstairs.

"Mr. Stanley? Mr. Stanley?" He went on knocking.

"D'ja find them, Harry?"

"I have to speak to you!"

"What is it? Jesus, I can't even have my massage without . . . Wait, I'll put on a bathrobe. That'll be all, Miss Collins."

Trish came out in her neat, starched white dress and winked at Harry Lee, who closed the door behind him.

Stanley Zeigler, flushed through the dark tan of his cheeks and bald head, sat breathing heavily on the edge of the massage table, holding a white silk robe tight to his belly under crossed arms.

"Well?" he asked.

Harry looked down. "I found them."

"So why the hell did you burst in . . . ? What? What's wrong?"

"Maxi is all right, sir. I found him sitting by the traffic light on Alton Road."

"Where the hell was Abe? Damn, I knew he was too frigging feeble to take the dog for a walk. What a dumb—"

"Sir, no. I went to the park then. Maxi started to howl. I found Mr. Zeigler in the bushes. Dead, sir. I think we—"

"Dead?" Stanley squeezed his arms tighter and rocked forward. "What do you mean, dead? How do you know? Maybe he's lying out there with a heart attack! Jesus, you just *left* him?"

Harry looked at his employer. Stanley looked and dropped his eyes.

"Mr. Stanley, I'm sorry. He's dead. He was shot in the head, sir. It was terrible."

"Tell me," Stanley said, looking at his wrists over his belly.

"There was a hole in the middle of his forehead, sir. And the back . . . I'm very sorry, sir. The back of his head just was not there. I don't wish to describe more. Should I phone the police?"

Stanley rocked on the edge of the massage table. The red had drained from his face and his tan went from bright brown to lava gray. "Oh, my god, my god. My poor cousin."

"I'm sorry, sir," Harry said. "You were close."

"Close?" Stanley wiped his forehead with the back of his hand. "No, we weren't that close. Harry, don't you see? Someone mistook Abe for me. *I* walk Maxi there every day. We look alike. They thought he was me. They thought the poor feeble schnook was me."

"Sir, nobody wants to kill you."

Stanley shook his head. "You don't know my history, Harry. I keep telling you I have lots of enemies. That's why I hired you."

"Yes, sir. Should I call—"

"Yes, of course. Call the police. My god, poor Abe. I *dared* him to walk Maxi. I teased him into it!"

Harry Lee stopped at the door. "Mr. Stanley," he said slowly, "you would never do anything bad. You are a pussy-cat."

CHAPTER 4

He put his right hand lightly on his wife's shoulder. He pushed his fingers between her shoulder and collarbone and pressed, released, and pressed. Her head moved toward him with a small sound, "mmm." She breathed deeply again, so he slid his fingers over her shoulder and shook her. "Mmmm, mmmm, no," she said, holding to sleep.

"Karen," he whispered, continuing to shake her. "Karen," he said, sitting up and bending over her. He put his hands on both her cheeks and shouted, "Karen!"

Her eyelids opened, her eyes rolled. She shivered. "No, no, no, no," she said, and then, "What? What? What is it?" and was awake.

Schwartz lay back and looked up. Eyes widened to the dark, he counted twelve rosebuds around the ceiling boss.

"Karen?"

"Yes, what is it? Why did you wake me?"

He turned onto his right side and put his mouth to her ear. "You wouldn't . . . I had this terrible thought. You wouldn't strangle me, would you?"

"You woke me in the middle of the night to ask if I wouldn't strangle you?"

He moved his head directly over hers. "Please. I know it's strange, but please tell me. Just, I mean, seriously."

"I'm to take this question of my strangling you at—at . . . What time is it?"

"I don't know. Around four."

"At four in the morning I'm to take it seriously."

Schwartz nodded.

Karen coughed. "All right, Len. No, I wouldn't strangle you."

"Thanks. That means a lot." He lay back and closed his eyes.

"Len? You know how sometimes something gets you up in the middle of the night, some stupid little thing? So you're awake and you find you have to pee, and you pee and it's a sort of compensation?"

"Yes."

"I don't have to pee."

Schwartz sat up. "I have to take a shower." He felt at the base of the bed for his robe.

"Don't you want to say something?"

"Oh. Sorry about waking you."

"And what about 'good night'? Wish me 'good night and sleep well, Karen.' "

"Good night and sleep well, Karen darling."

"Mmmm," she said.

Under the shower, Schwartz shifted from one foot to another and turned it so hot he had to run in place to keep from scalding. He threw back his head, letting the spray run into his nose and fill his mouth. He gargled, spat, turned the shower to cold, and danced about slapping his chest, ass, belly, and thighs. When he rubbed himself with the heavy bath sheet, he felt clean, loosened. Now maybe he'd sleep. He switched off the bathroom light and stepped into the bedroom.

His right foot was kicked forward and he fell so fast nothing came from his mouth but a sucked "Oowa." Knees pinned his upper arms, hands were at his throat strangling him.

God! She was strangling him! His throat burned, his eyes went hot and teared.

"Stop!" Schwartz croaked, and managed to bend one leg across the front of her shoulder. Then he understood the joke, but his laughter took most of his remaining breath and he became frightened. His forearm jerked up; he caught at some material and pulled down with all his strength. There was a ripping sound.

"Oh, I'll really get you for this," Karen said, slowly toppling off him, her hands too loose to choke, pulling him now by the back of his neck.

Her gown tore open as he rolled over with her, so that he ended up with his face in her bare belly. He stretched his hands up and caught her wrists, pinning them to the carpet, and he licked his way—belly, breasts, and small of her neck—up to her mouth.

"You," he said, feeling his heart thump on hers. "You really scared me!"

"Scared you stiff," she said, laughing, relaxing under him, so that he let her go of her wrists and she dropped her arms over his shoulders and ran her hands down his back.

"You know what I'm going to have to do about it, don't you?" he asked, speaking low and so close to her mouth that his lips, forming the words, brushed hers.

She said, "I hope so, darling," and spread her hands on his back and pulled.

Later, back in bed, she pulled his arm behind her neck and rested her head on his chest.

He said, "I love the hair under your arms. It turns me on."

She turned and pulled at his chest hair with her teeth. She said, "Like this does me."

"Even with the gray mixed in?"

"The gray's sexy, spicy salt and pepper. I love you."

They lay quietly in the dark.

"Are you relaxed, Karen?"

"Mmm. Might even get to sleep."

He looked up. Maybe they weren't roses; maybe the boss had been painted so many times over a century that what had been, say, jonquils had thickened to these blobby buds. "Karen?"

"Mmm."

"That business I woke you up about. It's part of this fear I have."

"Fear of me getting some sleep?"

"No, seriously. I almost got Bob Malinowski killed last week because I was so jittery. I can't work, I can't sleep until it's resolved."

"What, what's resolved? What are you talking about here in bed now at . . . at ten minutes past five in the morning?"

"When Juan Montanares died, Roberto Cruz took over the drug business. He runs it from Miami, but it's big here in New York, too. I think he may have a contract out on me."

Karen pushed up onto her elbows. "Why should he want to kill you? You didn't kill Montanares."

"But they knew I'd taken a bribe once from Montanares, so to Cruz and the others I was a cop owned by their organization. All wrong, but that's how they saw it."

"I still don't see—"

"I was there when Montanares died, so Cruz might *need* to kill me to establish his authority as absolute boss with his other charming associates who might want the position."

"Yes, I see a kind of sewer sensibility in that. But what can you do?" she asked, turning on her side.

"I have to confront Cruz, ask him straight out. The only way he'd tell me, if at all, would be face-to-face. What's making me so paranoid is *not knowing*. Gallagher agrees. So I'm going down to Miami Beach. We've called down there already so that I can get some unofficial police help in making contact with Cruz."

"When will you go?"

"The day after tomorrow, for as long as it takes. A few days, a week or ten days at most."

"And you couldn't have told me this at dinner last night or breakfast tomorrow . . . this morning?"

"I'm sorry. I always seem . . ." He sighed. "Anyway, that's why I asked if you were relaxed."

"So that you could tell me your worries about a gangster killing you?"

"Yes."

"Darling, you needn't be worried anymore. He won't be able to."

"Why?"

Karen lifted herself to look down tenderly at Schwartz. "Because I'm going to kill you myself, right now!" she screamed, and began strangling him.

CHAPTER 5

"Of course you should phone her," Karen called from the bathroom, her voice juicy with toothpaste.

Schwartz regarded the turquoise bathing suit he'd just thrown into his suitcase and knew there would also be time to see his aunt. He sat down at the bedside table with his address book and dialed.

"Aunt Rose? This is Lenny. How are you, dear?"

"Lenny? Oh, Lenny. I'm not well, thank you. Where are you?"

"Brooklyn. I'm coming down to Miami Beach tomorrow on business and I'd love to see you. What's the matter?"

"It's not my health. It's Abe. You remember Abe Zeigler, my dear friend, your distant cousin. You met him here, I'm sure. He's dead."

"Oh, Aunt Rose, I'm sorry."

"Yes, yes. We just buried him. He was murdered."

"What?"

"Shot in the head. My god, Lenny, they showed me photos. Do you know what that looked like?"

"Too well."

"Oh, yes, your job. Lenny, he was a man who never hurt a fly. And that Abe should be murdered and the police do nothing . . . I can't understand it. Lenny, I just cannot understand!"

"I'm sure the police are doing what they should, Auntie."

"If they were doing what they should, Stanley Zeigler would be under arrest instead of running around everywhere pretending to be the chief mourner."

"*Stanley* Zeigler?"

"Another cousin. Abe was killed when he was out walking Stanley's dog. Stanley is, forgive me, a dog himself. It was Stanley they meant to kill. Or maybe worse, maybe Stanley had Abe killed."

"Aunt Rose! What are you saying?" Schwartz looked at Karen, who had come into the bedroom, toothbrush in her mouth.

"Stanley Zeigler is a crook. It's well-known. A fast dealer. Listen, he used to boast of knowing Meyer Lansky! Lenny, do I sound crazy, senile maybe? Lenny?"

"I'm thinking, Aunt Rose. No, you don't. You sound full of grief and anger, but so you should."

"All I can say is it's very strange, as well as horrible. The police ask the most obvious questions over and over. They don't seem to listen to me. Is that because I'm a woman, an old woman?"

"No. That's how we work. Simply, methodically, repetitively. You just have to trust us. Them."

"Oh."

There was a silence.

"Aunt Rose . . ."

"What?"

"Maybe, yes, some of it *is* probably because you're a woman and older."

"Thank you, Lenny. I was beginning to think it was me."

"Aunt Rose, I'll try to help you. But I have to tell you it's going to be very unofficial. Police from one place never work on cases in another place."

"Oh?" she said. "The movies always have the cowboy sheriff helping the city police or the black Detroit officer working out in Hollywood."

"Sure. And the movies always have a little mouse beating up a cat."

"I see. Well, I'll wait for your call. Tomorrow?"

"Tomorrow."

"Lenny, I *must* be losing my mind; I never even asked how Karen is."

Schwartz looked up. "She's fine. Her teeth are very clean."

"Send her my love. Lenny, I'm miserable. So thanks for being such a wise guy and for calling me at 11:30 at night. It makes me feel that I might still be alive."

Schwartz put down the phone and hooked his arm around Karen's thighs.

"I heard," she said. "How awful. How's she coping?"

"Miserably, terrifically. Like me: I miss you already. Karen, is that the toothpaste, or are you just foaming with desire?"

C H A P T E R 6

In the mid eighties when the Florida condo boom went bust, Roberto Cruz was able to pick up for under five million dollars the top three floors in the beachward wing of Broadmoor, a bleak concrete blockhouse of twenty-two stories at Bal Harbour. Its zigzag frontage had narrow windows, irregularly placed, and its ocean side was slit by long balconies deep enough to hold their doors in perpetual shadow.

Cruz used the penthouse floor for small-group entertaining. For larger parties the apartment opened into his home on the twenty-first floor to make a seventeen-room duplex, where three hundred people needn't rub shoulders. The twentieth floor was separate, the center of Cruz's operations. Four of his associates—bodyguards—lived there, and its electronic security systems, with private elevator to his separate four-car underground garage, had cost him another two million.

Had Cruz known that his Eden had the name of an infamous British prison for the criminally insane, his pleasure in

26

Broadmoor wouldn't have changed, for it was not the name but the abstract notion of a setup worth, as he said, "at least fourteen million dollars real money" that gave him pleasure.

Events, however, weren't abstract. Having called for new business, Cruz sat in the frigid air-conditioning of his boardroom frowning down the fifteen polished feet of teak table. At the other end of the ruined rain forest, his brother-in-law Jaime pulled from a pale yellow alligator briefcase some horse-racing forms. Jaime tried to smile them away, then used his hands, shoved them back in, and took out a torn piece of brown envelope. "Okay," he began.

"Wait." Cruz stuck his arm down the table and pointed. "Is that your report? A fockin' piece the back of some envelope? Jaime, this is a big business. Look at this place. This is the center of a big business. You get the horses and the leather garter belts out of your head now. Get serious, Jaime; I mean, *por Dios*, show yourself a little respect!" Roberto let his arm drop. His fist made a thick thud.

"Hey, I do. Roberto, I do. I mean, the business, you, the whole works. I just didn't have time to take this down any other way. And, anyhow, you say we don't want records of any of this," Jaime said, lifting one shoulder and side of his mouth so that his challenge managed to retain a cringe.

"Damn it, Jaime, I want *proper* reports, typed on white paper, to go into the shredder." Cruz raised his eyes in appeal to the four large men who sat two each side of the long table, but they hadn't been hired to respond to eyes raised in appeal. He put his hands down before him and imagined the thin neck of his brother-in-law between them. "All I'm asking is that we shred business reports. Not envelopes. Not pages off the fockin' *Daily Racing Form*. Now go on."

"Yeah, well, about an hour ago I got word from Port-au-

Prince that about forty families, about two hundred people, mainly businessmen and lawyers and doctors, have been missing—now wait for this—since the morning after Bob Williams sailed out of Puerto Plata. You see? He's using the boat for this other business, Roberto, not just ours—maybe, you know, for his other backers. Anyway, he picked these people up near the border, and now he must be trying to run them into the States.''

At the other end of the table, Cruz was nodding at his folded hands. ''Williams isn't gonna come anywhere near here after ripping off our two million. If he's picked up those Haitians, he's working another scam. He's gonna take their money, too, and fockin' drown them and get to Mexico and move on from there.''

''Oh, Roberto,'' Jaime began.

''Shut up,'' Cruz said, still looking down. ''But that's good work, Jaime. That's more like it.''

''You think he'd dump women and kids?''

''Sure, he's a professional. Right?''

Jaime nodded. ''Right,'' he said uncomfortably.

Cruz looked up. ''What's the name of that boat?''

''*Sport King,* '' Jaime said quickly, pleased to be on top of it.

''You don't have to yell, Jaime. I know we got walls here three-point-three-feet reinforced concrete but there's no wall between us now. We're in the same fockin' room!'' Cruz yelled. ''Anyway, we'll just see where this boat turns up. But Captain Bob's not gonna let his crew go. He's not stupid. And now he must be scared, you know? So don't give me any more shit about waiting for rednecks to show flashing big bucks. But you got a good lead there. You got something else?''

Jaime leaned forward. ''Else? No.'' He thought for a moment. Tracing the rednecks still seemed like a good idea, but he didn't want to piss Roberto off. He knew what: "Oh, we got that delivery later—"

"Shut up. That's not on the agenda. We got an agenda here that's about *new* business. So I got some." Cruz paused; he rolled his fingers on the table. "You interested?"

"Yeah, sure. Just, you know, go on, Roberto."

Cruz shook his head. Things never . . . "A well-located friend of ours tells me that shithead Lenny Schwartz, that homicide dick from New York, is coming down here."

"Schwartz, that one with Juan when he snuffed it?"

"Yes. I don't know what that little wise-ass fock thinks he's got on us comin' down here, but he gets me nervous. He's a flake, Jaime, even for a cop. A weirdball. I want you to set up a special welcome for him. He's staying in that shithole the Neptune Plaza, down South Beach. Typical. He thinks he's gonna lie low. Jaime, arrange him a welcome to make him lie very low, get his ass out of our backyard."

Jaime laughed. "I got just the boys for it."

Cruz adjusted his necktie. "Okay, we got no more new business, so this meeting's adjourned." He watched his brother-in-law stand and put the envelope into his briefcase, look across at him, pull the envelope from his briefcase, and point to the door.

"Right, Jaime. We shred our reports. And no more back of envelopes, and no more focking half-ass ideas about finding rednecks. But the Haiti stuff was good. You took yourself more serious, you could do things, Jaime. I mean, look how you fockin' dress for business, pink faggot sweater over a yellow shirt with green pineapples and red pants."

"The sweater's 'cause it's too cold in here. If you didn't wear those suits . . ."

Cruz walked around the table. "That's not what I'm saying. Listen, will you? No one's gonna take you serious, you go around dressed like some Calle Ocho pimp!''

Jaime, near the door with the four big men, turned. ''But Roberto, I *am* a Calle Ocho pimp.''

Behind his back, Cruz held the piece of white paper from which he'd given his report. It was blank. He twisted it and twisted it between his hands.

Were Schwartz omen prone, the check-in area at LaGuardia would have convinced him that walking was the easy way down to Miami. Large Hasidic fathers rushed from counter to counter while their large families waited by heaped bags and boxes, wives in clumps, children in scatters playing tag.

Schwartz took his place in line behind a distinctly Palm Beach couple reading matched copies of *Vanity Fair*. The man turned, shook his head slightly, and said, "They make quite the zoo out of it, don't they?"

Schwartz had no particular zeal for Hasids, but looking into the man's fair, exclusive smile, he found himself pulling back on his sports jacket so that his gun and holster showed and asking, *"Fahrsteit Yiddish?"* upon which the man turned back to his own glossy world.

But this unloaded gun of his, this bigot buster, proved the second holdup. Schwartz, aware of security arrangements, had brought the necessary documents, as well, of course, as his police ID. The young man at the desk, of crew cut and bland face and permanently perky smile, kept repeating, "Uh-huh, uh-huh, I see, I see," and phoned for his supervisor.

Schwartz said, "I only have five minutes to make the plane."

"That's all right, sir. Your flight's delayed for forty-five minutes. But you won't make that anyway. You'll make the next one, the 12:15."

When Schwartz asked how he could know he'd miss a flight in fifty minutes, the young man insisted it had nothing to do with firearm security, merely that Schwartz had no seat on the flight.

"No seat?"

"No, sir," said Perky the smiler, "that flight closed out twenty minutes ago."

Schwartz thought to point out that he had a reserved seat, that he'd arrived at the airport two hours early and stood in line for one hour and fifty-five—no, two hours, now. He thought better and said, "Double booking? Airline deregulation?"

"That's right, sir!"

Then, through a door behind the counter came a dark man with a tragic look. He checked the ID, the documentation, the gun, and the bullets in Schwartz's briefcase. "It's all in order. Take it through the metal check and hand it to a crew member on boarding. Look," he said, raising his arm as slowly and solemnly as the Commendatore's statue. "Look at this mess. I hope you came right up to the desk, Officer?"

Schwartz said he hadn't.

The supervisor put out both hands; Schwartz awaited something from *La Forza del Destino*. The supervisor said, "If I had to stand in a line like this, I'd kill myself. Have a nice flight."

When the same sort of production took place at the metal detector, ending, two phone calls later, with the arrival of the same supervisor, Schwartz still continued to defy the fates. The supervisor shrugged. "People . . ." He sighed, and walked off trailing his morose ellipsis.

The gun business went well on boarding, and the plane doors closed only ten minutes after scheduled departure time, so Schwartz was cheered. No stupid superstition would deter him. One hour later, in the middle of the line of planes awaiting takeoff, he wondered if by faking grand-mal foamingly, rigidly well, he might be taken off the airplane for a pleasant ride by ambulance.

Eventually the plane took off; five minutes later, the captain made a heavy weather announcement suggesting everyone stay seated with seat belts on. For the fat man in the window seat next to Schwartz, this was the signal for a continual cycle of gettings-up and squirmings-past and squeezings-back-in again. Not so for the woman in the aisle seat on Schwartz's other side: at each new sign of turbulence she tore at his arm, letting go only to calculate her rosary.

A few minutes later, at 2:15 in the afternoon, Schwartz politely asked a flight attendant about lunch.

She answered in *Luftsprech*: "There'll be a bar service following the sale of airline souvenirs. We don't serve lunch after two, sir."

"You didn't put it aboard? But this was a 12:15 flight. The airline suggested being at the airport by eleven. I was actually there before nine. Overbooking. Airline deregulation."

"I know. Isn't it awful?" she commiserated, moving off.

"Not to mention union breaking with related undertraining, understaffing, and . . ." Schwartz stopped talking and watched her go toward her galley of T-shirts and umbrellas and inflatable airplanes, any of which probably flew better than this one.

By 3:30, Schwartz had decided that the airline's meanness

in not serving lunch was probably a good thing. The flight was
so consistently air-pocketed that a quarter of its passengers sat
intently bent before their vomit bags waiting for the plane's next
wrench, their next retch.

Finally bumped down through storm clouds onto Miami's
runway, the pukers were still applauding a landing remarkable
only for failing to make the plane burst into flames, when the
announcement came that mechanical problems at the landing
gate would necessitate passenger debarkation a short distance
from the terminal where the busses would be waiting. And on
behalf of Captain Hook and the entire crew they hoped to serve
them again, real soon.

But Schwartz had landed safely: omens were for myths and
idiots.

When the airplane doors opened, the passengers filled their
lungs with air that hit like the hot wet towel of cliché, the one
used to wipe old jet exhaust. Some became sick again where
they stood. Others made it out the door and down a few steps
to hang over the handrails. At the top of the stairs, Schwartz
thought he could make out airport buildings, vaguely, somewhere to the east.

He waited until the first three buses filled and left, and
then, with a half-dozen other clever, unsicked-up dawdlers, took
the empty fourth bus. But the move wasn't clever enough or the
buildings were only eleven miles away, so that he didn't avoid
the baggage scrimmage.

Schwartz pushed to the carousel ("carousel," so miserable
a word here, suggesting as it did merry-go-rounds and the
laughter of small children). A very large box swung out and
scraped his shin. ("No, nothing. Ouch, Jesus! No, I'm fine,
thanks, everybody.") And there, finally, was his suitcase.

It was being opened by a middle-aged man apparently
wearing nothing beneath his baby-blue sports jacket but a *chai*,

a great golden mound of a *chai*, a *chai*mound as big as the Ritz.

"Sir, this is mine," Schwartz said, turning over the label on the suitcase and pointing to his name.

"Oh, sure. Sure. The case looked so exactly like mine. You know, I hope you didn't think . . . Say, you think maybe I *need* someone else's *schmattas*? Take it, take it, it's yours *so much*!"

All right, it had been a lousy flight. But now, with his suitcase, his problems were over.

Almost. There remained the wise guy at the car-rental agency who insisted that Schwartz at least take a look at the special deal this month, the Stingback Ray Scorpion, a real fun car—he's in Miami for fun, right?—with double sunroofs and hexaphonic (hexaphonic?) stereo. Right out there, the chrome and red one, and no kidding, sport, a great bargain.

Schwartz didn't know what to say. He looked. He knew what to say. "Is the driver supposed to pimp for the passenger, or is it the other way around?"

The salesman looked at his computer screen and mumbled, "Yes, sir, we do have the four-door Ford available."

Schwartz drove from the airport scowling. The car he followed out had a bumper sticker saying "Florida, the Gunshine State." The sky was gray over the peeling Orange Bowl, gray blue on MacArthur Causeway over the ocean-liner parking lot, and clear blue as he turned onto Ocean Drive along Miami Beach. The furrows smoothed over his eyes.

His smile began along the park, beside the little deco buildings. There was the Beacon, there was the Breakwater (there was the one about it being the Miami Beach maternity hospital). Happy buildings, human-scaled—two stories, three—the details like on liners from the thirties. These were swing-era rhythms in pastel.

He passed the Edison, the Leslie, the Carlisle and Cardozo.

Maybe he should have stayed down here. He turned left at the
top of the drive and then right onto Collins.

Well, at least where he was staying he was alone; Karen
wouldn't have liked it around here. He pulled into the Neptune
Plaza parking lot and wondered what Karen would say. She'd
say it was something Walter Gropius would have left in an air-
sick bag.

In his mind he tried to argue with her. He looked up and
saw how the hotel's purple and maroon bits set up a tension
with its lime green, how its electric-blue tower seemed fringed
with sea foam. Then he saw the foam was cracked plaster and
he went to check in.

The hotel lobby was even more bizarre then he remembered.
The padded rose plastic benches surrounding the mirrored As-
syrian columns (Assyria, Illinois) were more time-warped, kitsch
in aspic. People who spoke mostly Spanish were asking questions of people who spoke mostly Yiddish and getting answers
they understood.

The desk had Schwartz's reservation at the weekly rate,
had a top-floor beach-side room, and had a telephone number
for Schwartz with the message, "Please phone Officer Gomez."

He certainly would. The purple elevator opened to the
eleventh-floor corridor whose ring and strip fluorescent lighting
paled against the walls' bright blue, beneath the ceiling's yellow. He was whistling "The Miami Beach Rhumba," imagining what Karen would name these colors. Short-circuit blue?
Maniacal canary?

His room was colored with a certain tasteless splendor in
rose and gold and yellow and blue—these, like the room, in no
particular order. But it was relaxingly seedy with a big working
refrigerator and a seawall of saggy venetians. He set down his
bag and briefcase and pulled up the blinds.

And there, through twelve years' unwashed windows, was

the sea. The ocean! Miami Beach was his, with long sunset shadows thrown across the sand by buildings every bit as cuckoo as the Neptune Plaza.

Schwartz, in the bathroom of rust-stained green tile (Nile green? bile green?) washed his hands and face and looked into the mirror. He'd better call this guy Gomez. Between his thumb and index finger he pinched his chin into a cleft. No, he'd never look like Robert Mitchum. Still, here he was, feeling—how could he put it?—very okay, very forties RKO.

He sat on the bed and dialed. "May I speak to Officer Gomez, please?"

"This is Officer Gomez, Linda Gomez," she said. "Inspector Schwartz?"

"Yes, hello."

"The department detailed me as your unofficial contact. Do you want to meet now?"

"Why not."

"Say, half an hour, the Riptide Bar?"

"Where's that?"

"Know Wolfie's?"

"Sure."

"A couple doors down on the same block."

"Good, thanks. Oh, how will I know you?"

"Cops always know cops, Inspector."

"So do robbers. See you there, Officer Gomez."

Schwartz stripped, showered, and changed. Gomez: she'd be short, dark, round-faced, and stocky. Definitely "one of the boys." Fine.

Because he thought he might be continuing on from the bar, Schwartz drove the few blocks up Collins and parked on Twenty-first. He walked back around Wolfie's, passed the cigar store, and looked up at the dull red neon flickering RIPTIDE. Inside was a long, dim narrow room filled with an oval bar.

One side was up a few steps at the bartender's shoulder, where an old man in a white yachting cap sat next to an old woman with bright yellow hair and a red Hawaiian shirt. At the lower, street-door end, two men in blue T-shirts saying "Beach Plumbing" sat drinking boilermakers. On the other side was a big kid in a Dolphins net T-shirt nursing a small beer, and a few stools down Schwartz recognized another cop.

Officer Gomez had short black wavy hair and large brown eyes and was rather different than he'd imagined. Rather pretty. Beautiful, actually, if you were into that sort of thing, which he was desperately trying to stay out of. That was not to mention her figure. To mention Officer Gomez's figure was not how to stay out of that sort of thing. He went over to her absolutely not looking at her short skirt and long legs, wondering how, if he absolutely wasn't looking, he saw them.

"Officer Gomez."

She smiled. "Inspector Schwartz."

They shook hands. Hers was smooth and cool. His own felt to him made of horn, about to vaporize. She brought a wallet from her handbag and laid it open below the bar across her thigh. Her ID seemed all right, but shouldn't he inspect it closely? No, no. He took out his own badge wallet, showed it to her, and sat down.

"Gin and tonic," he said to the bartender. "You?"

"My drink's good. Look, I don't particularly want to call you by your title if you're here low-key."

"Call me Lenny. May I call you, uh . . ."

"Linda. Please. Well, you must be some heavyweight to get this unofficial attention."

"A hundred and sixty-four pounds, dripping wet," he said, somehow thinking of Linda Gomez dripping wet. "We've always helped out on any requests from your department."

"Do you know the Miami area?"

"I thought I knew the beach some, but I've never been in here."

"This place is as much old beach as Wolfie's."

"So I see," Schwartz said. "Those folks across the bar are obviously from Central Casting, and the place could be used without touch-up in any respectable film noir. Of course, I don't much look like Mitchum."

"No, you don't. You're good-looking, though, in a kind of nice, ugly way."

"Shucks, enough talk about me, ma'am," Schwartz said, paying for his drink. "Tell me everything about you."

"All right. My parents came to Miami in the early fifties from Cuba, both doctors. They're retired now. My full name is Linda Bonita Alicia Favela-Gomez, but it won't all fit on the name tag. That makes my mother unhappy. What also makes her unhappy is that I didn't become a doctor. I graduated from Miami with a degree in social psych and went right into the Miami police. I made it to sergeant there, but started over to be with the Miami Beach police."

"What's the difference?" Schwartz asked. The house gin tasted like Vitalis.

"The difference is that we sometimes get to arrest them. About fifteen percent of that force is under indictment. We have a small force here, under three hundred. A nice, clean force."

"What section are you with?" he asked.

"We don't work that way. We form case teams so we get to cover about everything. Of course we also have special duties. Mine's weapons and physical combat."

Schwartz looked.

"That's the idea. I don't have to look exactly like Arnold Schwarzenegger to get by. I like a .357 Magnum Ruger GP100. What about you?"

Schwartz scratched his head. "I go for rational discourse. If forced, I have an old .38 I've had fitted with a safety."

She looked at him with an ironic smile. "I've never heard of a .38 with a safety."

"I'll show it to you sometime," Schwartz said, happy that he hadn't prefixed his comment with "Come up to my place." He said, "I mean, I really don't like guns. Which reminds me: can you tell me if this 'Florida, the Gunshine State' bumper sticker is satirical?"

"No, I think it's probably worn with pride down here. Somewhere on that vehicle you'd probably find an NRA badge. Damn NRA. I know weapons. We need much tighter gun control to keep the bad guys from forming armies. So I guess I've told you all about me now."

"Not at all. You married? Do you have children?"

She shook her head. "No kids. Married at twenty-one, divorced at twenty-four, five years ago. He was Miami police, too. Something else I left across the bay. Just immaturity. Lust was love and love was everything, for almost two years. What about yourself?"

"Married for twenty-two years, a son in his second year of college."

"Is your wife beautiful?"

Schwartz laughed. "Yes, she is. And smart and funny. She writes books on art."

Linda sipped her drink and looked away across the bar. "Well, this isn't the greatest town for finding bright, straight, unattached, honest, not-too-sexist males of the species. Sigh, sigh." She turned back to Schwartz and smiled. "Did I start whining? It's, I guess, that I trust other officers, even ones from the big bad city of New York."

"You didn't whine. And thanks for the trust."

"You're very welcome. Now, how can I be of help, unofficially?" She sipped her drink through a straw.

"I need to make contact with someone down here called Roberto Cruz."

Linda's straw dropped from her mouth, her mouth stayed open.

"Did I say something?" Schwartz asked.

"Only *Roberto Cruz*? Is this homicide or narcotics or both?"

"Neither. This isn't a case; it's personal. I want to meet with him and have a private talk. That's all. So if you could get me a contact, someone or someplace, I'd be very grateful."

Linda put her hand on Schwartz's on the bar. "Our department, Miami's, the county and the state, not to mention two or three federal agencies, have been trying to nail Cruz for three or four years now, ever since he started running the Miami end of the Montanares syndicate. And now that Cruz is the big boss, he's even harder to get at. Oh, I can show you where he lives, maybe even pull one of his unlisted phone numbers for you, but that's not going to get you close to him at all, believe me."

Schwartz looked at Linda's hand. It felt warmer now. She drew it away. "Well, that would be a start, Linda. Would you?"

"Sure. He lives in a fortress up the beach in Bal Harbour. I'll try to pull a phone number for you, but Chief Pearlman will have to okay that."

"Good. What about places where Cruz hangs out—restaurants, clubs, racetracks? Our records have him as a pony fan."

"I don't know. Let's take it a step at a time. Can I ask what personal business you have with Cruz?"

Schwartz watched her uncross and recross her legs. She couldn't be that tall; her legs looked long because they were that wonderful shape. . . . He said, "Chief *Pearlman*: only in Miami Beach, I guess. Even in New York, I'm one of the few Jews of any rank in the department."

"It's no bar to advancement here, as long as you speak Spanish. My ex is a Jewish cop."

"One of the unindicted?"

Linda smiled. "Honest enough." Her smile dropped. "But a bastard, a spoiled brat, a mama's-boy misogynist."

"Ah. Ready for a drink?"

"Thanks. Vodka Collins."

Schwartz ordered. Up on the back wall a televised basketball game was going on unwatched, the sound turned down. A fishing net hung on the opposite wall before what, even in the gloom, could be seen as a very badly painted mural of crashing waves—the riptide, he imagined. What exactly was a riptide? Two tides? A tide against a current? Two opposing forces that made whirlpools? She'd let the question of his business with Cruz drop. He put the money on the bar. "Why don't we have dinner, if you're free?"

"Thanks for the drink. No, I'd like to, but I won't have dinner with you, thanks. Like what you said about your wife, some men say I'm nice looking and smart and even funny. But unlike your wife, Lenny, *I'm not your wife.*"

"Yes. *Claro*, Linda. *Muy claro.* I guess you'll make contact as soon as you have something?"

"I'll call you tomorrow. Here's my card," Linda said, standing, her head at his shoulder height. She looked at the hand Schwartz still held out, put out both of hers, and flat-handed pressed his hard.

Five minutes later Schwartz sat in his car in the dark. There was something in that handclasp, some way she'd actually sent a shock, a nerve jangling, up the length of his arm. It was

almost soft enough to turn him on, almost strong enough to
break every bone in his hand.

He drove back to the Neptune Plaza. Maybe the fantasy
just went with the territory. He'd have supper, call Karen, and
go to bed.

The front parking lot was full, so he pulled into the side
street, turned at the beach end, and came up to park. He heard
the squeal of tires and looked to see the taillights of a car coming
at him. He watched it swerve back into his space, rock forward,
and stop.

Schwartz backed down the street. He'd had enough travel
confrontations for one day. He found another parking space,
pulled in, and watched three young men pushing and slapping
each other out of the car, then walk yelling and laughing up to
Collins.

He locked his car and walked up along the side of the hotel.
He stopped at the other car: it looked just like the one the
agency wise guy tried to rent him, the Shark Tarantula's Ass,
or whatever. No, all in all, he'd done pretty well today, had
been right in ignoring bad omens.

Looking up at the moon and stars to give an ironic wink
at that heaven which wasn't there, Schwartz saw some movement at the top of the hotel. He saw a paleness knocking out
the sky. The top of the hotel was falling down on him. He threw
his hands on the low car roof and vaulted, rolling to the other
side, and fell into the street. Masonry smashed down on pave-
ment and steel. Small pieces of cement rained on his head.

He stood up with slightly scraped hands and shook the dirt
from his hair. He looked up. Nobody. Nobody along the street.
It could have been just a bit of bad luck, a bit of unrecon-
structed deco testing his lack of superstition, but he ran up the
street and around through the full parking lot and up the stairs

into the hotel lobby. And after he'd sat for ten minutes he knew
it had either been an accident or was too well planned, so that
its perpetrators would have gone right down to their hotel room.
Of course, he could start checking arrivals and departures, but
that was no way to remain just another guest.

Schwartz went to the desk and informed the management
that a large piece of their hotel's parapet had just missed hitting
him. Part of it was now on the sidewalk; another part, happily
a large two-hundred-pound part, could be found on the roof of
the brand-new pimpmobile it had pressed into the steering
wheel.

The management hoped Schwartz would accept their sin-
cere apology. Schwartz hoped the other driver would believe in
omens.

C H A P T E R   8

"Rose Fine. She sure is." His childhood joke went through his mind as he walked up Collins Avenue toward the park at Twenty-first Street to meet his aunt. Not his aunt. Rose was a second cousin on his mother's side, but had always been Aunt Rose to him. And always he set her in the Brooklyn Public Library, that grand, Grand Army Plaza building where eventually she became the head librarian. When he was six or seven, she'd shown him how the building was designed so that its great, curved entrance was the spine, the two wings out from that the open halves of an enormous book.

It seemed to him he'd gone there every day after school for years, always looked into her office, into those bright hawk eyes over the small beak over her smile, and then went to find his books. The arrangement he had with Aunt Rose was that he had the complete run of the place providing he could explain what he was doing, how each new section he went to worked, the sort of books and journals it contained.

Even angry, she'd been a teacher: when she found him reading something "rough," as she put it (he must have been

45

eleven; it was *Cry Tough* or maybe *The Amboy Dukes*—and after
he argued that it was real and exciting; he'd left out mentioning
his autoerotic enchantment), she'd thought and given him city
novels of Upton Sinclair and Sholem Asch to read which he'd
then read and liked and forgotten, and the Thomas Wolfe short
story "Only the Dead Know Brooklyn," which he'd then read
and hated and thought was pointless and remembered almost
verbatim.

And there she was, Aunt Rose, at the corner of Twenty-
first Street, with a cane and shorter and squarer than in memory
but with the same bright bird intensity beneath the white bun
of her hair.

Schwartz ran the few steps to her, put his arms around her.
"Aunt Rose!" He found tears in his eyes.

"Lenny, dear. How are you? Let me squint at you. You
look good." She cocked her head. "Tears? You're still a sen-
timental idiot?"

"Yes. How are you?"

She started walking down Collins. "Oh, I'm terrific. Come
on, if I stay still too long, I tend to lock. Terrific. My thyroid
condition is such that once the weather goes over sixty-eight
degrees, I sweat something like those hydrants they used to open
in the summer in Brooklyn. But I come from a thyroid family.
And my cataracts grow just about as fast as I have them removed. But, then, I come from a cataract family. The Cataract-
Thyroids, a distinguished double-barreled family. My hearing
problems seem my own original contribution."

Schwartz leaned his cheek down to hers. "If you can catalog yourself like that, you really are in great shape. Aunt Rose,
I was just remembering the Brooklyn Library, how its architec-
ture would fit in here at Miami Beach."

"Yes." She nodded. "You're still the polymath policeman."

They passed a restaurant in whose window a woman lifted the handle of a hot press and took out the Cuban bread.

"Lenny, do you know that the Concord Cafeteria is gone? They've sold half of it to an Argentinian restaurant that isn't too bad if you stay away from their fried-cow specials and concentrate on the nice tango records. I'd be all right, Lenny, but for Abe's death. You didn't know him well, did you?"

Schwartz frowned. He remembered a quiet, boring man, well dressed. "No. The only Zeigler I remember was Uncle Morton from Argentina, the diamond merchant."

"Another cousin. Abe Zeigler was my best friend. I knew him since I was a child. After I came down here on my own, when Sid died, Abe was so good to me. Really. I know what you think of retired stockbrokers, you with your lefty radical father from the union, the communist."

"No, Aunt Rose, the communist was Maurie, Aunt Celia's husband. My father was the lefty radical from the union, the social democrat."

"Of course. My memory. Wait!" Rose pulled his wrist and stopped at the curb. The light was with them.

"The light's green, Aunt."

"Sure, but it's been green too long. At my pace I need the entire light. I'd have thought you'd figure that out, detective."

"I'll try to be more observant."

Rose spoke in a low, pleasantly gravelled voice. "I know people thought Abe a quiet, self-centered man. He wasn't. He wasn't an intellectual like my Sidney, may he rest in peace— my god, may both of them rest in peace, but Abe was a kind and companionable and good man, a real philanthropist in his way."

A small curbside wind swirled Rose's white and green polka-dot dress. Her shins were mottled white and blue over her dark brown tan. The light changed.

"Come on," she said. "Then there's Stanley, Abe's first cousin, my third cousin, and I suppose, your fifth cousin. Do you know him?"

"No, I'd never heard of him before you mentioned him on the phone."

"I'm going to try to be fair, Lenny. You're not missing much." She smiled. "See how fair I am, already?"

"Are we walking too fast or too far, Aunt Rose?"

"No," she said, glancing at people her age sitting in chairs set out before the hotel across the street. "Walking is good for me. Stanley Zeigler is—there, that was the Concord Cafeteria. You know it's closed? You remember it?"

Schwartz looked into the empty half of the building—long, dark, endless. "I remember pieces of marble cake in there the size of breeze blocks."

"And heavier," Rose said, stopped by the window. She began to laugh. "I'm not . . . Wait, I'm not laughing at my own joke but at my telling you the same thing about the Concord twice in two minutes! I don't think I'm senile, Lenny; I'm just so distracted with Abe's murder. So, back to Stanley. Stanley came to Miami Beach at the start of the war, the Second World War. And for fifty years now he's been doing shady property deals, trades, buying, developing, speculating."

Schwartz said, "Well, it's not a noble calling, Aunt Rose, but it is the way of this particular world, isn't it?"

Rose began walking again, the end of her cane coming down so fiercely that but for its rubber tip it would have struck sparks off the sidewalk. "Not as Stanley Zeigler does it. There's not a year he hasn't been in court."

Schwartz held her arm to slow her. "Aunt Rose, just what is it you think Stanley has done?"

Rose stopped. Two old men in straw hats passed her and looked her over. Both had long unlit cigars in their mouths like

the pacifiers of a second childhood. The shorter of the two had
the drag-and-shuffle walk of a stroke victim; the taller held his
arm.

"What are you looking at, Lenny?"

"Nothing."

Rose smiled sadly. "You're afraid you'll come to this? You
will, and if you're lucky, you'll have someone to hold up or to
hold on to." She shook her head. "Oh, dear, forgive me. I get
so bitter. Look, I think Stanley was the one they meant to murder. It was his dog, the place he always went at that time, and
if you didn't know them well, I suppose they looked something
alike." Rose began walking slowly. "Stanley knew such people!
Abe had this family loyalty, so twice a week he went to Stanley
and they played Scrabble or cribbage. But I couldn't stand it
there. Abe knew and never pressured me to go. He was very
gentle and understanding like that."

"Aunt Rose," Schwartz said, trying to speak clearly but
keep his voice low, hoping Rose could hear, "I can check the
records, I suppose, to find what convictions Stanley has. But
to be frank, I still haven't heard anything from you to suggest—"

"Whores and gangsters," Rose said.

"Excuse me?"

"You heard me." Rose looked down at the sidewalk, appearing to concentrate on her footing. "The last time I was at
Stanley's preposterous house was two years ago. A party. He'd
begged Abe to bring me. So I went. The place was full of whores
and gangsters. Call girls, perhaps, more accurately."

"Oh, Aunt Rose, how could you know that?"

Rose shook her head. "You mean how could *I* know about
life because I was a librarian? Shame on you. Do I question
your cultural knowledge because you have a career in homicide?"

Schwartz threw up his hands. "You've got me. I'm sorry. But I am trained to ask dumb questions, and if you want my help, I'm afraid there'll be more of them."

"All right," Rose said, suddenly breathing hard. "Listen, we'll sit on that bench for a minute. No, no, I don't need help, now. I might ask your help getting up again."

Rose sat heavily and wiped her brow with a large handkerchief initialed "AZ." Schwartz sat beside her and felt the sweat under his shirt.

She turned to Schwartz. "I haven't asked what you're doing down here, you'll note. Some terrible business?"

"Mildly terrible."

Rose looked across the avenue to the small residential hotels in whose front patios the aged sat and schmoozed or stared or snored. "So boring, so boring," she said. "You know, as I grow older I'm convinced that only those people we call 'characters' *have* any character."

Schwartz nodded. "It's dumb-question time. All right?"

"Sure. Fire away, slowly and dumbly, if you must."

"I do remember Abe. I don't remember him as much of a character."

"That wasn't a question," Rose said. "It also wasn't so dumb. In public, Abe was very reserved, taciturn. When you knew him very well, as I did, he had character."

"And Stanley?"

"Loud, vulgar, a braggart. Stanley is a caricature, not a character."

"I forget, Aunt Rose: are you agnostic or an atheist?"

"What sort of a question—all right, Mr. Policeman, I'll come quietly. I'm both, ambivalent, thinking there is no God and thinking that I don't know."

"But you live at the Marlowe Court Hotel, a very kosher establishment. Why?"

"Abe was agnostic and lived there, too. Like him, I lived there because it was and is a very well run, very clean place. And when, about seven years ago, they sold off the top two floors as condominium apartments, Abe suggested I buy one. He bought a larger one on the top floor. Nothing flashy, but nice. And I bought a one-bedroom apartment on the floor below. Abe was very clever that way. The price was good and I've never regretted taking his advice. As to kosher, we don't, we didn't often eat in the hotel restaurant. I remember our teasing the management, asking them why they hadn't named the Marlowe Court for another Elizabethan writer—for Francis Bacon?"

"Was that Abe's idea?"

"What does it matter? I think it was my idea."

"And what about Stanley; would he know his Marlowe to save his bacon?"

Rose rocked forward on the bench, motioned Schwartz's arm away, rocked forward again, and on a shaking arm pushed up onto her cane. "There. All on my own. Pretty good."

Schwartz walked at her side. "Very good, except you didn't answer my question about Stanley."

Rose grimaced. "I don't think he'd know." Rose ungrimaced. "Maybe he'd know. I didn't say he was an idiot. Who knows what he reads? The man has a bodyguard. Lenny, does an intellectual need a bodyguard?"

"Metaphorically, that's an interesting question."

They walked by the larger seaside hotels; they passed the Marlowe Court, walked on, crossed another street, and came to a clump of palm and seagrape surrounding a fountain.

Rose pulled his arm. "Let's stand in this shade for a minute. Then we'll go back to the Marlowe."

The fountain was an Aztec god in mock lava, perhaps the god of ersatz. A fallen god, Schwartz thought, watching the

water trickle through one eye socket and run down the porous
excrescence of its jaw, hit the clump representing its loincloth,
and splash to disappear, at last, off its single toe. Schwartz
looked up. A long black-windowed limousine was coming slowly
along Collins, tight to the curb.

"Aunt Rose, are you ready?" Schwartz asked, and looked
back down the avenue.

The limousine had climbed half up the curb. Its motor
revved.

"Rose!" Schwartz yelled, pushing his aunt up toward the
fountain in the growing noise.

Schwartz tipped Rose onto the mulch and fell over her.
Black steel doors hissed by, whipping the leaves and the fronds.

"Are you all right?" he asked.

"Mister, are you all right?" asked someone.

"Is the lady all right?" asked another.

"I'm all right," Rose said. "I'm all right."

"She's all right. I'm all right," Schwartz said.

"They're all right, it's all right," someone called.

Schwartz helped Rose to stand. He handed her the cane
and brushed the chippings from her side. Through its hollow
eye the lumpish god continued to cry placidly.

"Mister, so help me, another foot and you—"

"Another foot?" another bystander put in. "Another *inch*
you would have been mincemeat! A madman, coming up on
the sidewalk like that."

"Anyone get the number?" Schwartz asked.

Headshakes. Someone said, "Probably a Florida license,
maybe."

"Meshugana!" another said. "They're all *meshuggah* with this
crack. They're cracked!"

"Thanks, we're all right now," Schwartz said, walking
Rose slowly past the two women and a man.

A few steps farther Schwartz asked, "Are you *really* all right, Aunt Rose?"

Rose nodded. "Yes, yes. That bastard, Lenny! Pardon my language. That bastard!"

"Yes, it was—"

"Stanley. That was Stanley!"

"What?"

"No, not in person."

"That was his car?"

"No, of course not. But I'll bet—"

"Aunt Rose, Aunt Rose." Schwartz patted her arm. "I'm terribly sorry. That was *my* fault. That was something to do with *me*, not you. Buildings are falling on me, cars leave the road for me."

"You're saying someone just tried to kill you?"

"No, no. That was a warning. Believe me, Aunt Rose, if they'd wanted to run me down, they would have."

Rose stopped, turned, and waved at the three bystanders. They waved back and walked on. Rose continued walking, faster now.

"Take it easy," Schwartz said.

"Why, I feel fine now, fine. Look, you stick to your theory and I'll stick to mine. Let me help you on this. I can do some research on Stanley."

"Abe and Stanley."

"Of course. Lenny," she said, nodding, "this hit-and-run, near-miss hit-and-run thing: would you believe it's woken me up, taken some of the shock of Abe's death away?"

"I believe it."

"So how can I help you?"

He said, "The first thing you might do is arrange for us to visit Stanley."

Rose squinted. "I suppose I have to. I can do it; Stanley

will see it as a rapprochement, the stuck-up fool. All right. But will you do one thing for me?''

"Anything, Aunt Rose.''

"I'm not your aunt, Lenny. I've wanted to tell you this for at least thirty years: please call me Rose. Rose.''

Schwartz bent to her cheek, kissed it lightly, and said, "Rose Fine. She sure is!''

"Mr. Schmaltz," she said.

BOOK

CHAPTER 1

If buildings fell and cars roared up the sidewalk in friendly warning, what would happen when Roberto lost his temper? For what else but Roberto Cruz's warnings could these be? Would he just have to wait until Cruz, who obviously knew his movements, decided he'd see him—if, that is, Cruz didn't decide he'd kill him first? But how had Cruz gotten onto him so quickly?

Schwartz had left Rose at the Marlowe Court and spent the next hour looking out the dirty windows of his hotel room at the ocean, wondering what to do. He sat down on the edge of his bed and did one plodding, basic thing; he phoned to check on lovely Linda Gomez, and was put through, finally, to the chief of police of Miami Beach.

"Hi," said the informal, distant voice, "this is Dave Pearlman. How are you doing, Inspector Schwartz?"

"Fine, thanks," Schwartz said, shifting to a less sagging bit of mattress. "I have a question, a little formality. I want to check that your officer Linda Gomez is who she says she is."

"Okay. Wait a minute, please. Here it is. You met with
Officer Gomez yesterday at the Riptide Bar between 6:15 and
6:55 P.M. and asked her for assistance in making contact with
someone. Should I read more details from her report?"

"No, that's fine. I suppose I wondered—"

"Yes, Linda Gomez is a very beautiful woman. She's one
of my best officers."

"Thanks, Chief."

"Of course. You know, you can come over here to see
Linda and her identification in person, anytime. You'd be very
welcome."

Schwartz thanked the chief and hung up. He went back to
the cloudy window with its clear view. The phone rang, inter-
rupting nothing.

It was Rose, calling to tell him they were to lunch tomorrow at Stanley Zeigler's, an invitation, she said, "far too
easily obtained, the mark of a guilty conscience," didn't he
think?

He didn't say. He thanked Rose for her good work, put
the phone down, and wished he could do some good work, too.
Even mediocre work would be better than this cloudy suspen-
sion.

The refrigerator coughed itself on, buzzed and shivered. The
air-conditioning tried to hum but couldn't hold the tune. The
phone rang under his hand.

"Lenny? This is Linda, calling from the station. Did I pass
the test?"

Schwartz coughed and hummed, attempting to camou-
flage himself as a hotel bedroom. "Shouldn't I have tested
you?"

"Sure you should."

"You passed."

"Good," she said. "How about your turn? I'm off work at five. Want to take a run on the beach?"

"How did you know I ran?"

"You *are* suspicious. Most fit officers run. No, actually it was a little double checking on *my* part."

"Oh? And did I pass?"

Linda laughed. "The ID, yes. This will be the physical."

He said, "I'll be waiting in my joggies at the beach end of Seventeenth, say 5:15?"

"You're on. 'Bye."

Schwartz wondered exactly what he was on. Nonsense! She'd said "physical" in an open, literal way; any undercurrent flowed from his own libidinal tide. He unclutched the telephone and started to change clothes.

Schwartz was doing leg stetches on the sidewalk when the car door slammed. Linda glowed in slink-pink spandex, a yellow cassette player strapped to her hip. He nodded "hi" and dragged his eyes back to his own tight calves.

"Pretty cute," she said, standing beside him. "Your joggies are just little black shorts. You *look* in good shape."

"You're taking all my lines," Schwartz said, straightening and regarding Linda's shimmer. "You look like any ordinary descent-to-earth of Pallas Athena."

As they walked onto the hardened sand, Linda said, "They're not such hot lines."

Schwartz clamped his mouth shut to keep from saying that hers were.

Linda pointed south. "We could jog to the point and back, just under four miles." She adjusted the thick pink sweatband at the top of her forehead.

"What do you generally do?"

"I go up the beach about three miles, sometimes more, and then come back. Do you want to do that?" She put on her earphones.

"All right."

"And I don't jog, I run. Okay?"

"Okay." Schwartz smiled. "What's the tape?"

"*The Best of Aretha.* You know Aretha Franklin?" Linda asked, her head in a tease tilt.

"One of those youngsters," he said, "newer than Guy Lombardo, even newer than Dick Haymes."

Linda pointed, Schwartz nodded, and they started to run, Linda setting the pace. It was fast. Even with the late-afternoon sun at his back, even running across the shadows of the ocean hotels, Schwartz immediately broke into a heavy sweat, only half of which, he assumed, was lust.

"Very good running surface," he shouted as they passed Collins Park, about half a mile up.

Linda turned, lifting an earphone. "What's that?"

"I said it's a good surface."

"It's great. This beach is the best running." She set back the earphone, smiled, and seemed to run faster.

She looked cool. Schwartz wiped the sweat from his eyes and saw how at the swing back of each arm her shoulder muscles stretched and the lines of her pectorals swelled up from her breasts. Swell images, thirty-six hours away from home!

Up past the Fontainebleau, Schwartz began to wonder when Linda would slow the pace. Then he began to understand that she wouldn't. He touched her shoulder. "You train with weights?"

She nodded and called, "For strength, not bulk."

He imagined Linda doing bench presses. He imagined this

far too well. He concentrated on the sweat trickling down his sides. Then he found himself looking at the light sweat on Linda's forehead and on the down above her full top lip and he knew he was looking too close. This wasn't a holiday. Oh, God, he didn't mean that it if were a holiday he could . . . It was with some moral relief that Schwartz began to feel a stitch in his left side.

For the next mile or so he grappled with its guilty stabs. Only two nights before he'd been grappling with his lovely wife on the floor of their connubial bedroom! Of course, his lovely wife had been trying to strangle him. A detail, a detail.

The two of them ran up the beach; passing other runners with aggressive consistency. Schwartz saw his heaving chest as shiny as Linda's spandex and only slightly less pink. Her head bobbed to her music.

She turned to him and said, "You run well for an old Guy . . . Lombardo fan. Shall we go up to the end of the open space and turn back at Surfside?"

"Sure," Schwartz gasped.

But halfway up the park his breath came easier and a looseness like cool water flooded his calves and thighs and filled his chest and shoulders. When they turned back down the beach, the wind on his face felt fresh and clean.

Linda's unitard was flushed dark pink with sweat across the top of her chest and over the ripples of her stomach muscles.

Schwartz pointed to her ear. "What's the song?"

"Aretha's 'Eleanor Rigby.' "

"All those lonely people," he said.

"How hip of you, Lenny."

Schwartz yelled in an old man's crackle, "Why sure, young lady. I even know it was a song by them young whippersnapper English lads—the Termites, wasn't it?"

A mile or so later Linda said, "You really can run."

"Thank you," Schwartz said. "I'm all right at hanging in.
Do you have any news for me?"

Linda blew a spray of sweat from her top lip. "I thought
you'd never ask. I have a number you can call where you can
leave a message." After a few more strides she added, "No
answer guaranteed."

For the last two miles they ran faster, neither one making the pace, both letting their nerves lead them. At Seventeenth Street they slowed to a jog, turned from the packed sand,
and walked off the beach between the tall scruff of Australian
pine.

When they stopped by her yellow convertible, Linda said,
"That was such a great run, especially the last few miles." She
brought a towel out from the car and wiped her face. "We ran
well together. You could have run faster and longer, couldn't
you?"

Schwartz was taking deep breaths, walking a small oval by
the car. "Not those first few miles, but by the end it was terrific,
something like your body's going so well it feels more than
physical; you're almost out of your body." He stopped by her
side and took more deep breaths.

She asked, "Want some towel?"

"No, thanks. I'm right at my hotel, here. What do you do
now?"

"Have a very sticky ride back home."

"Right. Well, I'll get that number."

She draped the towel around her neck. "Unless I could
shower and change here."

"Yes," Schwartz said so quickly that he looked down in
shame, adding, "so you could give me that contact number."
His feet shuffled at the non sequitur.

By the time they stepped inside the Neptune Plaza's elevator, Schwartz had caught his breath and reexhausted himself with a cycle of fantasy, fantasy repression, and more fantasy. He pressed button 11 and leaned back on the wall farthest from Linda. She looked down at her canvas tote bag.

Entering his room, she laughed. "Oh, wow, this is really sleazy, in a cozy sort of way. Or did I mean that the other way around?"

Schwartz pointed to the bathroom. "I'll wait."

Once she'd closed the door, Schwartz felt the full sexist, exploitative nature of his thoughts. If he couldn't let a colleague take a shower without imagining . . . Oh. Just because she was a woman! A woman so strong and smooth . . . He was some sort of mad dog. He should be fixed. He meant, he'd fix it, just take off his running shoes and socks and get into a bathrobe and put an end to these stupid, disloyal thoughts. He stood by the robe draped on the chair and pulled off his shorts and his jockstrap.

"Lenny."

Naked. Linda was facing him naked, dripping with sweat. Naked. She was. He was. Her hands were held out. Was this still his fantasy, so strong that . . . The least he could do for the field of amateur psychology was to test this. He did so by walking toward this possible fantasy of Linda with his hands out, too.

Next, the fantasy somehow had him moving through the air, his head and torso turning a slow half circle around his arm and shoulder which slid along Linda until she let go, when the floor sped toward his eyes and he crashed out of fantasy into the bottom of the bathroom door, head twisted, cheek stinging, shoulder and hip banged to the floor. He pushed onto his hands and knees and shook his head.

Linda turned toward him in a half-crouching position.
"Come on," she said, "you run well but how well can you
fight?"

Her thighs shone with sweat; it glistened in her thick black
pubic hair. This was crazy. He was already hurt. His nose, the
traitor, had completely bypassed his brain and was in direct
communication with his crotch. Was she crazy? Was he? Could
he still be failing to understand? Was this a new generation that
practiced such safe sex that naked all-in wrestling didn't mean
all in? Schwartz rubbed his shoulder and stood up, slowly, pain-
fully, erectly. He held his palms up. "Linda, this is way over
my speed, my depth. My god, you're lovely but I'm not, I
think, into . . . I hope—"

Her heel flashed out between his hands and kicked into his
chest. Schwartz slammed backward, crashed into the door. God!
Had she cracked his breastbone? He clutched at his chest. Tears
streamed from his eyes. "Look," he said, "you can't . . .
You're going to have the manager up here with all this noise.
I've never seen the manager, but I'm sure that even this place
has one."

Linda ran the back of her hand across her face, licked her
lips, and smiled. Schwartz recognized the smile from the lim-
erick about the tiger. "Lenny," she said, "I stripped for my
shower and looked at myself in the mirror and knew. You can't
deny it, can you?" she asked, pointing.

He looked down to where she pointed. No, he was a jolly
good fellow, that no one could deny. "Of course I can't, but I
can, that's just . . . You're very attractive, but I'm not playing
this game, Linda. So I'll take my shower first and you can cool
down out here."

As he turned for the bathroom door his eye caught a flying
blur and Linda landed on him, her arm around the front of his
neck. The well-strangled Schwartz went limp so that his head

slipped out, but Linda swung her other arm around and jutted her hip so that he tripped into her headlock out of balance, wary of the natural defensive instinct to wrap his arms around his assailant's hips. His assailant's naked, hard-soft sweaty hips.

"Nice move," she said, "going limp."

The headlock was powerful, painful, yet as his head pressed into Linda's wet stomach he sensed he hadn't gone entirely limp. This was exciting. No, he meant crazy wrong. He wasn't into all this. . . . "What if I give up, Linda? Say Uncle? *Tío?* Aunt?"

Her answer was a jerk upward of her hip and a swing of her locked arms so that Schwartz's head pretzeled his neck to the accompaniment of loud bone clicks. He said, "Ouch!" and "I see."

Now, though he still refused to play, to fight her, he had to put his arms around her hips to take the pressure off his aching neck. If only her smell didn't excite him so. He begged his nose to mind its own business; his nose immediately snorted that this was precisely its business. And then Schwartz had it: he'd break the rules, all the rules, and Linda, humiliated, would lose heart. And reassuring himself that it was the only way to remain loyal to his wife, Schwartz slid his left hand deep between Linda Gomez's gleaming buttocks.

Her humiliation took the form of lunging with Schwartz toward the bedroom door, where his head smashed so hard, he expected, when he opened his eyes, to be looking through into the hotel corridor. "Enough!" he shouted. "Damn it, enough, Linda!"

"Wimp."

"I'm not," he whimpered. "I'm just not into the Sacher-Masoch workout."

Linda spun him around and lugged him headlocked into the bedroom.

He said, "I really *could have* had you, then. You shouldn't move with—"

She'd let go and backed off. He straightened. Good. She'd come to her senses. "All right, Linda. No more now. You've hurt me, really."

"No pain, no gain," she said with the tiger smile, sweating, her breasts shiny, tan, and pink. Did Odysseus have these problems with Athena? But that, Schwartz thought, was more than *ten years* away from Karen-Penelope, not two days.

And then, when he was still in Homeric reverie, Linda hit him in the face, a right hook with a martial-arts knuckle whip at its end that shook the side of his jaw, reeled and sank Schwartz to his knees by the refrigerator. He held its handle and pulled himself hard up as he saw Linda's legs, still, damn it, so shapely, coming his way.

She was saying, "Is this the best the New York police can—" when Schwartz jumped forward behind the fridge door, throwing it open into her shoulders.

In the moment she staggered, Schwartz in his low forward momentum grabbed her ankles and pulled back. Linda's reaction was what he wanted: falling, she tried to twist away onto her stomach and Schwartz straightened, lifting her ankles and beginning a pivot on the ball of his right foot.

Linda grabbed at the desk leg as she came around but let go when it crashed into the fridge.

Schwartz began to pick up spin. "Your problem," he shouted as Linda's arm swung out of the fridge, pulling a bottle of seltzer and some green apples down on her, "your problem is that while you're a mistress of martial arts . . ."

Here, for two spins he had to pause; the centrifugal force was straightening Linda, lengthening Linda so that her hands and forearms smashed down the desk lamp, pulled shelves from the open fridge, and flapped off the bed ends.

"I'm just," he continued, spinning faster, dizzying himself, "a student of dirty street fights."

Linda started to shout, a long, low scream of a shout during
which Schwartz wondered: If he aimed her at the windows and
let go, would she fly out, turn around, and fly back in again?
No, he figured dizzily, so as he spun around to the bedside he
let go.

She moved in a horizontal high dive over the first bed into
the brass bedside lamp and crashed through it to the other bed,
arms into the wall.

Schwartz stood still as the room slowed its turns around
him. The room stopped and looked awful, beaten up. Linda
groaned and pulled herself over.

"Oh, Lenny."

What did she want now, an apology?

"You passed, Lenny, you passed. Fuck me."

She didn't seem to want an apology.

"Beat me, fuck me," she said, louder.

"Shh," he said.

"Fuck me, tie me up!" she yelled.

He felt he had to keep her quiet, felt he had to stop the
brawl, felt she felt so good. He was dazed, he lied, beside himself, so he went to Linda on the bed, pushed the lamp off to the
floor, and warned his nose there'd be a *serious* talk about this,
afterward.

Afterward, they seemed literally stuck together. Was that
dried sweat, was that Schwartz, now with a back doubtless full
of red tiger smiles, too bruised and aching to dare move, or was
that merely Schwartz too thrilled by Linda, these voluptuous
muscles locked their whole length to him? Linda unwrapped
from him, pushed back, and said, "Wait, baby, wait."

Schwartz lay back, his head turned to the window. The sky
over the ocean had darkened to blue purple; farther out, a

massed roll of clouds was violent gray, pink-tipped in sunset, right out of the C. N. Wyeth illustrations of his childhood. Ah, but this wasn't his childhood, this was his married and disloyal early middle age. And he knew he was a shit who could have stopped this kinky hanky-panky any time he wanted. But he—

"Baby."

Baby? *Was* this his childhood, some time-warped fantasy of an infantile adulthood?

Not time-warped. It was Linda, standing at the bed end with a pair of handcuffs and some rope. Just plain warped.

He thought best to make ordinary conversation. "What's that rope?"

"It's a jump rope. Handcuff me, tie me up," she said, and added, in a whisper, "Whip me, please."

"No, Linda, sweet wild strong girl, not in the slightest, thank you," Schwartz said, rolling over with a moan and rubbing his shoulder and jaw. He didn't want even to think of his back burning bright, in the forests of the night. He stood and pointed to himself. "See? Not in the least; not my thing."

"Come on, please," Linda said with a disturbing lack of force.

"Enough! Linda, you are wonderful, beautiful, you have an amazing, I mean amazing body, every bit and all of it and you are intelligent and attractive, and no, I can't do what you ask. What do you need that for? No, don't answer."

Linda came up to him, holding out the cuffs and rope. Was she going to cuff and whip him? No. He took them from her, went to the bathroom, and put them into her tote bag. Then he stepped into the shower.

Linda stepped into the shower. "Please?"

Schwartz sensed she was in her extremely submissive phase. "No, damn it!" he said. "Am I going to have to beat you up again to prove that I mean 'no'?" he asked, and knew it was the very wrong thing to have said. "What about that contact number, Linda?"

She began to lather his back and whispered in the rush of water, "What about that little safety on your .38?"

CHAPTER 2

As the gates swung open, Rose said, "What did I tell you."

What had she told him? Wasn't it something about Stanley Zeigler's sleazy sex life? Schwartz stared down the crushed marble drive along an avenue of silver-blue palm fans backed by parallel lines of royal palms. Beneath them on the lawns, thick clumps of bougainvillea burst like red and yellow fireworks. Fireworks: he wondered if he looked to Rose like someone recovering from a decathlon of sex with a fellow police officer. Well, less a fellow than a marvelously muscled woman who was not his wife. Oh, God. "What did you tell me?" he asked as the car crunched slowly on.

"Pretentious. Look how pretentious his house is."

The house, like others on the drive, was built of Miami keystone coral with a red tile roof. Unlike others, its three-story facade was gothic tracery, windows of gilded tre- and cinquefoil and a roofline bristled with quatrefoil spears. The porch before its vast oak door was framed by wooden pillars striped red and white, like mooring posts for gondolas. Schwartz pulled up before the palazzo and grinned at Rose.

She said, "He copied the Ca d'Oro in Venice!"

"And got the Ca-Ca d'Oro in Miami Beach."

Rose laughed and coughed into a handkerchief. She took a compact mirror from her handbag and squinted into it. "All right," she said, "this face is good enough for Stanley Zeigler."

Schwartz's face felt bruised but the bruises didn't show, probably no more than some marital trust he'd battered. He said, "Rose, we have to be polite so that Stanley talks to us."

"I understand," she said. As Schwartz helped her from the car she muttered, "Here he is."

Standing in the doorway was a man in his seventies, plump, tanned, bald, wearing a warm smile and hot-pink Bermuda shorts with a white knit short-sleeve jersey and white knee socks. His leather loafers were the same hot pink. "Well, well, well. Rose, it's so good to see you," he said, opening his arms and leaning his head to hers.

Standing very straight on her cane, Rose moved so that Stanley lightly kissed a mother-of-pearl earring.

"Stanley. Stanley Zeigler, Lenny Schwartz. Lenny, Stanley Zeigler," Rose said with the warmth of a long-distance operator.

Stanley grabbed both of Schwartz's hands. "Well, well, well, well, well," he said, beaming.

"Nice to meet you," said Schwartz, his hands continuing to bob in Stanley's strong grasp.

"So you're the famous New York police detective. Your mother, may she rest in peace, was *the* most beautiful woman." He dropped one of Schwartz's hands and flourished his own past Rose. "Present company excepted, of course."

Rose walked past him. "Thank you very much, Mr. Malarkey. May we go in now, or are we lunching out here on the Grand Canal?''

Schwartz couldn't help smiling as he said, "Rose?"

Stanley shook his head. "No, no. A clever woman. I love wit." He winked at Schwartz and shrugged. "She hates me. What can I do?'' And he swung Schwartz's hand toward Rose, who was disappearing into antiqued oak.

They entered a cavern of a hall on whose marble floor, a checkerboard in pink and black, Rose stood, her head nodding in disdain. Above her hung a glass-flowered chandelier so vast, its manufacturer could have employed the population of Murano for much of the eighteenth, no—Schwartz reassessed—early-twentieth century.

Stanley tapped Schwartz's arm. "Lenny, if you're interested in art—"

"He wouldn't be here, Stanley," Rose finished.

Stanley smiled and wagged a finger at Rose. "The murals are by Tozzi. He did them in 1950 and '51. Lived here ten months doing them. A genius! A big elephant of a man, but my god, were the ladies crazy about him!'' Stanley turned to Rose. "Sorry, dear."

"Oh, think nothing of it; just be yourself," she said, making "yourself" sound like something one took a dog out to do.

Schwartz attempted to place the name Tozzi. Around the cavern walls fluttered a tutti-frutti fluff of 1950's gondolas and pink Salutes, camp campaniles, and dodgey palaces. "Tozzi?"

"Angelo Tozzi," Stanley said, looking at his walls with pleasure. "A genius, a follower of Tiepolo."

Rose gave a short cough. "The genius must have been following at quite a distance."

Stanley looked at Schwartz and winked again. "Don't mind Rose. Enjoy like I do. Life's too short."

"*Some* lives are too short, Stanley," Rose said with closed eyes. "So may we please go to one of your playrooms now and sit?"

"Follow me, follow me," said Stanley, and with a bounce step led them through a tasseled baldacchino of gold leather into a space so hugely bright white that Schwartz had to blink to focus.

Stanley announced, "The Florida room."

It wasn't true, Schwartz thought. The state was larger and not so overdecorated.

But Rose, sitting slowly into an armchair of white leather said *out loud*, "Florida, schmorida, what could be horrider? This is the Vatican throne room as designed by Sinbad the Sailor."

Stanley laughed. "Well, at least I'm ecumenical."

But not economical, Schwartz continued to himself, looking at the twisted marble columns that leaned from the room's six corners supporting a trompe l'oeil tent roof of concrete painted and molded to look like white leather, the walls ditto, billowed out, except for the farther wall which was fifty feet of glass doors before the long swimming pool and smaller tent trompe cabañas, all backed by an improbably emerald lawn sporting red, pink, and yellow hibiscus like dandies' boutonnières. And behind this and the line of mixed exotic palms gleamed the wide blue cabin-cruisered waterway of Indian Creek and across it the high glitz of big hotels. Schwartz found it vulgar and very cheerful from where he sat, a white leather sofa so deep his feet dangled like a little boy's.

Stanley hovered, bouncing and rubbing his hands. "Rose, Lenny, what can I get you to drink? Tomato juice, Rose? You still drink that, am I right?" He turned and yelled, "Harry! Harry!"

"Tomato juice with a few ice cubes and a bit of lemon would be nice, thank you, Stanley," Rose said in a voice so quietly cold that Schwartz could hear his spirit drop. He encouraged himself with the observation that Stanley, who seemed to understand all Rose's insults, was still buoyant.

A tall, white-jacketed Chinese butler entered.

Stanley smacked him on the back. "This is Harry Lee, my butler, chauffeur, valet, whatever. Harry, you remember Rose Fine, poor Cousin Abe's friend? And this is a relative I've never met before. Say hello to Lenny Schwartz of New York's finest, a famous and tremendously high ranking officer, so you better behave."

Lee nodded to Rose and Schwartz. Schwartz nodded back, witnessing his tourist's cover, never more than a loincloth, lifted shamefully. Recognizing this metaphor displaced from the last night's kinked Olympics, Schwartz dropped his eyes to the floor, which turned out to be tiled with pink whirling through white, looking like nothing in the world so much as certain welts, like nothing in the *welt* so much as—

"Cat got your tongue?" Stanley was asking.

Schwartz thought no, *that* was last night, too. "No, sorry, I'll have a white-wine spritzer, thanks."

Stanley gave Rose's order and added, "My usual dry sherry, Harry. I'm a real Englisher that way." He turned to Schwartz to continue so that it might be out of Rose's hearing. "My ulcer. They don't let me have a real drink, at least not before dinner." He turned and followed Harry. "Hey, and Harry, put some good music on, some Nellie Lutcher or Louis Jordan or something."

Schwartz wondered if Nellie Lutcher was even earlier than Dick Haymes, wondered why he wondered and knew at the same time and wanted to leave the room and call Karen to confess and . . .

Stanley sat opposite on a white, papally proportioned armchair. "Rose, you know this, I think," he said, "so don't answer. Lenny, what do you think my nickname for Harry is?"

"For Harry Lee. Is it 'Bruce'?"

"Hey, yeah. That's terrific!" Stanley leaned forward, his belly popping out before him like a half-white, half-pink balloon. "How'd you figure that?"

"Since he's your bodyguard . . ." Schwartz shrugged. "His muscles show through his clothes."

"Sure." Rose nodded, consciously now. "You see? Some 'ecumenical' guy, here. A Jew who thinks he's the Pope of Baghdad and needs a bodyguard is—"

"Please, Rose," Schwartz said, "don't."

Stanley waved his hand, the smile gone. "Wait a second." His tanned face flushed red, and he smoothed the top of his shiny head as if he had hair. "I may not be a police detective, but I know why you're here."

He stopped as Harry came in and served the drinks and a bowl of vast cashews, which neither Rose nor Schwartz wanted. Stanley leaned toward them but Harry set the bowl on the table next to Rose.

It seemed to Schwartz that if Stanley was hiding anything very well, it was his having anything to hide. As Harry left the room, from somewhere hidden in the concrete leather walls the Benny Goodman Trio played "Chinatown," perhaps by chance, perhaps by the wit of Harry Lee.

"Terrific stuff, huh? Teddy Wilson—is that delicacy or what?" Stanley asked. Then he looked at Rose. "Listen, someone like me with a house like this and a bodyguard is someone who fears for his life because he came to this town forty-five years ago and played rough in property and development and won most of the time, but made a lot of enemies on the way."

"Rough?" Rose asked. "Is that your euphemism for 'illegal'? Is that why you've been in court every year you've been here?"

"No, only twenty times." Stanley smiled. "By your reckoning that would leave twenty-five spotless years.'' He picked up his glass of sherry, held it to the light, and slowly turned it. ''And those twenty times, I won; not guilty, I was judged not guilty. I've had twelve successful countersuits. Some of those people are tough guys; maybe one of them would like to see me dead. So I have a bodyguard.''

''How many people do you employ in the house?'' Schwartz asked, a question seemingly plucked from the air-conditioning or off the convoluted wall.

''I have three people from outside—Beth my cook, who comes when I have company, and two very sweet Guatemalan ladies who clean, and Harry, of course.''

Schwartz asked, ''Who lives in?''

''Just Harry. Why? What's all this?''

Schwartz put his hand across his shirt and rubbed his shoulder, holding back the wince. ''I don't know. Just looking for ideas, I suppose.'' Rose squinted at him from the better of her eyes. Stanley gave him a wink. Schwartz felt ambivalent about his own complicity.

Raising his glass, Stanley said, ''Rose, I feel bad. I feel, like you, that Abe was shot by mistake for me. I want to drink to his memory and our loss. He was a good guy.''

Rose pulled the glass from her mouth. A thin line of tomato juice ran to her chin. ''You hypocrite, Stanley. You hypocrite! You wept at his funeral and now you sit here toasting Abe, but you killed him!''

The accusation, balder than their host, embarrassed Schwartz; he looked at Stanley as a Roman would look at a plump prisoner as the first famished lion trotted into the arena.

Stanley had turned beefsteak-tomato red. He sipped his sherry, made a face, and rubbed his stomach. ''My ulcer was acting up, but still, I shouldn't have let Abe walk Maxi. I said he couldn't handle such a big dog. But Abe insisted. So how should I know this would be the one day in forty years someone would be gunning for me? I told Abe the dog was too big and there was too much traffic, but, Christ, could I say 'and, besides, you'll probably be assassinated'? Listen, Rose, Lenny," Stanley said, turning to Schwartz, "I told all this to the police in great detail. They haven't been around to question me again, so maybe that proves something? And, I'm ashamed to have to put it like this, my sending Abe out to be killed *instead of me* doesn't make any sense. You tell me, Lenny; you're the professional. Abe, he should rest in peace, is killed and the next day it's in the papers and on TV and the killer and whoever had the contract out *know* they didn't get me. So how does that save my neck? Tell me that?"

Stanley wiped his neck with a paper napkin, looked at the napkin, and shook his head. Then he stood and walked over toward Rose, whose hand went up as if to fend a blow. Stanley took the nut bowl and offered it to her. She coughed and shook her head and Stanley took a fistful of the cashews and brought the bowl over to Schwartz.

"So tell me," he said.

Schwartz took an inch-long cashew. Cashews were paisley-shaped, but Stanley and Rose wouldn't be very interested in that right now. "Yes, I agree, Stanley. If you were at risk, Abe's death would make no difference; you'd still be at risk."

Rose dabbed at her chin with a napkin. Her hand shook. "Maybe," she said in a low voice, "maybe, Stanley, you had Abe killed." She looked out toward the pool, shutting her eyes to the glare.

Stanley slowly shook his head and fell back into his chair. "Rose, that's just crazy. I don't kill people, even people I hate. And I liked Abe and Abe liked me. Jesus, Rose, you know that. You don't like me but Abe did. Abe was a nice guy."

"Nice? Nice?"Rose was pushing herself up on her cane. "He was wonderful, a real gentleman. You're not in the same class, you with your women and . . . Oh." The cane handle wobbled beneath her hand.

Schwartz went and put his arm around Rose, supporting and hugging her. "All right, Rose. It's all right. That's enough."

"Ah, Rose," Stanley said, getting to his feet again with much puffing. "Women? Well, I'm a single man and I don't see married women, so what's the—but okay, okay. As to Abe being nicer than me, fine. Sure, okay. But Rose, that has nothing to do with his death. Listen, you want the names I gave the police of people I think could have it in for me? You want them, Rose? Lenny, I'll give them to you."

Rose, still under Schwartz's arm, said, "Stanley, I really don't want anything from you, including information. I have my own sources. I, too, was a professional person. I *am* a thorough and professional researcher, and what *real* information is available on you, I'll find, I swear. I swear on Abe's dear memory."

Stanley said, "Good, all right, *azay mit glick*."

"I won't need luck," she said.

A gong sounded over Gene Krupa's heavy brushwork on "The Sheik of Araby."

"Lunch," said Stanley loudly. "Let's all go in and relax and have a nice lunch. Rose? Please?"

"Stanley, I'm sorry. I don't feel I can stay."

"Please," Stanley said.

Schwartz looked closely at Rose. The color had gone from her face under small clear beads of sweat, and she shifted on her feet as if trying to stir up circulation. Her legs were more strongly blotched than usual. "Stanley, I think Rose should really go home and rest now."

"Of course. Of course, if she . . . Rose, forgive me if I've said anything . . ."

Schwartz was shaking his head and winking at Stanley as they began to walk.

In the grand gloom of the hallway, Stanley told Harry, standing in a doorway, to hold lunch. "No," he added, "we'll eat in a minute—you, Beth, and me."

The last Schwartz heard from the palazzo hi-fi was the trio swinging into "Tiger Rag," which reminded him he certainly had not held that tiger last night; that is, he'd certainly held that tiger yet hadn't held himself from—her fearful symmetry. And, of course, she would have given him that contact number for Roberto without all her clawing or his, alas, pawing.

"Good-bye," Rose said to Stanley as Schwartz helped her into the car. "I'm sorry to have spoiled your lunch."

"No, no," Stanley said. "Just rest and be well, Rose."

As he walked around to Schwartz's side, he said, "Listen, Lenny, there were some things I couldn't say in front of her, you know? Look, if you're free tomorrow, we could . . . You like racing? I'll take you to the track, we can talk privately, you can cross-examine me, we'll enjoy ourselves. Call me later on it."

Rose held her tears until Stanley Zeigler's wrought-iron gates closed behind them. Then she cried in three loud sobs for about thirty seconds, after which she blew her nose, said "Oh, dear" to Schwartz's "There, there," and then sat silent.

As they came back onto Collins Avenue, Rose blew her nose again and said, "I blew it. I'm sorry, Lenny. You told me not to but I lost my temper and ruined everything."

Schwartz shook his head and smiled. "On the contrary, you were perfect. We were a great hard-soft team back there."

"You mean you *knew* I'd be? Despite your warnings I'd . . . I think I should be angry with you."

"I didn't know at first, but I generally find it's most useful when people are just themselves, however complicated and contradictory that is."

Rose gave Schwartz's arm a feathery punch. "So we're such a great team, what did we find out about Stanley?"

"Stanley was just himself."

"Meaning you think he was telling the truth?"

"Yup, but I'm keeping an open mind on this. I wish you would, Rose."

"All right. You're right: I promise to stick to the facts I can find about Stanley."

"About Stanley—and *Abe*."

"Abe? I don't . . . Yes, of course. What do we do now?"

"Now, as any police team would do, we go have a nice lunch at—" Schwartz stopped before saying "the Villa Deli," a favorite of the Miami Beach police, as Linda told him when their appetites had risen to food. And if Linda should be there . . . No, Rose had problems enough without his burning infidelity.

"A nice lunch at Wolfie's," he said. "Where else?"

Rose said, "The Villa Deli is good."

"That was really funny, Rose, your remark about 'lunching out there on the Grand Canal,' " he said, driving to Wolfie's.

C H A P T E R 3

Halfway across the paddock walk, just when he'd calmed down, Roberto Cruz looked over to the saddling stalls and his face began to swell. He pulled at the sleeve of his brother-in-law's bright yellow blazer. "Jaime, oh shit, look at the shine on the bitch!"

The girls were bringing up the rear, so Jaime did a slow, casual look around at the women strolling or seated in the paddock gardens.

"No, asshole, the horse, Colombian Dancer, the filly!"

Jaime stood on tiptoes and brought up his field glasses. "Could be some other horse. The Dancer will be all right. Stay cool."

"You tell that filly to fockin' stay cool, you want something cool around here!" Cruz said, taking off his sunglasses to wipe the sweat from his eyes.

Alva and Carmen came up to the men. Alva asked, "Are you starting again? Jesus Christ, Roberto, wasn't that scene in the Turf Club enough?"

"Oh, sure, I'm supposed to keep quiet when I win on the

first two races and we got the fockin' two-hundred-dollar bottle
of champagne open on the table and *then* Jaime says he forgot
to bet the daily double!''

Jaime looked down at his shoes, yellow and white in a
checker weave.

Carmen said, ''Come on, Berto, be nice. You won fifteen
hundred anyway, and me and Jaime paid for lunch.''

''I won fifteen hundred and your husband the jerk lost me
thirty-six grand. Thirty-six thousand dollars,'' Cruz repeated
slowly, replacing his sunglasses.

''Not that much,'' Jaime said, '' 'cause you'd gotta pay
tax, they take it out for the big wins.''

Cruz stopped walking again. ''They don't; it's gotta be
three hundred times more than the bet, jerkoff. Still,what's
thirty, forty grand compared to losing two million, right?''

Alva stamped a high heel into the ground and rocked on
her ankle. ''Damn it, enough, Roberto! We come out to Hialeah to have a nice time and you fuck it up. You want to make
sure your damn bets are placed right? Do it yourself.''

She was breathing hard, chin forward. Her necklace, dia-
monds spelling ''Alva,'' jiggled with the emotion.

''Oh sure,'' Cruz said, less loudly, ''I got to do everything
myself. You want something, I got to do it. *I* got to make big
contributions so that *you* get to sit your fat ass in a good box
back there in with all the old Florida money.''

Alva tugged down on the short skirt of her white suit and
glanced at a passersby. ''You think my ass is too fat?'' she asked
Roberto.

Carmen said, ''Her ass isn't fat.''

''She's got a great ass,'' said Jaime helpfully.

''Shut up, Jaime,'' growled Cruz. ''Alva, your ass is okay,
it's nice. Now let's go. I'm the owner: I'm supposed to show
up at the saddling, for Christ's sake.''

When they came through to stall five, the trainer was wet with the effort of trying to calm Colombian Dancer. He held the reins high up to the bridle, stroking the horse's cheek while Willie the stableboy tried an occasional dab with a towel at her lathered flanks. The trainer dropped one hand off the reins to tip his straw hat to the owner, his lady, his sister, and her husband. The jockey, Luis Perez, lifted his head to Cruz and continued swaying, spread-legged, refusing to notice Colombian Dancer until he had to mount her.

"Shit, Jeff," Cruz said to his trainer, "think she'll go?"

The filly rolled her eyes, raised her head, and swung around. Jaime hopped backward and went to the girls at the railing. Cruz looked down at the stain of horse sweat across the jacket of his light brown linen suit.

"Mucho calor, señor," said Willie.

The trainer swung the horse around and brought her forward a few steps. "She did this at Calder, remember? I think we should let her run it out. Luis won't let her do anything silly."

From the corner of his eye Cruz thought he saw Luis drop spit softly between his boots. He knew Jeff was right but he thought, Goddamn it—he hated paying a top jockey to exercise a horse, to be a fucking horse doctor.

Cruz came directly in front of Colombian Dancer. *"Oyez,* girl, *oyez, chica,"* he said, speaking almost into her nostril. *"Qué passó, ay?"*

For a moment she focused on Cruz and relaxed, her ears pricked. Then she wanted to rear, so that he had to step back as Jeff stepped in and pulled down hard. She started kicking back. Willie jumped away lightly. Luis Perez turned, hands still on his hips, and took a few deliberate steps.

Cruz saw the bright jackets of the outriders coming through

the clubhouse from the track. "Put on the saddle, Jeff," he said.
A small crowd stood by the railing to study the horses.

Cruz went to his jockey. "You all set, Luis?"

Perez scratched at the back of his knee with his riding crop.
"All set, sir," he said without looking up.

"What you think?"

"She's gone spooky. Give her the outing so it don't get to
be a habit. I'll see what she's up to before we even get to the
gate. Sorry. One of those days."

Cruz nodded. One of those days, he thought. He thought
Luis didn't know the half of it. Thirty-six Gs, to drop thirty-six
Gs because Jaime couldn't walk two hundred yards to the fifty-
dollar minimum window without sizing up everything in skirts
and forgetting the daily fucking double. He walked back to the
railing. He didn't want to hear any wisecracks from the crowd.

"Roberto, Jesus, she's foaming at the mouth now!" Jaime
said.

Before Cruz could speak, Carmen elbowed her husband in
the side. "Jaime, give Berto a break, will you please? Even
these people watching don't say it so loud. It's so obvious, you
know? A little fucking *tone*, Jaime. A little *tone*, you know what
I mean?"

"You listen to my sister, moron," Cruz said to Jaime, and
he watched the sad business of his filly being saddled up.

She tried to buck, to rear, to throw her head, but Jeff kept
her in small circles before the stall, reversing the recircling, while
Willie threw on the saddle and tied the cinch. Then Luis jumped
on without checking and the saddle slipped and Luis jumped
off with a disgusted expression. Then Jeff undid the buckle and
pulled the cinch three inches tighter when the filly wasn't blow-
ing out. Cruz saw the sweat come off her in a heavy spray.

Then he saw the other horses walk off dry, not, he thought,

gone nuts. They allowed their owners a little pride, a little dignity, for fuck's sake. Behind him a loud voice said, "Now here's a certain loser, Las Palmas Farms, used to be Wild Palms Stables, not a bad stable and sired by King of Colombia, a big winner—Flamingo Stakes and the Turf Cup—and out of Carmen Dancer, another good runner. And you'd find in the *Daily Racing Form* it had a pretty good record. So if you didn't actually come out here and see this, you might be tempted. Will you look at that sweat!"

Cruz heard another voice ask, "Is the horse sick?" He froze.

Alva put her arm around his waist. "Here comes the cobra face again. *Now* what is it?"

The first voice said, "Not sick, Lenny, just so crazy nervous that all the energy's gone. She'll get to the starting gate exhausted, plotzing."

Then the second voice said, "It's wonderful out here, the vine covering these stalls. What is it?"

"Orange trumpet, I think," said the first voice.

A third voice said, "Excuse me, not orange trumpet."

"What then?" asked the first voice.

The third voice said, "I don't know, but I know those aren't trumpets up there. Flowers like little orange fingers, maybe. Like fingers sticking out."

"Thanks. Well, what horse does look good to you, Stanley?" asked the second voice.

Alva was staring at Cruz. He shook off her arm. When he turned, his nostrils were flared and his forehead seemed to roll out over bulging eyes.

Lenny Schwartz was as he remembered him. Short, wiry, with dark kinky hair curled back of his ears and those same quick flaky eyes. He was wearing a loud orange and blue and green tropical shirt and was staring back at him.

Cruz lifted his head at two bodyguards, Paco and Jesus, who moved in to a few feet behind Schwartz.

"Hello, Roberto. I'm glad I bumped into you."

"You make any moves, Schwartz, you're in trouble."

"Me? All I want is to talk to you for a few minutes. I left that message yesterday. Didn't you get it?"

Jaime came up to the railing pointing across at Schwartz.

"I got it," Cruz said. "How'd you get that number?"

"I had to work for it," said Schwartz.

"Yeah," Jaime said, smiling. "It's Schwartz the hymie copper from hymietown."

Schwartz turned to the very red-faced man in a navy-blue blazer next to him. "Stanley, I'm not going to introduce you to these sportsmen. I'll see you back at your box."

When the man walked off, Schwartz turned back to Cruz. "Roberto, how come you end up with a flunky that still says 'copper'? No one has said 'copper' since a bad movie in 1957. I didn't like Jaime in New York; I still don't down here in Jaimetown. Did he sell you that horse, Roberto?"

Cruz's face deflated. He laughed. "That's about the only fockin' thing he hasn't done to me today." He looked at the women and lifted his head. "Take a walk, girls."

The women gave Schwartz quick, sour looks and took a walk with pointed-toed high heels polka-dotted with mud.

"What you staring at, Schwartz?" Jaime asked, leaning over the rail.

"I thought you might want to introduce me to the ladies."

"Up yours. You didn't want us to meet the old fat guy," Jaime said. He rolled a toothpick with his tongue across his bottom lip.

Schwartz looked down into his race program. "Well, I know Roberto likes his privacy."

Jaime said, "And we like our women kept away from police scum."

Cruz put his hand on Jaime's shoulder and pulled him back. "Go watch the filly in the ring, Jaime."

Jaime pulled up the double Windsor knot of his necktie, gave Schwartz a look, ran his hands over the side streaks of his hair, and left.

Cruz came close to Schwartz across the railing and turned his head away to watch the horse wind through the ring and out between the crowd. He said, "You're right, I like my privacy. I like things real quiet, too. What do you like, Schwartz?"

Schwartz kept looking down into the program. "I like my life."

"Yeah? Okay, we'll talk. Next couple of days. Someone will call."

"Good," Schwartz said. "Terrific track here, very nice. It's too bad about your horse."

Cruz shrugged. "An unlucky day. She's not so bad. Nothing like her sire, though. That was one fockin' fast horse."

Schwartz looked up from the program. "Is King of Colombia your stallion?"

Cruz shook his head. "I wish. I don't even have a little piece of that."

Schwartz said, "Never mind, Roberto. Cocaine's the real king of Colombia and you've got a big piece of that."

Without looking at Schwartz, Cruz walked away to watch his horse lose the third race of the day at Hialeah. He thought Schwartz was the same cool cocky bastard.

Schwartz continued to lean against the railing and then, when his legs stopped trembling, walked off.

CHAPTER 4

Stanley Zeigler had been bois-
terous and intimate and charming until the chance meeting with
Roberto Cruz. Afterward, his loudness was a sound barrier that
Schwartz finally had to break.

It was after the seventh race, when a track attendant had
stirred the flamingos to flight. Up they'd gone in a flapping
flurry, beating so hard the air could be heard whistling and
creaking across the lake. Up and up, hundreds and hundreds
in a slow pink spiral against the milk-blue clouds until, at the
point they seemed massed to fly free, down they broke, a ragged
pink cloud raining to earth where they squawked and stalked
each other or settled to cleaning their feathers with beaks like
bent black clipping shears.

Stanley said, "Not bad, huh?"

"Very nice, if a bit artificial," Schwartz said. "Like you,
if you'll pardon my saying so, since the third race. What's bothering you, Stanley?"

Stanley removed the seven-inch unsmoked Corona Corona
from his mouth, rolled it in his fingers, and said, "Three quar-

ters of the guys here still smoke cigars, you notice? Half the old ones have been ordered not to but some of them, like me, still need the heft of it, some weight, the taste. Sure, I could mouth smaller, cheaper cigars, but I'd lose the heft, you know? I throw away three of these a day. An expensive but relatively harmless habit now. The guy you talked to over at the saddling stalls? He's been pointed out to me. Cruz, big drug racketeer. He should be shot. I don't like thinking you're on the make, you know, on the payroll.''

Schwartz turned his tub chair in toward Stanley's. ''I'm not, Stanley. I once did something bad—greedy and bad—and I'm trying to clear the last of it now, end it. I don't know why I'm telling you. I'm supposed to be suspicious of you, on Rose's behalf, but I'm not finding it so easy.''

Stanley slapped a heavy hand onto the back of Schwartz's. ''Well, well, well. You're okay, a *mensch*.'' He nodded for a few moments, put the cigar in his mouth, and took it out again. ''Rose Fine has this picture of Abe as the perfect man. She wouldn't admit it, but I think she had like a schoolgirl crush on Abe. Maybe she wasn't even aware of it. So what can you do? We're all strange. But I meant what I said: I liked Abe. He was a nice guy, but not perfect, not, anyway, what Rose thought. Look, he had a girlfriend. It didn't bother me, of course, but Abe was a very stiff sort of character. The one time I brought it up, he denied it, so I let it drop.''

''How did you know he did?''

''I saw her, bumped into him with her once, a few years ago down at that stone-crab restaurant on Key Biscayne. He went gray as an old fedora and said she was his broker. Can you imagine? This was a looker, dressed to show it, and at least thirty years younger than Abe. I was with them maybe two minutes but I knew the sort of brokering she was doing with Abe. After that, I didn't see them. Abe probably laid low, no pun intended. I remember he said she was Sally? Maybe Mary; I don't remember. But you know who might? You ask some longtime staff at the Marlowe Court, I'll bet you could find something.''

Schwartz asked, ''Did you tell this to the police?''

''No. They didn't ask, so I didn't think it was—to tell you the truth, Lenny, I didn't want Rose possibly learning about it. What good would it do?''

''You like her.''

''Yeah, sure. She's bright and funny. I wish she liked me.''

''She's bright, yes. I think she's going to find out the worst about you, like she says,'' Schwartz said, smiling, watching Stanley's eyes. ''But maybe that's because you insist on pretending to be a tough guy.''

Stanley shook his head and put the cigar in. ''I may not be so tough, but compared to Abe, it's a hundred to one they meant to bump *me* off.''

''So why isn't Harry Lee here with us?''

Stanley rolled the cigar, still in his mouth, between two fingers. ''What do I need with Harry when I'm at the track with a big shot from the New York police? Which reminds me, Harry will be back with the car. If you want to beat the rush, we should go now.''

They beat it, even with Stanley stopping to pick up ''just one more great kosher hot dog they got downstairs,'' and when, in front of his home, Stanley asked Schwartz in for a drink and Schwartz said he couldn't, Stanley insisted he let Harry drive him down to the Neptune Plaza.

Schwartz sat up front. ''You drive well,'' he said. ''Do you like being a chauffeur?''

Harry nodded. ''I like my work; Mr. Stanley's the best employer I've ever had.''

The high white Rolls rolled quietly down Pine Tree Drive.

"Tell me something about yourself, Harry."

Harry kept his eyes on the road. "Here's something: I don't talk about myself."

"All right, tell me something about Stanley. Do you think Abe could have been killed by mistake for Stanley?"

Harry turned off Twenty-third onto Collins. "That's a two-part question, sir. I wouldn't know why Abe Zeigler was killed. I do know he wasn't mistaken for Mr. Stanley. Mr. Stanley likes to talk tough but he's . . . he's a pussycat."

The car drew into the Neptune Plaza drive and stopped.

"Thank you for the ride and your opinions." Schwartz opened the door. "Harry, do you have any sort of a . . . ? What I mean is a—"

"Eighteen years ago I did two for unarmed robbery. That's all. That's what you mean, isn't it?"

"Yes, thanks. I suppose Stanley knows."

Harry's placidity cracked in a grin. "I have to keep him from bragging about it to his friends." He gave Schwartz a short wave as he drove off.

At the desk Schwartz picked up a message envelope. It was from Linda and said: "COMING TO *GET* YOU."

He could flee; he could barricade his door. He could call the police—yes, he could call Linda.

He went up to his room and called Karen.

"Fine," she said. "How are you getting on?"

He told her of Rose, of Stanley, of Roberto and Jaime at Hialeah, even of strong and mainly silent Harry Lee. He didn't mention Linda because Karen wouldn't . . . Karen would understand immediately. He didn't understand, and he felt, with the relief of returning dignity, that *he* needed to understand, first.

"So maybe," he said, "I can wrap up this Cruz thing in the next few days. What I can do for Rose in that time, I don't know. Not much, I think."

Karen asked, "Are you getting help from the police down there?"

"Why shouldn't they help me? I mean, no, what I'm actually getting"—here, a few steamy images of what he'd already been getting fogged his brain—"is a sort of, you know, friendly cooperation, up to a point, that is."

Karen remarked on his attention to ambiguous detail. But she understood: that was the nature of his occupation, or did she mean his preoccupation? Then she said, "I miss you."

"I miss you, Karen. I miss you, I really do." And saying it, he really did, very much, with a sort of sob swallowing that made his "Good-bye, darling" a near yodel.

But no sooner had he put down the phone than his conscience, always a sucker for guilty wordplay, pointed out that he did in all good faith miss Karen—missed by the distance between a lie and truth.

Schwartz was thinking of a crushing rebuttal to himself when there came an athletic knocking on the door. When he opened it, the friendly, cooperative police officer looked at his long face and said, "Hi. Don't you like me anymore or are you feeling remorse because you wouldn't really, *really* tie me up?"

She was wearing jeans and a short-sleeve button-down shirt and looked funny and pretty and so concerned that Schwartz felt his sadness lift. He warned it down, pecked Linda's cheek (was he supposed to shake her hand after that battle of appetites? Shaking her hand might be the signal for a few preliminary body slams) and he directed her to the armchair in a neutral corner whose arm, were there some charity, should have been in a sling. He turned the weakened desk chair toward her and sat down.

"I can't," he began.

"Yes," Linda said, "I know. I went nuts the other night. I got into some sort of lonely, competitive desire frenzy and pulled you in. Date rape. Worse. I spent a pretty miserable yesterday, I can tell you, hombre."

Schwartz waved his finger in a downbeat, conductor of his own honor. "I'm not trying to get off that hook. I frenzied with you plenty, half the two it took, who were taken. But no more. I'm married and so that was very bad."

Linda nodded. "Right, right. But there are still two questions. Please?"

"Of course."

"My health's fine. How's your health?"

Schwartz looked at her.

"Your blood?" she asked.

"Ah? Oh, yes, oh, God, yes. I'm so old-fashioned, or do I mean just old, I guess, that I . . . Yes, my blood's as good as recent medical science, say that of two months past, can guarantee. And since then I've been with no one but my wife."

"Whose health . . . ?" Linda said, waiting and dropping her eyes.

"What? Wait a minute here. Damn!" Schwartz was up walking to the window. "I'm sorry. That was very rude. I'm not used . . . She's healthy." He looked at the clouds piling to the southeast. "I hope your second question is easier than that."

"Maybe not. Do you want to go for a run on the beach with me now?"

Schwartz turned back to Linda. "I don't think there's much point—"

"I mean," she interrupted, "will you give me the chance

to show you that two nights ago was what I said it was and is over?'' She picked up her tote bag and pointed to the bathroom door, head tipped in question.

He thought that if she came out naked, he could simply leave the room. "All right, I'll have my run. Go ahead and change.''

When he heard the door shut, he called, "And then I'll change in the bathroom after you change," just to make sure she understood.

He needn't have. In a few minutes she came out dressed to run. She wore a slinky basic black, a black so down and basic that . . . that Schwartz quickly locked the bathroom door behind him and changed into running shorts and an excessively warm but stained and shapeless antifrenzy T-shirt. His hand locked on the doorknob as it came to him how Linda could now be *out there* completely naked, waiting for him in his easy-to-strip-off, rip-off running clothes with nowhere to run—she could block his getaway into the hall. He wondered how he'd handle this.

He needn't have. Linda was ready to run, carrying her bag to show she wouldn't be returning here to change. To change everything, again. Was he being too hard? No, he thought in the slow elevator down, he was avoiding all, or most, of that.

But once they started to run on the beach, his head stopped lecturing him on the wrongness of it all; that is, stopped sexually exciting him, and for Linda there seemed no competitive thrust. It was only the enjoyment of moving through the first half mile warming up, stretching out, then, in the middle, feeling the rhythm of the run through the swing of shoulder and hip and the hit of toe and front of foot that sprang back through ankle, calf, and thigh. They'd gone south to the end of the beach, turned at the rocks piled at Government Cut, and in the final half mile had found the second wind, much finer, richer than the first, in which their strides lengthened and their veins seemed charged so that wanting to run faster translated into motion with a weightlessness that felt like flying on earth, that had left them back at Seventeenth Street shaking their heads, silent and smiling.

He stood by the yellow Chevy convertible as she started the motor.

"How's the quest going?" she asked.

Schwartz said, "I called and asked politely, but what helped was bumping into the man at Hialeah, this afternoon."

"That's good. You like horse racing?"

"No, not really. I was there with a distant relative, Stanley." Schwartz tapped the side of the car. "Linda? I'd like to pick your brain about something."

"You'll have to pick some other time. I'm sticky and I am *going home* to change." She backed the car.

"What about dinner tonight?"

"I can't do dinner, thanks. I could meet you later, at about eleven." She pulled the car forward into the street and stopped.

"Sure, great. Where?"

"Why not South Beach? The Edison usually has good music, if you like."

"Sounds good. The Edison at eleven."

She pulled away slowly. "I take it you want to talk professionally."

"Absolutely," he said, watching her drive off.

Fifteen minutes later, looking into his bathroom mirror, shaving, Schwartz thought of the run on the beach and such tender desire for Linda flooded his stomach and upper chest that he cut his chin. He watched the pale line turn red and the blood thicken into one big drop. As he lifted his chin the blood ran down his neck.

If this were true feeling, he'd better cut his ties and cut his losses. He'd better cut his throat.

He washed the blood off. By the time he finished shaving, his chin and neck were red again. He stepped into the shower and turned on the cold tap, which ran its usual Okeechobee-mud lukewarm. Well, the algae in the water might clot his blood, or eat it off.

He felt that what he felt for Linda was masturbation. What could he mean by that? He turned to let the water silt his back. He could mean that he was a cop and she was a cop, that he liked to run and she did, that she was beautiful and . . . Yes, he was beautiful, he thought. So it was hetero-projection, Narcissus looking into the pool and seeing the White Rock girl.

And now he felt better, having reduced his infatuation to something like an Orange Crush, wholly in love with Karen, his wife who didn't like running and wasn't a policeperson.

He dried himself, stuck toilet paper on the oozing chin, and dressed, aware of how immature it was to fall in love with someone for her running, how short term and short of breath that would become. Yet how did that sonnet run:

> Love is not love
> Which falters when the run becomes a walk,
> Or bends with rheumatism to remove—

Schwartz was reminded by this to call Rose at the Marlowe Court. She told him her friends at the Dade County Library were being very helpful, and, no, with many thanks just the same, she couldn't come out to dinner with him because she had a pile of photocopy to read through, and besides, she'd eaten supper earlier. He in his turn, suppressing news of his day at the races with Stanley, told her he was following some leads and said he'd call tomorrow.

Where should he eat? He wasn't hungry. In the desk with one broken leg (what had they done? when would the hotel find out and bill him?) next to his .38, whose custom-fitted safety Linda had yet to see—he meant *had not seen*; he really should stop thinking about her—he found Linda's home address and phone number written on the card she'd given him that first night in the Riptide Bar, how many weeks ago? Three days ago.

He looked at the card then turned on the radio and heard that tropical storm Melvin was winding itself up 1200 miles southeast in the Caribbean, not yet a hurricane, and would probably blow out, but the storm watch was on. He turned the dial. Salsa music. Roberto could have him killed here so easily. Schwartz saw his own body falling slowly, slowly down into the ocean, not ripped by great sharks but snapped at by snappers, *fressed* by small fry until he hit bottom, a completely *gefilted* Schwartz.

He looked in the mirror before going out. He didn't look scared: he looked tough and semitropical, except for the piece of toilet paper hanging from his chin. He managed to roll it off without breaking open the cut.

Downstairs, he saw the night porter, the night watchman, and the repairman, all the same middle-aged man in a T-shirt sitting on a stool. He walked over.

"Excuse me. Have you heard of an apartment house or condo block in Miami called Viscaya Heights?"

The man thought and shook his head. "No, *no sé*. Maybe ask Jorge, that young man at the desk. And mister, you know you are bleeding in your chin?"

Schwartz thanked him, pressed his handkerchief to his chin, and asked the same question at the desk.

Jorge's eyebrows went up. "Yeah, a cool place, down the end of Brickell. I wouldn't mind living there. Someday. Costs a bomb, like half a million for one bedroom."

"Thanks," Schwartz said, giving him a five-dollar bill for no reason he let himself think of. He looked into a mirrored pillar; the blood had congealed to a fragile crust. Dinnertime. He wasn't hungry.

He walked up Collins and went into the Riptide Bar. Except for a young couple much too smart for it, the bar was the same set with the same lot of extras and bit players. And why wasn't he one of them? He smiled a crooked smile. Because he was an *ex*-crooked cop at the end of his crooked mile? Because he could and they couldn't tell, before the end of its first bar, the Ravel quartet? And wasn't his *need* to tell it, his need to *tell* it, the clearest sign that he fit right in here with the losers and braggart nebbishes, here where watered drinks would be an improvement?

The man across the bar well was telling the bartender, "Why, of course guns are natural. What they are, see, is just the best way to throw stones."

Sure, Schwartz replied in his head. And following that logic, plutonium and tritium are natural. And, bartender, give that man a whiskey and heavy water, on me. And good night.

"Good night," Schwartz said, leaving the bar. Outside, he looked into Wolfie's and decided he really wasn't hungry. He walked down by the Gaiety Burlesque and stopped. The poster said tonight's live show starred Busty LaFoxe. The photo showed a naked woman cupping her abnormally large breasts. She could not contain them. They spilled over, covering the back of her hands. Linda had large breasts, normally large— large, he supposed, especially for a body-building athlete. Karen's breasts were large. He wondered if he'd do less damage if he'd been another sleazey customer of this establishment, a supporter of pornography rather than a head pro-feminist who fucked around?

It was sad. He sighed and walked down Collins. People

were sitting out here on the humbler side of the street on small porches and patios, on chairs of solid plastic or chairs of aluminum tubes with plastic strapping. Most of the people were old, talking in English, Spanish, Yiddish, or Russian, or reading under humming neon lighting with newspapers and books up to their eyes. One man in a Cubs hat held a paperback out at the end of his straight arm as he might have held a stereopticon back in his childhood. Some of the old people had dozed off, chins down or heads tipped to the side, their day as done as yesterday.

By the time Schwartz reached Ocean Drive he himself felt eighty-four years old and decided to go into the spruced bar of the Leslie for a drink. Three Bombay gin and tonics later he came out feeling his forty-two years, fuzzy and still sad.

Why sad? There was the bright half-moon that sailed the clouds over the palms, There was the ocean shining like dark silk. And here was Miami Beach. He swung his arm toward the pastel buildings. This place should cheer him: it was a city made of Necco Wafers. He liked that. That was pretty good, "Necco Wafers." He'd tell that to Karen—Linda, he meant. It was ten o'clock. He wasn't hungry. The people he passed looked happy, men and women, women and women, men and men arm in arm. They all looked like reasonable couples, honest with each other.

At the signboard outside the Edison, Schwartz began to smile. It read FOR TWO NIGHTS ONLY—THE LEGENDARY TOMMY FLANAGAN.

He went in and stood, waiting to be seated, listening to Flanagan's solo on "You'd Be So Nice to Come Home To." "Very true," Schwartz said under his breath. The maitresse d' showed him to a table. A waitress asked in a whisper what he'd like.

"I'm very hungry."

They didn't do food after 9:30, but he got a bowl of peanuts with his Bombay gin on the rocks. He watched Flanagan's duo partner, a tall very young looking man, lean into his solo with concentration and then arch away, head back from the baroque curl at the top of his double bass. He seemed to Schwartz to be trying too hard, an attempt to match the master he accompanied. How could an ordinary police officer live in Viscaya Heights? The duo was playing the melody line. Flanagan's head showed over the piano, white fringed around his *café con leche* dome. His playing was intricate and poignant. Karen would be so nice to come home to. Schwartz joined the applause as the duo went off for its break.

Schwartz ate two peanuts and found he wasn't hungry. Something was wrong. Even if that cornice had fallen of its own decrepitude, there was still the sidewalk's malicious limousine. And then there'd been nothing. What linked with that? It was twenty past ten, Friday night. Where would he be? Schwartz wondered, going to the pay phone at the end of the bar.

He put in a quarter, dialed the number with the reverse-charge code, and asked if a call would be accepted from Mr. Schwartz. Then he heard Kitty Gallagher say, "Sure, yes," and "Hello, Lenny? Wait, here's Tom. Tom, come on! All you have to do is reach over—"

"Lenny? Where the hell are you? You throwing a party?"

"Hello, Tom. No, it's a place, a club. Tom, who'd you tell down here that I was coming?"

"I spoke to Pearlman, the chief, told him you were coming down on private business but we'd appreciate any assistance he could give, if you asked. Yeah, that's it. Why?"

"Nothing. Just some confusion on my part."

"Oh, well, sounds like business as usual. You're sorely missed in the department, so hurry up and get killed, or even better, sort it out and get back here," Tom said. "That was just my little joke; Kitty's set to bring out the rolling pin."

"Tom, what do you think of Pearlman?"

"Dave Pearlman's a good man, Lenny. Clean as a whistle."

"All right then, thanks. 'Bye-bye." Schwartz hung up thinking of police whistles: under the shiny chrome, white saliva and black crud.

He sat down and kept drinking the gin on the rocks because he wasn't hungry. Everyone in the Edison seemed beautiful, handsome. But would Linda's *mind* be so nice to come home to? Didn't she have too nice a home to come home to, too? The gin seemed very nourishing.

The second set began. Schwartz finger-bopped the table to Flanagan's towering, fluorescent runs on "Poinciana." Then Linda was sitting down, sliding her chair next to him.

"How are you?" she whispered, leaning.

She smelled of frangipani. There were big pink cabbage roses printed on her tight-wrapped black chintz dress.

"Starving," Schwartz said, eating a peanut.

Linda drank white wine and listened to the music. Schwartz looked at her. Her thumb hit silently against her forefinger on the two and four beats, so that was in her favor. What the hell was he weighing up?

A bartender appeared at the table and bent over Linda, who hugged him. "Linda, baby, you are looking *so* beautiful, hon," he said. "Just had to tell you. Got to fly back to the bar. 'Bye, baybeee!"

Schwartz thought of telling Linda the story of the man who goes into the New York dive in the thirties and is amazed to see the two big Arts, Rubinstein and Schnabel, sitting in a booth. "Maestros," he asks, "what are you doing here?" And Rubinstein, pointing to Tatum being led onto the bandstand, says, "We've come to hear *that* Art; he plays the piano much better than we do." Yes, that would be a nice little culture test for Linda. He put down his glass. He was a shit to think of such things.

"Poinciana?" Linda asked.

He nodded. So she knew it, even in the improvisation. Jesus, what was wrong with him! All she was doing was being herself. Her very beautiful and musically knowledgeable self. Did she know the lyrics went, "Poinciana, your branches speak to me of love"?

In the applause she asked if he'd been drinking. When he said he had but that wasn't a problem, she said, "Wait," got up, and went out through the swinging doors back near the pay phone.

Yes, the telephone. What had he meant to ask?

Linda came back with a sandwich and potato salad on a plate and a fork and napkin. Schwartz ate while the duo played minor-key blues—fast, dark, and allusive, and he looked at Linda until she turned and asked, "What is it?"

He leaned close to her and whispered, "Thanks for the turkey sandwich. How do you get to live at so fancy an address on a policewoman's pay?"

"That isn't your business," she said calmly.

"Correct."

She looked up at the musicians on stage behind the bar. Then she looked back again at Schwartz. "My parents gave me the down payment. They said they might as well give me an inheritance when I needed it. After my divorce, they didn't want me living someplace where they'd worry." She looked down at her hand on the table. "Retired doctors, remember? Not poor. Is that all right, nosy?"

"I should have figured it out. I'm sorry, Linda," Schwartz

said, looking for her eye. "I didn't think of it because, I suppose, I want to think the worst of you so that I don't . . . to keep from . . ."

"Don't worry about it," she said, and put her elbow on the table and her cheek into the palm of her hand and shook her head.

Schwartz said, "I'm sorry."

She said, "I don't understand why we had to specially meet for this."

"No, not this," he whispered. "After this number, let's go."

He touched her hand on the table. Just that, just a touch saying sorry, an end to innuendo. Linda was a colleague from whom he wanted assistance. Flanagan was playing "The Lamp Is Low." Whether she knew it came from the Ravel pavane meant nothing. Schwartz motioned for the bill.

When they were outside, he took a deep breath of the warm ocean air and told Linda he would have been drunk but for the sandwich. They crossed Ocean Drive and sat on the park wall, backs to the beach.

"Look at those buildings," he said. "A city made of Necco Wafers."

"What's that?"

"They were—maybe they don't make them anymore. They were little . . . Nothing, really. I wanted to see you about a case, the murder of an old man named Abe Zeigler, probably a professional job, a few weeks ago?"

Linda ran her hand through the back of her hair. "Yes, I know about it. I'm not on it but a friend is. What's your interest?"

"He was vaguely related to me, though I didn't know him. An aunt of mine here in the beach was very close to him and asked my help. And I've said yes, whatever that means. So.

Any information you could pass on?'' Schwartz felt calmer,
talking like this. The rest of it was nonsense.

''I don't know more, probably, then you already know.
There's another relative, isn't there?''

''Stanley Zeigler.''

''Yes.'' She nodded. ''He seemed a likelier victim, I remember my friend saying. And there were no witnesses coming
forward and a good chance there were none. That's about it.''

Schwartz swung the heel of his loafer back onto the stone.
''And nothing's turned up in the victim's past, or the cousin's?''

Linda stood and smoothed the back of her dress. ''Not as
far as I know. I suppose the case team is still digging.''

Yes, Schwartz said. He walked along with Linda, wondering if they now looked to others like honest and reasonable people? They were, now. He said he hadn't any hunches more than
that the key seemed to *have* to lie in one or both of the cousins'
pasts.

Linda shrugged. ''There are some pretty crazed hit men
down here, junkies working for bargain prices, and wrong vic-
tims have been known, so even your sensible hunch could be
wrong.''

They stopped at Linda's car. The half-moon was high,
green white, and tilted.

''Thanks, Linda. If you hear anything else, I'd appreciate—''

She broke in. ''Up to a point. This *is* an ongoing investigation.''

He nodded and closed his eyes, feeling tired, and accepted
the lift to his hotel.

When she stopped the car to let him out, she leaned to kiss
his cheek and he was kissing her, sleepy, mouth on open half-
moon mouth, honestly but not reasonably like colleagues.

Going into his hotel with her, he saw the sleepy, lopsided moon. In the elevator his head fell down onto her hair. Tilted sleepy. Half-moon, half head.

Half-aware of the tote bag she'd brought up, Schwartz saw it wasn't a bag of tricks. Linda came out of the bathroom and slipped under the covers next to him. And what was it, he asked his drowsy self, that they were doing? Was it honest to call it making love, this slow gentle holding, these enfoldings, a somnolent sliding so that he looked into her long, half-closed eyes? It wasn't reasonable to call it merely lust. It seemed he didn't stop but slowly slid himself in her to sleep.

He dreamed of a slow turning and wrapping. Was it, he dreamed, a dream of a dream?

Schwartz opened his eyes. It was still dark. He couldn't move. He was handcuffed, tied up, and tied down. He was wide-awake and frightened.

"Shhh," said Linda, rising as a black shape from the bottom of the bed. On her knees she straddled him and said, "Don't be afraid. This won't hurt."

It didn't.

C H A P T E R 5

The pain in his head felt like a hangover, but Schwartz knew it was his conscience beating his brains out. When he'd first woken, he hadn't felt it. There'd been no sign of Linda, no signs of the ties that bound. Perhaps it had been an enchantment. He propped himself on his elbows. No, the only magic had been Linda's apparent ability to store three hundred feet of clothesline in her little tote bag. Then electric drills began to whir out in the hall and the headache crashed inside his skull like surf.

Work was the answer, work that kept away, as Voltaire said, those three prime evils: boredom, vice, and thoughts of himself, Karen, and Linda Bonita Alicia Favela-Gomez. So, after a *colada* of Cuban coffee had zapped enough caffeine into his blood to stun his hangover, Schwartz set out for Marlowe Court to cultivate old employees. If he ran into Rose, he'd raise lies.

No one working in the lobby looked older than fourteen. Of course, if they'd started working here when they were four . . . The young woman at the desk said she'd only been there a year and hadn't known Mr. Zeigler, "that poor gentle-man," very well. But Mr. Zeigler took a swim every morning, so maybe George, out at the pool, could help.

Under the morning's overcast, the Marlowe's pool was empty, shaped like a stylized Tudor rose, or maybe a club on a playing card, a swimming club? At its far end shuffled a very old couple at shuffleboard. Schwartz watched. It was cutthroat shuffleboard, his jaw and her jaw locked on their dentures as, remorselessly, they knocked each other's disks out of the scoring triangles. Terrible, wordless attrition, the daily ritual that kept them together, clenched in matrimony. Schwartz pulled his eyes away; the man who'd appeared with the mop had to be George.

"Mr. Zeigler," he said, "was a delight, a great tipper. If they were all like him, my job would be wonderful—I'd retire tomorrow." George beamed at the end of his mop.

"Anything else?" Schwartz asked. "The family knows so little about him."

"Nope. A nice, generous guy." George bent to scratch a bare foot. "Well, have to get this mop around the pool before ten."

"I'm sorry you couldn't tell me more, but thank you, George." Schwartz handed George a twenty-dollar bill.

"Thanks. Big tipping must run in the family."

As Schwartz turned to go, the mop handle tapped his shoulder.

"Look," George said, "I really liked the guy. I wouldn't want to say anything. . . ." He stopped and pointed to the street with the mop. "You want to know something, maybe you go next door to the Sheldrake pool. Mr. Zeigler went there, too." George got busy with the mop.

Schwartz strolled out to the beach, walked a bit, returned, and crossed to the back of the Sheldrake, a fifteen-story beige and three-tone green hotel designed by a refugee from the Bremen Line. Why should Abe Zeigler frequent a second swimming pool?

The Sheldrake's pool was more elaborate: a long cabaña building topped by a sundeck, ending in sentinel showers at the gateway to the beach. He'd look around.

"Hi there! You over there, yes. Hi. Do anything for you?" yelled a bright voice. It came from shadows at the hotel end of the cabañas, from behind a counter piled with towels. Above it was a signboard crammed with regulations, the largest lettered of which, number 17, read TIPPING IS RECOMMENDED. Behind the counter, Schwartz now saw, was a young, bouncing man with sandy hair and eyes thinned in a smile.

"Hi, I'm Toby," he said as Schwartz approached. "I run the pool here. Want a lounge and towel? You've got a great choice of position at this hour. You a guest?"

"No, no to all of that, thanks," Schwartz said, deciding, despite the pool's constitution, he'd make up his own rules as he went along. "I'm looking for some information. Have you worked here long?"

Toby, who appeared dappled pink, said, "Long? Only twenty years! I run this place. Listen, I know everyone here, I know their children's names, their grandchildren's names. They love me. Every year they come back and bring me presents from New York, Chicago, Cincinnati. I run the cleanest pool on the beach, and I mean the whole beach!"

Toby leaned through a lower pile of towels, his toe bounce speeding up, slightly blurring his appearance. "Listen," he said, "I'm not Jewish but I can even talk Jewish. Sure. They rent a cabaña for the season, I know whose private chairs are whose. You could rent a cabaña. They play cards inside in the bad weather—gin, canasta, palooki, mah-jongg. I'm like family, here for them all the time."

Toby wasn't young. Close up, Schwartz saw his burned

skin crosshatched with fissures and his hair sandy up from white roots. Toby said, "Listen, I can see you're not just anyone off the beach."

"I've just come off the beach," Schwartz said.

"Sure. Listen, anyone comes in here, they've got to see me. I keep them out, the riffraff off the beach." Toby stopped and suddenly barked, "No riffraff! I run a very tight place here. See those prices on the board? They are *nothing*. A tenth of what I make here. Less. They think the world of me, my people here. Sometimes they want to tip so much, I have to refuse. Know what I'm saying?"

Schwartz felt he had even less idea of what Toby was saying than did Toby, who was breathing hard, his neck set down between permanently lifted shoulders in a frozen shrug.

"Was Abe Zeigler a good tipper?"

"Abe Zeigler was . . ." Toby seemed to notice Schwartz. "Who am I talking to?"

"I'm Mr. Schwartz, a relative."

"I see. I'm Toby. Everyone calls me Toby. They all love me. Listen, they really think the world of me here. You know what I mean?"

The question hung like a paper bag filled with water.

Schwartz said, "Mr. Zeigler?"

"A perfect gentleman. If everyone was like Mr. Zeigler—"

"You'd retire? I mean, was he a good tipper?"

"Good?" Toby yelled. He came around the counter into the light, where he appeared discolored, as if his tan hair dye had run over his body and his natural red skin was trying to flash this message through. He took a plastic armchair, drew it back, and pushed it forward. "Did you see what I just did?"

"I, yes. I believe I did."

"*That* was five dollars from Mr. Zeigler!"

"Was that one of the tips you thought too much?"

Toby said, "Listen, I'm like a son to them. Family."

"Toby, why do you think Mr. Zeigler would swim at his own hotel pool every morning, a hundred yards away, and then come over here?"

"He liked it here," Toby said. "They all do. I run a quality establishment here. Ask anyone."

"Did Mrs. Fine, a Mrs. Rose Fine, come here with him?"

Toby bounced faster on his white shoes. "I don't know a Mrs. Rose Fine."

"His cousin, an older woman, walks with a cane. Are you sure?"

Toby's tans were consumed by red. "I know everyone by name here. Listen, I know names they forget. They forget a grandchild's name and they say, 'Toby, what's the name of my daughter's second boy?' and I say, 'Richard, Richard is Lisa's second son, Mrs. Feldman.' "

Toby was livid, his voice swelling to a choked yell. "I tell you there was no Mrs. Rose Fine here, Mr. Schwartz. Not with Mr. Zeigler, not with anyone. No Mrs. Rose Fine! I know them all! They're crazy about me here because I run a tight establishment. Know what I'm saying?"

Schwartz felt it was time either to rent a lounge chair for the morning or to change tactics. "Toby, I'm not only Mr. Zeigler's relative, I'm also a detective with the New York police, an inspector in homicide." He showed the wallet. "So please look carefully at the badge and identification card so that you're sure I am who I say."

Toby simmered down from roiling red to embarrassed tan stains. Toby didn't know his New York police from his Miami Beach elbow. "Yes, sir," he said. "How can I help?"

"Just answer a few questions, please. Did Abe Zeigler come here often?"

"Four, sometimes five times a week. He kept a cabaña. Still does."

Schwartz was dealing with a madman. "Still does?"

"Well, no, of course, he's dead. He was a tipper, I can tell you. I was like a son—no, his friend has it. Mary."

"Mary?"

"Mary Smith." Toby tucked his T-shirt trimly beneath the rope belt on his bright blue pants. "Listen," he said to Schwartz who was listening, "I run a clean establishment. People behave themselves, fine. None of my business what they do in private behind the closed doors of their cabañas. Know what I'm saying? But no public fooling around here. It's strictly a family atmosphere. No riffraff allowed."

Schwartz touched the scab on his chin. "And Mary Smith is considerably younger than Mr. Zeigler was?"

"Oh, yes, younger," Toby said, winking.

"Toby, I see you're a man of the world. How would you describe Mary Smith?"

Toby tilted his head. "I'd describe her being over there."

"What?"

"She's over there on her own, last lounge this side."

"Toby," Schwartz said, "I think I'll just go over very quietly and have a word. No need for you to bother yourself or mention our talk to anyone." Schwartz held out a twenty-dollar bill, which was taken and slipped into a back pocket so fast that he was half unsure he'd given it.

"Sure. Got you, Mr. Schwartz. Hey, any time you want a swim, sunbathe, massage, I'll fix you up nice here. Towels, lounge, the works. Terrific. Ask anyone. The works!" Toby said, bouncing and heating up again.

Schwartz nodded. Toby returned to his counter, coral red, and began giving the works to a stack of towels, slapping them down and shaping them up as if they were Richard or Richard's mother Lisa or old Mrs. Feldman herself.

Walking along the side of the pool, Schwartz kept his eye on the wrapped figure of the highly pseudonymous Mary Smith, someone less likely to be taken in by an out-of-town cop. He sat on a lounge two away from where she lay in a white robe, the long visor of a white fishing hat pulled over dark glasses. Against the red lines of her lipstick, her skin, streaky white with sunblock, looked like a slab of bacon. A relative, he'd be a relative sniffing for money.

He moved to the lounge next to hers. She didn't move.

"Good morning. Are you Mary Smith?" he asked.

She didn't say anything.

"Pardon me," he said, leaning forward. "Good morning. Are you Mary Smith? Is that the name you go by?"

She didn't say anything.

Schwartz didn't want to touch her. That would be rude. Besides, for all he knew, that sunblock was a sticky trick; she could be a white tar baby.

"Hey," he said.

She didn't move but spoke: "What the hell do you mean, 'the name I go by'?"

"Well, Uncle Abe referred to you as 'Mary Smith,' but then, he was such a cautious guy. Nice but, you know, very old-fashioned." Schwartz put on a sweet, nostalgic smile.

A white silk arm lifted; a finger with a long red nail pushed back the visor; a dark lens turned slightly in his direction. "Referred to me? What do you mean?"

"Oh, always nicely. He clearly thought the world of you. In his letters. I could tell—"

"Who are you?" she asked, pulling her knees up and turning on her side.

"Leonard Schwartz, Miss Smith. I mean, if your name is Mary Smith."

She swung her legs over the lounge and sat up, pushing back the hat so that its visor pointed skyward over thick hair several shades of yellow. "Just stop this name business, will you?" She removed her sunglasses. Her eyes were small, brown, and blinking. "Mary Smith is my real name. And you say you're a nephew of Abe's?"

Schwartz nodded. "No. I called him 'Uncle' because he was an older generation. We're cousins, actually. Well, we were cousins. I wasn't able to make his funeral. It was terrible, all that, how he died. You must have been . . . Well."

"Yes. Awful. And I couldn't even . . . You're sure he *wrote* about me?"

Schwartz smiled. "It wasn't so much what he wrote, you know, more like between the lines how I got the feeling you made him, his last years, you know, very happy, very . . ." He looked down at his feet. "Worth living."

Her feet showed red-lacquered toenails from under the strap of wooden clogs.

"He never mentioned you," she said. "You're not from around here, are you?"

"No, New York. I had to be down this way on business, so I thought . . ." He shrugged. "Actually some other relatives asked me to . . ." He shook his head.

She put on her sunglasses again, took her hat off, and shook out her hair. It fell to her shoulder in thick waves, beautiful hair despite the silly yellows.

"What are you trying to say, Mister . . . ?"

"Schwartz. Lenny, please call me Lenny. Mary, may I?"

"Sure. But what's the head shaking?" she asked.

Schwartz looked unhappily toward the pool. "Look, I didn't want to, but, you know, family. Even my wife started. See, Mary, Abe didn't leave anything to us, not a nickel. Not that it mattered. But it was strange, not even a *little* something. So, anyway, we thought, they did, that you'd maybe be able to . . . Well, you know, explain that if he lost his money at the end, or something—"

"Screw you!" she said, standing, pulling the robe tight around her full figure. "I gave that man six years of my fucking life and I can tell you he wasn't exactly the world's greatest company!"

"Oh, please," Schwartz said, standing, his hands out in conciliation.

"Please, nothing," she said. "I don't know anything. Oh, he tipped big, but that was just to show off. He was as tightfisted a bastard as I've ever met. I'm sorry, but you come and accuse me—don't think I don't know what you mean with your little fucking smiles and compliments, guy. I wasn't born yesterday, guy!"

She slammed her hat on. It pulled her hair up and out so that her head looked like a straw doll's whose face the kids have crayoned and chipped.

She leaned to Schwartz and said, "Yes, Abe left me a little trust. Too damned little. But it's all legal. And if you think you or any of your miserable family are going to get a penny of that, you've got another thing coming."

Schwartz took a step back and said, "I see. And his lawyer, uh, I forget his name now. . . ."

She laughed. "His lawyer," she said, "is Melvin Weinstock. And I guess you *aren't* from here if you don't know that name. So you can take a flying leap." She laughed again. "Or you can see his lawyer first and *then* take a flying leap."

Mary Smith clomped down to the towel bar, where she leaned over to Toby and pointed back to Schwartz. Toby shrugged, his hands up, his face incandescent even in that distance. When Schwartz heard her loud "What?" he knew Toby's allegiance had naturally gone to the steadier customer, and it was time to say good morning to Aunt Rose.

Rose adjusted her thick bifocals, rubbed her eyes, and readjusted her bifocals. "Look at what I've waded through," she said, pushing at two six-inch piles of photocopied newsprint on the dining table. "And you know what?" she said, grabbing at Schwartz's arm for emphasis.

He had to ask. "What?"

"I've found that Stanley Zeigler is guilty—of being a capitalist, an aggressive, acquisitive, manipulative, close-to-the-line sailing capitalist and nothing more. And I don't believe that's a crime in this country."

Her eyes were tired, occluded; her pupils were swimming in milk.

Schwartz patted her shoulder. "The punishment for that crime is you get to be president, or at least secretary of labor. As they used to say in Brooklyn, Rose, you done good."

Rose pulled away from his arm, his sentiment. "Would you like a cup of tea?" she asked.

He said, "A cup of tea, you got maybe a lemon with it, would be good."

"Why the stage Yiddish-English, Lenny? You don't even speak Yiddish. You think because I do and I'm old and live in Miami Beach that I'll think it cute? I don't. It's junk sentimentality and it's condescending!"

Schwartz stared at her.

She sighed and limped into her kitchen, hanging her cane on the serving bar. She said, "I'm sorry. That's just sour grapes. I *so* wanted Stanley to fit my prejudices. Well, I shouldn't take it out on you. Look, a real tea glass."

Schwartz walked a circle. Rose's apartment was full of books and photographs. It was bright, spotless. She said she had a woman in once a week for heavy cleaning. He could imagine the hours it took with her pains and limitations for the rest. "Let me get tea," he said.

"Don't be silly. You know it's good for us old folks on our own to keep busy. Within limits. I wouldn't like to have to read through all that junk again." She put down the kettle, then reached with shaking hands for the glass in a holder and a mug printed with a woman's head.

"Who's on the mug?" Schwartz asked.

Rose put tea bags in the glass and mug. "Clara Schumann. Lenny, I found out he's a philanthropist. Stanley, the tough guy. He never said a word to me—nor, evidently, to Abe about it. And I thought he was such a braggart. Can you imagine?"

"I think so. Is this Uncle Sid, Rose?" Schwartz asked, pointing to a photo of a double-breasted, long-nosed gentleman he seemed to recall.

Rose looked in the direction of the photograph. "Sure. Don't you remember?" She took the whistling kettle off the hob and poured.

"I remember he was very quiet."

"With you. He was quiet with all children. He told me that because we couldn't have children—which was not his fault—he felt abashed in their presence. Sidney was a good man. Not so silent, either. Sugar?"

"Just lemon, thanks, like I asked for in stage Yinglish," Schwartz, walking by bookcases, said loudly so Rose could hear.

"Some terrific photos here. This is a lovely one of Mother and Dad with you two. Is that the Botanical Gardens?"

Rose brought the teas to the serving bar one at a time. "You know it is," she said, "like I know you're just *dying* to snoop in the bedroom. All right, Mr. Detective, I'll make a deal." She stopped and began pulling herself onto a stool. "Wait. Strange how sometimes sitting up on this stool, half-hanging, can be so comfortable for me."

He came to the bar and sipped the tea. It was too hot. "What's the deal?"

"Curiosity. I want to see how good a detective you are. You can go into my bedroom for five minutes, but you can't touch anything."

He started to laugh.

"Then," Rose continued, "you come out and tell me what you know that you didn't know before. And I don't mean the 1967 Librarians' Association Award." She leaned forward, braced on the bottom of her forearms, circled the mug with waxy, half-translucent fingers, and blew across its top.

"You're on," Schwartz said.

"But there's a catch."

"Which is?"

"Which is that we both have to tell the truth."

"Oh," he said, taking his glass of tea, "*that* catch. You're still on."

He came out of the bedroom sipping his still-hot tea.

"Is that five minutes?" Rose asked.

"It's about three minutes," he said.

"I see: you're showing off."

Schwartz came up close so Rose could see him, to where the pupils swam out from the depths of her eyes. He said, "I came out because I couldn't find anything except that Librarians' Association Award."

She lay her hand on his so that its tremble ran to his veins, as if trying to give him her age. She said, "Don't forget the catch."

He looked out the window across to the Sheldrake. It was an upended liner. The smokestacks would have stuck out from the ninth or tenth floors. "You and Abe."

"What? I couldn't hear. My hearing."

He repeated, "You and Abe."

"Abe and I," she said. "It was the closet, wasn't it? I can't bring myself to get rid of his clothes."

"No. You said I couldn't touch anything: I took that to include closet-door handles. It was the photo of the two of you on the dresser. I guessed it was Abe because he looked something like Stanley. Fitter. It was the way you looked at him, Rose. That wasn't just good friendship."

They sipped tea.

He said, "Come on, Rose, that catch was for both of us. Why'd you set up this little game? Why couldn't you tell me?"

"I was afraid you'd laugh. I mean . . ." Her hand flapped. "You'd find it grotesque."

"That an older woman needs love and companionship?"

She shook her head. "Oh, Lenny, not that. It was even to the end so sexual. He was a very fit and virile man. Of course it was my vanity, but that also kept me going."

He said, "That's good, too. Rose, nothing's wrong or shameful about it."

She sipped tea and nodded. Clara Schumann's ringlets shook. "I suppose," she said. "But the truth, the catch, is that but for the sex I don't think . . . I don't know. Abe Zeigler was not such a fascinating fellow. Decent, yes, attentive, but a bit dull. He was interested in business and business and business."

Schwartz smiled.

"Oh, sure," she said, "and in monkey business, too."

Schwartz thought of Mary Smith, a few hundred feet north. More monkey business and another testament to dull old Abe. "Rose," he said, "were you mentioned in Abe's will?"

She nodded. "A few photos, mementos. Sure."

"That's all?"

"What do you mean?" she asked. "He had enough for his needs, but Abe didn't have a fortune. It turns out that he had less than he let on. What he had, like his apartment upstairs and some stocks, goes to two nieces in New York, next of kin."

Schwartz moved to Rose's side of the bar. "How do you know?"

"How? Actually—this is in confidence—we have the same lawyer, so he told me."

"Melvin Weinstock?"

"No, Bernard Sonnabend, Abe's lawyer, my lawyer. Abe put me onto him when I moved down here," said Rose.

"Oh," said Schwartz, suppressing the stagier "Oy-oy-oy."

CHAPTER 6

The lights of freighters making south for Miami, inside the stream, appeared like spots of yellow on the sea, two panels of blue ink from the twenty-first floor of the Broadmoor. Alva Cruz, who'd changed her name from Alva Martinez by deed poll rather than by marriage with Roberto Cruz (who hadn't taken the hint but seemed content with, if not flattered by, this imitation) looked out past the balcony.

She spoke into the glass door at the reflection of the others watching TV: "Well, there's no hurricane, no nothing out here, whatever Channel 7 Weather says."

"It's a thousand miles away, Alva," Jaime said. He rotated the toe of his baby-blue shoe to look for scuffs.

Carmen shifted on the sofa and said, "So? All she said was there was nothing out there."

Cruz turned from the TV and narrowed his eyes at his sister.

Jaime inspected his other baby-blue toe. "Anyway," he said, "what kind of jerkoff name for a hurricane is *Melvin?*"

Alva turned. "M. It's M because that's after L. That was

Lavinia, L. It's how they number them.'' She turned back side-ways to the glass and moved her hips so that her buttocks tucked in.

"Will you all shut up about the weather so I can hear the fockin' weather?'' Cruz said.

Jaime slid closer to his wife and said, "Anyway, it's not the same. It's stupid giving them men's names. I mean, you can't remember them. Now Carol—Hurricane Carol was one fuck of a storm. See what I mean?'' Jaime dropped his hand onto Carmen's pink-silked thigh.

"What about Hurricane David, then?'' Carmen asked. "The one that flattened Jamaica. What was that supposed to be, an April shower?''

By the door, Alva twisted her head to look over her shoulder.

Cruz said, "Frank. That was Frank, not David,'' without taking his eyes from the screen.

"You're crazy, Berto,'' said Carmen. "That was David.'' She pushed Jaime's hand off.

"Frank,'' said Cruz.

Alva was turning back and forth, head over her shoulder. Her palms pressed into her buttocks. "Hey,'' she said, "I don't care what any of you say, my ass has really gotten fat. I mean, Jesus, it's enormous. Look at this dress, here, in back. It's sticking out like some kinda fuckin' *awning*!''

Carmen said, "David.''

"See what I mean?'' said Jaime. "No one remembers a hurricane with a man's name.''

Cruz pounded the table by his chair. "Will you shut the fock up all of you? You made me—look, the fockin' weatherman's gone now because of all your noise. Jesus.''

Jaime said, "No, he would've gone anyway, Roberto.''

Carmen laughed.

Cruz stood and picked up the remote control.

"No, wait," said Alva, slapping alternate buttocks as she walked. "I wanna catch this Channel 7 Newsflash."

Carmen said, "Shit, those poor Haitians. Who'd do a sick thing like dump them there without water?"

"Those white sheets," said Alva, pointing, "they must be covering the dead kids, don't you think?"

"Shut up, Alva," said Cruz, taking a step toward the five-foot screen.

"Yeah, shut up, Carmen," said Jaime.

Carmen said, "You tell me to shut up once more, I'll rip your fucking eyes out, Jaime."

Cruz sat down on the sofa next to Jaime. "You hear the name of that boat?" he asked quietly. "You hear what I hear?"

Jaime nodded.

Cruz said, "Girls, take a walk."

"Hey," said Alva, pounding the back of her hips with her fists, "we wanna watch."

Cruz stood and rerolled his shirt sleeves. "We got maybe fifteen fockin' TVs here. We got four fockin' living rooms! Get out of here!"

Carmen stood. "Come on, Alva. The company here really sucks."

Cruz lifted a muscled forearm and pointed. "Jesus! Out!"

"You want me, boss?" asked the on-duty bodyguard, putting his head into the room.

"No, Jesus, not you," Cruz said. "Just, that's it—out."

Alva gave a last look back to see how she was bringing up her rear and closed the door.

Behind the bar, Jaime poured brandy over ice in a tall glass. Cruz pressed a remote button and the screen dimmed to pearl and slid up into its slot. "You celebrating, Jaime?" he asked, leaning against a bar stool.

"I think, yeah, it calls for a little drink, old Captain Bob turning up for us like this."

Cruz frowned. "Oh? I must have missed something. All I saw was these fockin' dying Haitian niggers was found after being put ashore four days ago, some desert island out in the Bahamas. And that reporter said doctors and lawyers and their families trying to get away from a new government they got. And he said they'd paid five thousand each and the boat was 'believed' to be *Sport King*. So where's your friend fockin' Captain Bob in that?"

Jaime topped his iced brandy with crème de menthe, watching it go from pale amber to mud green. "Now we got the cops, the coast guard, the fucking *navy* looking for *Sport King*. Don't you see? They're gonna fucking find it, if anyone can. And then we get a lead on Bob and the rednecks crewing for him and the money."

Cruz leaned across the bar. "Jaime, listen to me. You got half a good idea there. Let me show you how you make it all good. Okay, so Bob's got everyone looking for him. You think he's gonna let his fockin' crew walk off? Here's a man's got nothing to lose: ripped me off, ripped off—not the poor nigger Haitians—whoever was his backers on that, and here's a man must be shitting bricks if word's back to him about our little *message*. And Bob's already left these couple hundred people to die on some fockin' desert island. You think he's not gonna waste a couple rednecks or *Marielitos* crew if he has to?"

Jaime sipped his drink, narrowed his eyes, and thought. "Yeah, maybe. But if the crew is crazy, too, maybe they'll get Bob first. And maybe then—"

"No, Jaime." Cruz tapped his finger against a golden papaya on Jaime's shirt sleeve. "*Por Dios*, you gotta play the odds. Bob must have had the whole thing planned, you see? He has to be way ahead of those peanut-brained rednecks on this.

Okay? But not bad, Jaime, not bad. Times like this I think there's maybe more inside your head than a telephone book full of pussy.''

Jaime smiled; things were going good. "So you gonna have a drink?''

Cruz smiled back. "Sure. A drink of water, Jaime. That's what this news is worth so far.''

CHAPTER 7

Schwartz tried to calm himself by sitting well back on the limousine's plush seat, an arm over an armrest, trying to guess where he was being driven. The phone contact had said to be at the corner of Washington and Fifth at two in the afternoon, so even before the long white car had pulled up, he'd known they'd be crossing the causeway to the city. When they turned west of Brickell onto Seventh, Schwartz thought Roberto might be waiting at a Calle Ocho club or restaurant.

That would be all right because they wouldn't kill him there. Why not? The limo swung back onto Eighth at Twenty-seventh Avenue, still heading west. Perhaps they'd take the Tamiami Trail right out of town to a remote . . . At Southwest Fifty-seventh they turned south.

Perhaps Cruz had a Coral Gables house, a place that would make Palazzo Zeigler seem as restrained as a New England saltbox. At such a private place they could also dispose of his body. An acid bath, a trip with the small remaining bag of Schwartz out to the Everglades and . . .

He wasn't doing wonderfully well at calming himself. He could ask the driver, of course, but that would be foolish. The driver would say nothing.

Schwartz tapped on the glass. The driver pushed a button and said, "What?"

Schwartz asked, "I don't suppose you could tell me where we're going?"

"Right there," said the driver, pointing to a large carved parrot.

"Parrot Jungle?"

"Mr. Cruz will meet you inside."

Schwartz got out under the parrot and watched the limo park in the shade of a ficus tree. He told himself he couldn't have wished for a more public meeting place. He could have wished for a less silly one.

He told the ticket seller that the admission price was high enough to buy a parrot. Then he told himself to shut up and calm down.

Roberto stood, sweat covering his face, by a perch in the bird posing area, his hand up to a scarlet macaw whose white beak seemed to swing in a frenzy of indecision.

"Roberto," said Schwartz.

Roberto stroked the macaw behind its cheek stripes and said, "Let's walk."

Schwartz followed, awarding himself no detection prize for picking out Roberto's bodyguards from assorted Cub Scouts, moms pushing baby strollers, and a group dressed in lederhosen and Hasselblads. The guards, two dark-suited heavyweights, hung at the periphery of vision behind and before their boss.

Roberto strode quickly with a rolling gait, reminding Schwartz of his temper and strength, making him wonder if, with these other two, a more homey choice of site wouldn't have been Monkey Jungle, just up the road.

He saw Schwartz look at his guards. "Paco and Taco," he said. "They're okay."

Schwartz was sticky. Paco and Taco were undoubtedly okay for very bad business. The air was heavy in the gardens. Well, it was Roberto's time and place, Roberto's jungle. The path curved down into giant bamboo that clicked in the light wind way above.

"Look at this, Schwartz, a Moluccan cockatoo. Watch this," Roberto said, putting his finger into the cage, perch high. The bird rocked across sideways. It bent its puff-feathered, salmon-pink head to the finger, and Roberto scratched the back of its neck. The cockatoo curled in pleasure.

Schwartz felt foolish. Here he was about to ask for his life and the man was playing with birds.

"They're hand-raised from hatching," Roberto said, taking out a large white handkerchief. "They like you if you're quiet." He wiped his very wet face.

Beneath the fine gray linen jacket, Schwartz saw the shining wet of Roberto's shirt, both sides of the gray-and-pink-striped necktie. "You used to be very quiet, Roberto. I never heard you say more than a word or two around Montanares. Now you talk, you wear elegant clothes, own racehorses. You're a socialite, a fancier of fancy birds. You didn't happen to drop half a hotel on me or run a car at my old auntie and me the other day on Collins, did you?"

Roberto said, "I don't know about dropping anything. When cars go for you, maybe you should move—move out of town. I didn't talk around Juan when you were there because you weren't supposed to hear anything. Now I'm running the organization. I've got my own style."

He turned and walked to the next cage. "See this yellow-tailed black cockatoo? Very rare. I got a pair I'm trying to breed. I got an aviary over my place in the country. I come here to look at breeds I might want, get advice. I like doing things right, professionally. Do you, Schwartz?''

Roberto had just put his handkerchief away, but already the liquid beads were forming on his full-moon cheeks. He looked like a sweating cheese.

''Yes, I do,'' Schwartz said. ''That way things can be clear.''

Roberto watched some children running down the path and said, ''Let's keep walking.''

A flight of small green parrots squawked overhead, clambering onto a strangler fig. Schwartz could think of no best approach. He wiped his forehead with the back of his index finger and pulled his shirt away from his chest. They'd come into another climate in here, even hotter, wetter. He looked at air plants dangling off a dark mahogany. Parasites. What place was fitting for this business? The word ''unseemly'' came to him: his unseemly crime, the one he'd gotten away with, led to all this unseemliness.

Roberto was standing still, pointing with an upturned hand. ''What do you think?'' he asked.

Schwartz looked and said, ''I wish the Kodak sign telling us this was a Photo Beauty Spot wasn't here to spoil the photo beauty spot.''

Roberto narrowed his eyes. ''Most people who come here don't know shit. They do what the sign says, they go home with a pretty picture.'' He looked around. ''It's as quiet as we're gonna get it here. So what do you want with me?''

''It's not easy to say. You're so different than in New York.''

''Yeah, yeah, I move my lips and words come out. You said that.'' Roberto's thick neck ran crisscross rivulets of sweat.

''You know I didn't set Montanares up to be killed.''

Roberto brought up his wet handkerchief and pulled it

across his neck. "If you mean you warned him off, yeah, he told me. Hey, look at that big blue one! That's called a hyacinth macaw. A beauty. I got them."

Schwartz felt he was losing the sense of what he'd meant to say. "So you wouldn't have anything to settle with me. . . ."

"With you? I never liked Juan dealing with you. You seemed too fast and fockin' crazy, so I thought you'd for sure double-cross us, like lots of paid-off cops. But you didn't."

Roberto looked up into the trees. His jacket came open and the buttons on his shirt seemed about to pop. "Look!" he said. "Look at those two parakeets coming in. They been out."

"Out?"

"If they're not in cages, they can all fly out of here. Lots fly out, but they don't lose them. Like those. See, that's the female with the light red chest. His is bright red, but he got his back to us. King parakeets, good birds. Yeah, they could fly off, but they always return. They got it made here and they know it: right trees, food, shelter. Everything they need." Roberto looked around for his guards.

He could have been a banker, the owner of a car agency, or a county tax collector, this medium-size, sweating man with the round smooth face and neat black hair. His physical strength showed only in the tendons flared from his wrists into his white French cuffs.

"I have to know—" Schwartz began and stopped. "Do you want to have me killed, to kill me?" He heard his heartbeat over the end of the question.

"Is that it? You saying that's why you come down all this way and hang around here, to ask me that? That's stupid, Schwartz."

Schwartz suddenly realized the question *was* stupid. "Yes," he said.

Roberto pushed his jacket back and put his hand on his

hips. He turned a full circle and again faced Schwartz. "I don't fockin' believe you. No way you're just here for that. I'll give you this: you got *cojones*. I wouldn't cry if I heard you were dead. But I'm not going for you. If you want to know the truth, you're not important enough to kill. You kill a cop, it better be worth all the fockin' heat it brings down. I don't go around making that kind of shit for myself. I'm a businessman and I want to keep the risks—and the costs—down. Even Juan, a cool guy, lost it at the end, started acting stupid, unprofessional. So, you got the answer to your question?"

"Yes, thanks."

"Hey, but just cause you got *cojones* don't mean you're gonna live forever. So you keep the fock away from me. Now I'm gonna go up and check out some new yellow-naped amazons up in the cages. Then I'm going back to town. I'll give you a lift."

Schwartz nodded. Roberto, now joined by his two big guards, disappeared up the path.

Schwartz was alive, they weren't after him. What was it, then, that kept him from any real sense of relief? Was it vanity, resenting that he was too unimportant to be killed? No, he'd always known himself *that* unimportant, had witnessed a few officers turn messianic and fulfill their self-prophetic sacrifices.

Schwartz walked slowly. A young boy was throwing stone after stone onto an alligator in a fenced-off pool. The alligator wouldn't move. From the other side of the pool a woman called and called in a flat voice, "Come on now, Jimmy Roy. Come on." Jimmy Roy wouldn't move.

There was no joy in this business. He'd been through the classical phases: guilt and, finally, confession to his son about the bribe. And much good that had done. He'd told Jake three weeks ago and not a word in reply. Still, Jake hadn't killed himself or, worse, dropped out of college. Very funny.

A loudspeaker announced five minutes to the next show in the Parrot Bowl. Schwartz stood aside to let two wheelchairs pass. They held two wizened children in hard hats. They were twisted, brittle, and smiling.

All right, he reasoned, guilt and confession, and he wasn't even the Catholic. Karen was the lapsed Catholic. So what more? Contrition and—ah, yes—restitution. Yes?

He walked to a large cage. He knew: his crime kept him close to these criminals, these *other criminals*. But it was more than identification.

"Here, birdies, birdies," Schwartz called to the multicolored clusters on the bars and shelves. He put his fingers to the cage. A bird lifted from the back and dived. He jerked back his fingers just as the beak clacked the wire.

The cage filled with mad beating wings, screeches, screams. One solitary bird above him swayed back and forth in the midst of the tumult, repeating, "I'm a good boy! I'm a good boy!" Schwartz named him Schwartz.

He stepped back and the cage came to rest. Punishment! Of course, that's what he sought. *Amazona ochrocephala oratrix,* it read. "Mexican Double Yellow Head." Except for the Schwartz bird, a Jewish-American double yellow head. "Schwartzbird, 'bye-'bye," he sang.

Roberto came over. "You talking to them?"

"Yes, I'm like you, Roberto. I'm not only for doing things professionally, I'm for the birds."

Roberto was wearing a fresh shirt, jacket, and pants. Fresh sweat rolled down his forehead. He said, "Montanares used to think you were very funny. I don't. So you come with us, you can sit up front. We got some business to discuss."

That was fine with Schwartz. Roberto sat in the back of the limo with Paco and Taco, and Schwartz sat with the driver who was probably called Macho. He tried not to imagine what business was being discussed in the backseat, how many this business would destroy when finally harvested, refined, shipped, cut, rocked with ammonia, and sucked into lungs. Punishment.

The car rolled under a tunnel of fine green leaves along a grand avenue of old ficus.

Schwartz thought. Karen once said the company of these criminals was a form of punishment for his guilt. But wasn't the idea that the punishment, if you were truly sorry, cleansed you of guilt? And just whose moral orders had he taken down, bad waiter at life's crummy table?

Or was it restitution he lacked? But didn't his restitution to society lie in his never-ending battle against crime?

Schwartz began laughing out loud and pretended he was coughing into his palms. Perhaps the really moral moments came to you only in cliché. Cliché, the epiphany of spirit? What would happen if he said all this to Roberto? Would Roberto kill him then?

No, Schwartz thought, looking out at the downtown towers, it was simple: he hadn't enough punishment or socially acceptable punishment. So did he *need* Roberto to punish him, and was he in this way unhappy because Roberto wouldn't kill him? No, no, that crime didn't carry the death penalty, even down here in frying Florida.

He was tired of all this. He looked at his watch. Only five? Schwartz felt he'd been without sleep for days. The sky out over the ocean looked very dark and tumbled.

He'd take a swim and shower. And then he'd call Karen and tell her the good news and ask why it didn't make him happy. Yes, as if he didn't know what guilt he'd feel talking with his loving, betrayed wife. He shut his eyes.

The car stopped. He opened his eyes. One of the guards opened his door. He was smoking a big cigar.

"Here you are, Schwartz, Miami Beach," Roberto said

from outside. He too smoked a big cigar, standing in the narrow street.

An alley?

The driver pushed over and said "Out" and Schwartz knew. He started to shake. His stomach turned and went very hard. He swallowed and pulled himself through the door on useless legs, feeling the driver's gun in his back. The guard pulled him up. The other guard walked over.

Behind them, Roberto blew out a big cloud of smoke. "This is it, Schwartz," he said. "No more."

Schwartz thought they were subtle, for gangsters—sadists who'd let him fly off like this for a while to think he was free. He let the driver pull his arms behind him. What was in his back now was the driver's knee.

The guard bent and blew cigar smoke in Schwartz's face. Just before the first punch his weak kidney began to ache. The punch came so fast and hard it felt like the driver's knee had gone through his back into his stomach. Schwartz opened his mouth. Cigar smoke. Then the guard without the cigar was in front of him. The bile rose into vomit with the second punch. The wet on his leg was his pee. And just before the third, Schwartz felt the corners of his mouth lift in a smile.

BOOK

CHAPTER 1

Fingers traced over his closed eyes and down his cheek. Karen. It was hard to open his eyes against the light; they seemed pasted shut.

He said "Karen" and "water."

Her hand slid under his head, fingers stroking his hair. A glass was at his mouth; he felt his lips tremble against the water.

"Here, drink," she said. "It's Linda. The doctor said you were very strong to come through without a burst spleen."

Spleen. Karen. Schwartz drank. The a/c rattled and the fridge hummed on. Where? "I didn't feel strong," he said. "I must have smelled strong. I thought they were going to kill me, Karen."

She stroked the back of his hand with her finger. She traced the veins. "Linda, Lenny. It's Linda. Maybe you smiled because they didn't kill you. I came to Emergency when I got the call. You smiled when you were unconscious and sometimes when you were sleeping. I'd wake in the chair and you'd have this sweet smile, so that it was hard to imagine the beating you'd taken. Hard to see it, too, a very professional beating."

Schwartz remembered. His stomach hurt when he breathed. He held his breath: his stomach hurt. He opened his eyes. The curtains were drawn in the hotel room but long bars of light stuck in through the gaps. He slowly turned his head. Oh, she looked tired and lovely. But it was Linda.

She stroked his shoulder. "How do you feel?"

"Did you . . . ?" His voice was cracked dry. "I mean, are you officially guarding me or . . . ? Thanks. You don't, I mean, have something better to—"

"I do," she said, laying her hand lightly on the sheet between his legs, "but you're in no shape for it."

He tried a smile and closed his eyes and set his head back. There was an alley and sirens; he'd regained consciousness with sirens. And a terrible stink of tobacco. He'd seen the rear of buildings—all cubes and rectangular setbacks. Then he'd thought something about how even the alleys of South Beach were art deco. Something . . . yes, he'd tell Karen: a meeting of cigar rot and ziggurat. This wasn't Karen.

He opened his eyes. "Linda, what did you say to the police?"

She leaned over him, wiping the corners of his mouth with her fingertip. "I said I'd ask you when you could speak. I figured it had to be Cruz, but I thought you'd want to tell it—or not."

"Good. Thanks. Oh, did *I* say anything?"

"Not very clear. Once you groaned something about 'two lawyers' and 'two no sense.' I took that down. It must have been, I don't know, about three in the morning." She put her hand over the yawn suggested by the memory.

He swallowed. "Does Karen . . . Was my wife called?"

Linda looked at the fridge. "No. When the doctor said you'd be okay, I thought maybe you'd want, wouldn't . . . No, I didn't call. That was okay, wasn't it?"

"Okay, sure," Schwartz said. Sure, he could call Karen himself. Or not call to worry her. Or himself, especially. He pressed a finger into the side of his stomach, bit his lip, and hummed to disguise his moan. "Two lawyers? That's about this other . . . Can I eat anything?"

Linda stretched. Her blue Police Athletic League T-shirt pulled up over her blue jeans. "There's yogurt. That'll be good for you."

He said, "About these two lawyers and this other thing, the Abe Zeigler killing. Would—"

There was a knock on the door."

Linda said, "That'll be your aunt Rose. She called earlier and I told her."

Rose came into the room followed by a man carrying a large paper bag. She tipped him, he left, and Linda set the bag on the table by the fridge. She shook hands with Rose. They said something out of his hearing. Rose came over to the bed.

Schwartz tried to push himself to a sitting position, but the pain laid him halfway back onto the pillow.

"No, don't on my account," Rose said.

Linda came with another pillow and plumped it behind his head. Rose bent and pecked his cheek.

"Here, Mrs. Fine," Linda said, bringing a chair to the bedside. "I'll wash the fruit."

"Fruit?" Schwartz asked.

"Fruit," Rose said. She looked at Linda taking the bag into the bathroom and said, "Thank you. Yes, a bag of fruit. Plums, apples, bananas. Listen, just because I'm not your schmaltzy stereotype doesn't mean I have no feeling." She tried to find a stable place along the bed to lean her cane, then laid it on the edge of the sheet. "You remember basic English lit, don't you, Lenny: the difference between sentiment and sentimentality?"

"Rose, don't make me laugh; I know it'll hurt. Yes, I remember. Thanks for the sentiment not in excess of what the occasion warrants. For the fruit, too."

Rose smiled. "I suppose I shouldn't ask what happened?"

"No." He shook his head. "I ran into some trouble—with my stomach. Nothing to do with our investigation. Other detection."

Rose leaned forward and very lightly touched his arm. She said, "I'm sorry. I can see you're in real pain. That's the hardest thing with pain: you'd think it would make you sympathetic to pain in others. But unless you work very hard, it just seems to make you selfish, locks you away in yourself. So. Okay. Let's play our detective game again. This time, I'm it."

Schwartz smiled. "Rose, you're something. All right, we'll play. What rules?"

She looked toward the bathroom door. "I come in," she said. "I don't touch anything, I look around with my half-blind eyes, and I tell you something I didn't know before."

"Right. How long do you want?"

"I'm ready," she said, dropping her voice.

Schwartz dropped his smile and asked, "Well?"

"Are you sure you want to play, Lenny? Remember the catch?"

He said yes, trying to keep his breathing steady to control the pain.

Rose nodded toward the bathroom. "Her, your colleague."

Schwartz asked flatly, "What about her?"

"You and her," Rose whispered, her head coming forward quickly and moving back again like a bird, an old eagle.

"Rose, just because she's good-looking . . ."

Rose was shaking her head. "It was how she touched you

when she put the pillow behind your head. How you looked at her. Are you telling me I'm wrong?"

He said, "You're very wrong to say that."

"Yes, of course. It's none of my business. I suppose I've been spoiled because of the two men in my life. Sidney and Abe were both faithful, you see."

Linda came out holding a bowl full of plums and apples.

Rose whispered, "I suppose the truth is that most men are like Stanley and you."

Schwartz shut his eyes rather than scowl at Rose. How dare she come to his sickbed and be so damned . . . What was the word? Rude? No. Right? Yes. He couldn't remember even glancing at Linda when she put the pillow behind him, let alone looking lovingly, lustfully. Oh, did he . . . had he had an erection? No, that couldn't—

"Banana, Lenny? Rose? A plum or apple?" Linda asked.

He opened his eyes. Why had Linda said "banana"? And where had that bowl come from? Had Rose spotted the bowl, known this hotel wouldn't have provided it, and deduced that he and Linda had set up house? Schwartz tried to see around the room. What other signs of domesticity had Linda brought in—chintz curtains, embroidery, a bullwhip?

"How long will you be in bed?" Rose asked.

Schwartz shrugged and looked at Linda.

She said, looking at Rose, "It's question of working through the pain. The faster he can exercise, the faster the bruising—broken tissue and blood—can be absorbed and heal. He could be up and around in a day or two, if he can master the pain."

Rose said, "And you'll be around to help him, Officer. . . ."

"Linda, Linda Gomez, Mrs. Fine. I can make a few hours a day, between my other duties."

Rose took her cane from the bed and brought it smartly down to the floor beside her. "Well, it's good to know he's in such capable hands, Officer Gomez."

Schwartz watched Linda see red. Rose red. He shut his eyes. Good, nothing followed but an embarrassed silence. Their silence, his embarrassment.

"Lenny," Rose said, "I have to go. I'll call in the evening and we'll talk. You know." She added a dramatic cough.

Schwartz opened his eyes. "Thanks for coming, and for the fruit and consequences, Detective Fine."

Rose, thumping doorward with her cane, said, "You're entirely welcome, Mister Schwartz. Get well."

At the open door she said, "Good-bye, Officer Gomez."

"Good-bye, Mrs. Fine," said Linda. "Don't worry."

"Worry? Worry about what?" asked Rose, her voice gravelly with phlegm and suspicion.

"About Lenny. He'll get well soon."

"Oh," Rose said, *"that,"* and left.

Linda stood looking at the closed door.

Schwartz called, "What is it?" and lifted himself higher. Yes, there certainly were some fantastic pains to work through.

Linda came back looking down at the floor. "You tell me," she said.

"She knows. She came in, looked at us, and told me. About us, I mean. Us two. You were out, washing dirty bananas in the bathroom."

Linda looked at him. "She's jealous."

"No," he said, "she's old-fashioned. Angry. What do you mean, jealous?"

She sat on the bedside and pulled down the sheet. She began slowly rubbing his stomach. "This hurt?"

"No, it's good. What about jealous?"

"You're good for Mrs. Fine, you and your little investigation of the Abe Zeigler killing. It's obviously revived her."

He saw Linda in profile looking at his stomach as her thumb
drew back from her hand and pressed across the coiled dark
hair over the muscle.

"And that's all?" he asked.

"Well, look," Linda said, still watching her hand, "she's
your relative and who am I? Just a colleague for a few days, a
passing fancy fuck."

"No," Schwartz said, putting his hand on hers on his
stomach, "say what you think. *She* certainly did."

"I think you should be careful, Lenny. You know, with
this investigation. I'm sure there's nothing bad, I mean, no bad
intention in her, but she has her fantasies."

He ran his fingers down between Linda's. "You're not
exactly without fantastic elements yourself, Linda Bonita."

She lifted his hand from hers. "But I can tell where the
fantasy ends and reality begins. And now I'll massage your
stomach. Tell me what happened with Cruz."

Schwartz let his head go back into the pillows. Linda's
thumb crossed his muscles harder. The pain grew sharp then
fell to a steady dull ache. He said, "Nothing happened. That's
the strange thing. It was all anticlimax. I met him out in Parrot
Jungle, we walked to a secluded spot, and I asked him what I
wanted and he answered. And that was that. Then he offered
me a ride back and his three nasty companions beat me in an
alley."

"But they didn't kill you."

"No, they certainly knew exactly what they were doing."
Schwartz looked at Linda's puzzled expression. "Oh, I'd better
explain. I came down here to ask Cruz if he had a contract out
on me; I had reason to ask, but let's not get into that. And

Cruz said no, he didn't. And I believed, I still believe him.
There was no reason for him to lie. But it's true that when
they started to beat me, I thought he was lying. But then, I
knew . . . I get confused about there.''

Linda said, ''So say he was right and didn't want to kill
you. Why should he want to beat you?''

Schwartz shook his head. Linda kept a steady pressure over
his stomach muscles. The pain was there, bearable. ''There's
something else. . . .''

''Some more happened?'' she asked.

''No, no more, but . . . Wait.'' He shut his eyes and said,
''*Roberto* said, 'No more.' I remember now. He said, 'This is
it, Schwartz,' and then, 'No more.' And that's when I thought
he was going to have me killed. I thought he meant *I* was no
more.''

Linda kept working her thumb down deeper. She knew, he
had to admit, many things to do with pain.

''So?'' she asked.

''Maybe it was a way of saying we were quits. He didn't
like me being here. Earlier—that's right. Earlier, he said—''

There was a very loud knocking on the door.

''Your aunt coming to get me with her cane.'' Linda slid
her hand onto Schwartz's blue bikini briefs. ''We'll continue
the therapy later—much more seriously,'' she said, standing
and pulling the sheet back up.

Schwartz heard a voice: ''Well, well, well, well. Are you
the Miami Beach police these days, my dear? What can I do to
get arrested? Only joking. I'm Stanley Zeigler, Lenny's cousin.
His older, handsomer cousin.''

And then Stanley appeared, insisting Linda go first so
that his ushering pink fingers fluttered at her shoulder blades.
His other hand brought up a large brown paper bag.

"Stanley," Schwartz said, feeling exhausted, "good to see you. Have you met Officer Gomez—Linda?"

"Linda! Ah, a pretty-meaning name for a pretty-looking girl," Stanley said to Linda, who gave a sweet smile rather than the karate kick to Stanley's groin that Schwartz feared.

Stanley, beaming at the bottom of the bed, asked, "Guess what's in the bag?"

"Fruit?" Schwartz guessed.

"No, no," Stanley said. "Rose brought the fruit." He hit his head. "Oh, I forgot to say, it was Rose, bless her, who called and told me. How are you? You look terrible. Been out all night fighting crime?"

Stanley was laughing at his own joke, the stomach of his madras plaid trousers and blue silk jersey shirt heaving and sinking like an anchor buoy in a sudden chop. He hit his forehead again. "Sorry, incredibly callous of me. So what's in this bag but a brace of—" He paused and lifted out the contents. "A brace of bubbly wine to lift the patient's spirits." The two bottles of Dom Perignon were lashed together with green ribbons.

He thanked Stanley, and Linda put the bottles into the fridge. Then Schwartz asked for something to eat. Stanley sank sighing into the bedside chair, and when Linda brought two cups of yogurt, Stanley accepted one—"But only if there's enough, because my doctor would approve of all this live, natural Bulgarian bacteria, the fink."

Stanley put his spoon hand on Schwartz's hand, blobbing some yogurt. "So, you gonna tell me what happened?" he asked.

"No, Stanley, I'm not."

"Linda," Stanley called, "gimme back the bubbly! Only kidding. I understand that you can't tell me. But where are you hurt?"

"In the stomach," Schwartz said. He swallowed yogurt. Swallowing produced what felt like a foot-long tunnel of pain back from the top of his stomach.

Stanley threw up his hands. A dollop of yogurt dropped onto the sheet. "My god, if I was hurt in the stomach, that'd be three quarters of me in pain!"

Schwartz said, "But I hear you don't get in trouble. As a matter of fact, I hear you're a pussycat."

Stanley tried to look displeased. "Harry. Damn it, Lenny, that sort of talk can ruin a reputation."

"And Rose—"

"Rose!" Stanley shouted, and spooned yogurt quickly into his mouth. "Listen, Lenny, she not only called me to tell me about you, kindly enough—but she was *friendly*. Polite and friendly on the phone. What's come over her? One day she storms out of lunch at my place, next she's comparing notes as to which of us should bring you what!"

Schwartz said, "I warned you she was a thorough researcher, Stanley. She's had to revise her attitude toward your reputation."

For the third time, Stanley slapped his forehead with the base of his palm. "It's always in three, how I forget. That's the other thing. Reputation. I wanted to—" He stopped and leaned toward Schwartz. "Does the lovely lady have to stay to guard you, or can we have a few words in private?"

Linda said she had to go out to do some shopping anyway.

When she'd gone, Stanley stood, went to the window, pulled back the drapes, and stared out. Then he sat by the bed again.

"Lenny," he began, "this is certainly not the cleanest establishment. You could come and stay with me. No, I'm running off at the mouth, again. You know that tip I gave you about Abe?"

"Yes. It was a good one, very useful."

"I don't feel good about it," Stanley said. "Not that it wasn't true. But I got to thinking how I didn't give you a fair picture. All of us, we're complicated. You know, mortal. Look, I did Abe a disservice because there was something *else* Rose didn't know about him. A very good side: the guy was charitable, a philanthropist."

"If that's well-known—"

"No, no. Abe let it slip. No bragging, but he told me. He gave anonymously, you see, and from what I understand, he gave big sums. He didn't say, exactly, but sort of hinted."

"Big sums," Schwartz repeated. "Could we check?"

"That's what I wanted to tell you," Stanley said, spooning the remaining yogurt from the sides of the cup. "I felt so bad about just telling you that other stuff that I set up an appointment for us on my own with Cy Weinstock."

"Who?"

"Cyrus Weinstock. Mr. Philanthropy. Old Miami money. You never heard of the Cyrus Weinstock Foundation? He set it up. It's given away maybe three hundred million." Stanley began cleaning out the yogurt with his index finger.

"Any relation to Melvin Weinstock, a lawyer?"

"Sure. Cy's his father. That's one of the biggest law firms south of Washington. Anyway, I made the appointment for lunch tomorrow, not knowing you'd be like—" Stanley waved his hand at Schwartz's middle. "And Cy's such a hard man to see, and I don't know him that well, so that we were lucky to even get hold of him."

"I'll make it," Schwartz said, feeling he was going to fall asleep during any word now. "You pick me up. When?"

"Eleven-thirty, if you're sure . . ."

"I'm sure. It gives me something to—" The cup and spoon fell from his hand. He picked them up and handed them to

Stanley. "Thank you." He shut his eyes. He'd aim for that, tomorrow. Something to aim for. Luckily, he had a very good colleague. Nurse. Fancy passing fuck. Oh, God. At least there were mercies: Stanley wasn't onto him like Rose. Small ignorant mercies.

Stanley was touching his shoulder. "Listen, Linda's back. I'll call in the morning to check how you are before coming over." Stanley kissed his cheek. "Get better, boychik."

Schwartz opened his eyes.

Stanley moved his mouth to Schwartz's ear and whispered, "You lucky dog. That's some piece of ass police officer you're *schtuping*." He stood, winked, and left.

The lucky dog was too tired to protest. The door closed. Linda was beside him, wiping yogurt from his chin, his arm, the sheet, telling him to sleep. He wanted to tell her about something, about what Cruz said. He wanted to ask if he'd called Karen—no, called *her* Karen—but by then he wanted to ask in his sleep.

CHAPTER 2

By the time Stanley picked him up the next morning, Schwartz was ambulatory, though he knew it was more of a hunched hobble than an amble. Stanley's flamboyance was only sartorial: a seersucker jacket in broad maroon and white stripes, maroon trousers and white shoes, and a white shirt, much of which was covered with a monogrammed maroon SZ. His manner was subdued; once or twice he'd tap Schwartz's arm to say, "A great man. We're lunching with a great person," and then look silently out the window.

Schwartz sat rubbing his stomach, hoping the liniment smell would fade. What he was doing in yet another grand, white, chauffeur-driven car wasn't clear. Why was he still down here? He'd asked Cruz the question he came to ask and had received an answer. True, he'd also received a beating, but that could be thugese for "no hard feelings." His stomach certainly felt tender. Well, he wasn't hanging around just to please Rose Fine, with her clouded vision and pain-in-the-ass perspicacity.

And Linda? Ah. Schwartz did a deep-breathing exercise. Linda had massaged him, then put him through a series of movements and exercises that built to burning, screaming pain, at which point she'd allowed him to collapse into massage again. And so the cycle went, three times, until she collapsed for a few hours' sleep before her night shift. When she woke, he asked her what the police now thought about the Abe Zeigler case. She called, over the running water from the bathroom, that since there'd been none of the mess of a crazed junkie looking for drug money, no sign of robbery, their best guess remained a professional who'd been able to get very close, who probably had a silencer. Then Schwartz heard the shower run.

But when she came out and asked him what *he'd* found about Abe, he said, "Nothing," despite having started to tell her before. His unwillingness to share a lead seemed the defensive equivalent of Linda's name for what they were doing together.

Schwartz looked out the window. Ahead, across the bay, the city shone in white light. But southeast over the ocean the piled clouds were gray, streaked with brown. They looked mud-stained.

Had Linda taken care of him as she had for the past thirty-six hours as only a passing fancy? No, but he wasn't staying here for Linda. And if he thought the police were handling the Zeigler case so well, why hadn't he passed on what he knew to them? No, he didn't understand.

Harry Lee turned south on Biscayne Boulevard. The last time Schwartz had wondered where he was being taken . . . At least a philanthropist probably wouldn't beat him up. Schwartz asked where they were going.

Stanley said, "What? Oh, the Cultural Center. Listen, Lenny, this is a very special human being you're meeting."

"Ah," Schwartz said, curious now to meet the source of Stanley's lip-biting awe. And to Harry's question, Schwartz insisted he'd be all right climbing the stairs.

He wasn't. At their top he felt freshly punched and stopped to clutch his stomach and slowly straighten up. The plaza was a series of glares in the hot sun; water, tiles, tabletops. He reached into his jacket for his sunglasses.

"We should hurry, you know," Stanley said, shifting from white shoe to white shoe. "I don't want to keep him waiting. I'm not trying to hurry you."

They crossed the plaza toward people lunching under white umbrellas. A man held up his hand. He looked like someone— like Leonard Bernstein. When he rose and shook his hand, Stanley stammered something about how good, very good it was for him to see them.

The man turned to Schwartz. "I always have time for this man," he said of Stanley. "I'm Cy Weinstock. I know, you thought I looked like Leonard Bernstein. Someone once called me Bernstein on stilts."

They shook hands. "Leonard Schwartz, Mr. Weinstock. Yes, there's a resemblance, especially from a distance."

"I'm six-foot five-inches tall and I'm eighty-four years old, Mr. Schwartz, and I still don't stoop." He indicated they sit on either side of him. "I have all my own teeth, perfect hearing, and I use glasses only for reading. I've met Bernstein, of course. Nice guy. He said we looked alike as long as I stayed seated. His Mahler is incomparable. But have you heard this new *Pathétique*? Stanley? Pathetic, all wrong, all Mahlerized. There's a kind of conductor who wants to rewrite the music. Von Karajan. Have you ever heard his Wagnerian Brandenburgs, those sparkling streams made into some *Götterdämmerung* mud ocean? And Beecham! Tommy Beecham was the worst. I met him in London in October 1927. Tremendous ego, a great musical propagandist. Well, have you been to our new Cultural Center before?"

Schwartz said no.

Weinstock said, "I eat sharp at 12:15 so I've ordered for all of us. Hope you don't mind. Chef seafood salad and white wine, though I drink mineral water mostly, with a splash of wine. All right?"

"Wonderful, Cy," said Stanley.

Schwartz said, "No. I'm sorry. I've had some stomach trouble, so if you don't mind, I'll reorder."

Stanley looked at Schwartz. A waiter came with the dishes and bottles and changed Schwartz's order.

Weinstock drummed his fingers on the table until the waiter left. "So everyone in Miama's going crazy about this place. To me, don't you think, Stanley, it looks like a California shopping mall. A better one—Carmel or Malibu—but a shopping mall. They think you can just plunk down a second-story space between buildings called museums and a library and everyone in Miama will suddenly love culture and make it the heart of town!" He rubbed his long cragged nose and snapped back a lock of pure white hair from his forehead. "Culture? You know what Miama's idea of Shakespeare is? *Kiss Me Kate on Ice*, and only if it's tax-deductable."

Schwartz smiled. Stanley laughed and wagged his head.

"Look at this man Zeigler, Mr. Schwartz," Weinstock said, fingering a blue-and-white-patterned necktie behind the lapels of his navy-blue blazer. "He looks like a gangster, doesn't he?"

Stanley squirmed with delight until Schwartz said no.

"And you know," Weinstock continued, "if there were enforced laws of aesthetics, Stanley would be serving a life sentence for that ridiculous pile of pink garbage a bunch of Italian con men from New Jersey sold him." He raised a large solemn hand. "It's true."

Stanley tried to work up a bright smile.

"But it's also true that you get into a discussion of Yiddish literature with this man, get arguing, say, if I. B. Singer is really a better novelist than his brother I. J., and Stanley is sensitive and perceptive. And modest. Look at him blush."

Schwartz decided not to look at Stanley blush. He thanked the waiter for his fruit salad with cottage cheese and sipped mineral water. Stanley poured himself a second glass of wine.

Schwartz said, "Mr. Weinstock—"

"See this behind me," Weinstock said, tossing back his white mane, "this library the size of El Escorial? You know El Escorial, in Spain. This may be the most technologically advanced library in the world. A child of four could master its brilliant computer catalog. Unfortunately, a child of four has probably read all the books they have here. Visual aids, microfiche, tapes, videos, they have them all. But ask for something simple, some basic reading? I'm retired from the law now, Mr. Schwartz. Stanley may have told you I was a lawyer. My father started the first law firm in Miama in 1901. And I was saying . . . saying something . . ."

"About the library, Cy," Stanley said softly.

"Yes, so from time to time I still like to read Roman law. Go find it in there, Mr. Schwartz. Go! You won't find it."

"Stanley," Schwartz said, calling for reinforcement to breach the monologue. But Stanley was eating, drinking, and eating and drinking in Weinstock's every word.

"Mr. Schwartz, I'm not one of those people who doesn't speak his mind. I never have been. I'll tell you: I donate a little money here and there, and that sometimes makes people take me for a fool. There, for instance, they asked me for some money for the Fine Arts Center behind you. A good-sized donation: they suggested eight figures."

Weinstock paused so that his listeners might understand

just how much the lowest eight-figure number was. Stanley gave
a low whistle. Schwartz gave a low groan. Stanley looked at
Schwartz. Schwartz pointed to his stomach.

"So first I asked them what, exactly, they had in mind for
fine arts. You know what? Nothing. A series of traveling shows.
No concept of a permanent collection. Okay, so they had a nice
early Cézanne show last year, I'll give them that. But you know
what sort of exhibition you get most of the time?"

Schwartz understood he was not expected to guess out loud.

"Exhibitions of Italian furniture from 1910. Fine arts? You
could see that stuff in stores on University Place in New York,
on Atlantic Avenue in Brooklyn, for heaven's sake. If that's fine
arts, I'm . . . I'm—"

"Leonard Bernstein?" guessed Schwartz.

Stanley managed a simultaneous smile and glare.

"Yes," Weinstock continued. "So, of course, I gave them
a few million, the foundation did, but not the money they expected."

"A wonderful story, Cy," said Stanley.

Schwartz looked at Stanley. Stanley nodded and said, "Cy,
you know I mentioned how Lenny was unofficially looking into
the killing of Abe Zeigler?"

"Terrible. A terrible thing," Weinstock said, pressing his
napkin to his chin. "Mr. Schwartz, Miama has always been a
gambler's city, but we never had this absolutely savage, inces-
sant violence until the arrival of these Latin American gangsters. Those buildings there?" he said, pointing to the glassy
towers just south of the plaza. "They call that our 'cocaine
skyline,' huge enterprises built on drug money. It's an exag-
geration, Mr. Schwartz, but sadly based on fact. A new bar-
barism, a world where they—have you seen the news?—dump
political refugees on an island to die."

"Terrible, Cy," said Stanley. "What will happen to those poor Haitians? They say they might all be sent back."

Schwartz coughed and rubbed his stomach.

Stanley, red with effort, continued: "Cy, I wanted Lenny to hear from you about Abe."

"But Stanley, I didn't know him well at all. He was your friend," Weinstock said, busying himself with his lunch.

Stanley said, "I meant, I thought it would be interesting for Lenny to hear about Abe's philanthropy from you."

Weinstock set down his fork, finished chewing, sipped water, and then said, "Is this a joke, Stanley? His philanthropy?"

"Yes. You know, he let me know how he'd give anonymously, and—"

Weinstock stopped Stanley with a lift of his large hand, the conversation's traffic cop and traffic. He leaned forward and put the hand on Stanley's bald head. "Mr. Schwartz, do you know why I love this man, *love* this gauche, garish man? Because he's got a heart of twenty-four karat gold. Pure as gold. Do you know how much money this man gives to good causes?"

"Cy, come on," Stanley said, going maroon as his monogram.

"He gives most of his income. Sixty, seventy—what is it, Stanley, seventy-five percent? More? *This* man," he said, taking his hand off to leave Stanley free to look away, "gives and gives and wants no publicity. *Here* is a philanthropist. Okay, so I give eighty-five million for a new wing at Mount Sinai. But I get it named the Cyrus Weinstock Cardiology Research Wing. I admit it. I have that sort of vanity. But not this man."

"Cy," Stanley said. "I haven't come here for . . . Lenny, don't listen. I don't give these tremendous amounts like Cy. I give what I can, and you notice how I don't exactly go hungry. It's no big deal. But Abe, Cy. Tell us about Abe."

Weinstock nodded. "Very well, since you insist, Stanley.
Mr. Schwartz, Stanley's heart is not only as pure as gold but
obviously as soft. Ten years ago in January we kicked off a big
building fund-raiser for Jackson Memorial Hospital with a five-
hundred-dollar-a-plate dinner at the Fontainebleau. You remember, Stanley?"

"Yes."

"Someone, not you, recommended Abe Zeigler be invited
as a potential big donor. I'd never heard of him as one, but
naturally we're always looking for major new sources of fund-
ing. So I call him myself and he says he's heard of me—mine's
not an altogether unknown Miama name—and he says he'll
come. Well, it's the usual dinner: floor show, celebrities, and
fund-raising speeches. I had Abe Zeigler seated right up with
myself and the president of the hospital board. Now, sometimes at these affairs, someone forgets to pay until he arrives
and it's time to take out the checkbook and donate. And he
then adds the five hundred dollars or whatever to his check and
that's that. Well, that was Abe's case. But I certainly didn't
know it, and besides, I was too busy trying to make conversation with him."

Schwartz tried very hard to imagine Cyrus Weinstock con-
versing.

"Stanley," he continued, "I love you and I'm deeply
shocked and sorry at your loss, but I must say your cousin was
a bore. A bore, a dullard, and a philistine. But I thought he'd
be good for maybe a quarter of a million, maybe more. So after
all the speeches, the time for checkbooks came and I remember
Andy Shaw, on my right, writing a check for half a million,
and I wrote one for let's stay ten times that. And I tried to look
at Abe's, but he was covering it up. I thought, very nice, the
man's modest. So after the dinner and making a big fuss saying
good night and thanking Abe, which I might say he acknowl-

edged like some sort of Medici prince, I asked Andy what Abe had given. Guess what? Five hundred dollars.''

Stanley said, "But—"

"Wait!" Weinstock directed. "I thought, of course, that Abe misunderstood. He paid for his dinner and Andy will get a check from him later. But nothing happens. So Andy has him over to the hospital for lunch, shows him all around, and finally asks him what he thinks he'll be able to give. And Abe says, 'Give? I already gave five hundred dollars for a lousy twenty-dollar supper and you expect me to give more?' And Andy's mouth is still hanging open when Abe walks out. And that was the first and last *donation* your cousin ever gave.''

"No," Stanley said, the color so drained from him that he looked like stone.

Schwartz put his hand on Stanley's arm.

"No?" asked Weinstock. "You want to ask Andy Shaw? Want to ask Myron Bernstein, Bob Church, Oscar Vergara? I never told you, Stanley, because I saw no reason to make trouble. But now you asked me to tell you, so I had to tell the truth.''

Stanley pushed up from the table. "Excuse me, Cy. Where's the men's room?''

Weinstock nodded.

Schwartz asked Stanley if he was all right.

"Sure, fine," he said. "How's your stomach, Lenny?''

"Better, thanks, Fine," Schwartz said as Stanley walked away.

Weinstock said, "So, Stanley says you're an important New York police officer.'' He smiled handsomely.

Schwartz nodded. "Sure. And I hear you were a great lawyer; I'll bet you clobbered your opponents.''

Weinstock nodded benignly, pushing his hand through his hair. "So they say, young man.''

"I hadn't thought Stanley one of them. I'd say he was a real fan, Mr. Weinstock."

A fast frown waved over Weinstock's large and noble forehead. "Mr. Schwartz, I hope I've been of some use to you."

"You have, thank you."

They sat in silence. The air was very close, hot. Schwartz ate a slice of cantaloupe. Weinstock glanced at his watch.

"I believe," Schwartz said, "your son is a lawyer. Melvin Weinstock. Is it your firm he's with?"

Something strange was happening to Cyrus Weinstock. Schwartz lowered his sunglasses to look. His mouth was hanging open and his pale olive face was growing dark. His large brow moved like a wave machine.

"You know Sonny—Melvin—my son?" Weinstock asked in a voice half its usual volume.

"No," Schwartz said, "I've heard his name mentioned."

"Sonny's firm is Weinstock, Trujillo, Weinstock. Have you heard of that?"

Schwartz shook his head. Weinstock, Trujillo, Weinstock sounded like a line by George S. Kaufman.

"It's a continuation of my law firm," Weinstock said. He sighed. "A continuation of my father's. But *I'm* not a Weinstock in that title. The day Trujillo became a full partner I removed my name; I'd already removed my presence. But Sonny had been expecting this and had set up Roberta, his wife, as a nominal partner so that people would assume one of the Weinstocks was me. It was all legal. Roberta could practice law in Florida. She hasn't in the thirty years since she passed her bar, but she could. So, Mr. Schwartz. My son . . . my son, as I still insist on calling him . . ."

Weinstock slapped his hand on the table. His eyes shone.

"Mr. Schwartz, what do you think of a son who works in the same office with his father and doesn't speak to him for nine

years? Is this a normal man? For nine years before I retired we
sat in adjacent offices. And naturally I'd occasionally go to ask
him a question, to say something. And he wouldn't answer! I'd
be standing there waiting for an answer and Sonny would call
in his secretary and say, 'Tell my father . . .' Tell my father!
Can you imagine? I wouldn't let the staff be so humiliated, so
before the poor secretary could repeat anything, I'd reply directly to Sonny. Can you imagine? Is this normal, Mr.
Schwartz? That's what I'd like to know: is this normal?''

Schwartz said, "It doesn't sound normal."

"He's sick. Sonny is a sick man," Weinstock said, his voice
now back to its authoritative boom.

"Why do you think he doesn't like you?" Schwartz asked.

"You know what some people tell me? They say it's because I settled only two million dollars on Sonny when he came
of age, like on his three sisters. The big money I put into the
foundation. But they're wrong. It's not the money, not that
Sonny isn't greedy, Mr. Schwartz. He's greedy, he's greedy.
But he has so much money now, probably more than I ever
had. No, no, he hates me because I'm an honest man, and
when I saw what he was becoming, I warned him and told him
I'd have no part in it.''

Weinstock grabbed Schwartz's hand and squeezed. His grip
was still strong.

"You know," he said, "sometimes you can say things to
a stranger you couldn't to friends or family. Family. Ah. My
wife died many years ago. I have three fine daughters, but they
have their lives and families far away from here. So I end up
with my son. My only son. And he ends up . . . You don't
know? You don't know who my son's clients are, what kind of
a lawyer he is?''

Stanley came back to the table still pale. Schwartz looked
at him.

"I'm fine," he said. "And don't let me interrupt you. I shouldn't really have more than one glass of wine."

"Yes, good," Weinstock said, turning back to Schwartz. "He's my own son, but he's . . . Mr. Schwartz, if Sonny's clients were suddenly off the face of the earth, the earth would smile."

"Oh, come on, Cy," Stanley said, reaching for Weinstock's arm.

Weinstock lifted his arm and brought his fist down. "Come on, nothing! What do you know, Stanley? You don't have children. What can you know of the heartache?"

Stanley looked down and said, "Nothing, nothing, Cy."

"An only son, Mr. Schwartz. My son, I don't pretend otherwise. So what can you do? You're a father, you love your son. But I don't *like* him. I've tried but I never really liked him. He was always a . . . *pisher*, a slob. So, finally, what you love, even, is the memory of your hopes for your son, not the man himself. Not the sick man, not the rotten lawyer with his disgusting gangster clients. There!"

Weinstock's arm shot out toward the skyscrapers. He looked terrible, like Moses pointing at the idolators. "Sonny helped build that skyline."

"Are you saying that your son has no legitimate clients?" Schwartz asked.

Stanley said, "Lenny, please."

"No, Stanley," Weinstock said, "Why must I be silent? If Sonny has a client with less then twenty million, I'm a monkey's uncle, Mr. Schwartz. And if one of them has made the money legally, I'm a monkey's aunt."

"Jesus, Cy, I hate hearing you talk about your son like this," said Stanley, his eyes wrinkled in pain.

"Stanley, when my son faces the law, faces *justice*, I will not be one of his accusers. I know what I know, but I'm his father. Mr. Schwartz, Lenny," Weinstock said, his voice breaking, "you know the tragedy? Sonny was first in his class at Columbia Law. The pity is the waste, Lenny, the waste. He could have been maybe as good as me. I suppose that technically, he's still brilliant."

Both Stanley and Schwartz picked up their water glasses to look away from the white-maned old man wiping his eyes with the paper napkin.

"I'm sorry, sir," Schwartz said. "It's very sad."

"Sad," Weinstock said, nodding his head with new energy as if the word were a tonic. "Yes it's sad. But I've achieved enough and can give enough to others to have great satisfaction in life without my son." He wiped his hands briskly with the napkin and dropped it. "Well, Stanley, I have an appointment to get to, so I'll be going. The lunch is taken care of, of course. My pleasure."

They stood. Weinstock took Schwartz's hand in his grip. "Pretty good for an old man, eh? I believe I'm still stronger than Sonny. I was four years on the varsity baseball team at Cornell. None of this freshman-exclusion nonsense back then. You look in good shape, young man. But Sonny? Sonny was always such a slob. A physical and moral slob. You know, it's always been difficult for me to believe he has my genes. Well. Good talking with you, Mr. Schwartz."

He turned to Stanley, patting his shoulder. "Take care. Get some of that belly off, Stanley. You'll live longer." Cyrus Weinstock strode away with the gait of a young man.

They sat down.

Stanley shrugged. "This business about Abe: we shouldn't breathe a word of it to Rose. God, I feel awful, dragging you out of bed to hear such stuff."

"Don't. It was useful," Schwartz said, patting Stanley's seersucker. He began to understand why he was staying in Miama, Miami.

Stanley chewed a breadstick, sadly. "And I never knew that about Melvin. My god, I feel sorry for Cy, a distinguished man with such a lousy son. What do you think?"

Schwartz rubbed his stomach. "I'm sorry for myself and I'm sorry for the crap you took. And I'm sorry for anyone with such a monster for a father."

CHAPTER 3

Schwartz told Stanley he'd stay on for some business he had. He didn't tell him it would consist of sitting on his own over a warm, flat glass of soda water wondering what business he had.

He looked across and decided the plaza wasn't bad, just pretentious.

Business: he had a murdered man who was a bore, a dullard, a philistine. Nothing there.

The trouble with the plaza was its assumption that the social spirit of Italian Renaissance street life could be created on a second floor between Miami's high-rise car parks.

Business: he had a murdered man who was a show-off, a cheapskate, a liar. Nothing much there.

He picked up the glass, turned it, looked for any bubbles, and set it down. But he had a murdered man who had two mistresses, two lawyers, two estates: he had a man with two lives. And Sonny Weinstock, lawyer to the very dirty rich, might be the man who knew, if anything, too much about one of them.

Schwartz crossed the plaza to the phone booths. Perhaps

phone booths were an advance over fifteenth-century Siena, Ra-
venna, Gehenna. Perhaps not, he thought, during the fifteen
minutes he spent bent under the plastic dome (his stomach hurt:
why have hairdressers design phone booths?) wheedling and
wheeling toward Weinstock the Younger.

The first phone voice, the receptionist's, was standard:
honeyed noncommitment. The second, from within the office,
was passionate with procrastination. And the third, the one to
which Schwartz added, besides his relation to Abe Zeigler, his
relation to the New York Police Department, was a voice—to
smorgasbord his metaphor—he heard look down its nose at him,
a voice braying with an affected English accent that made "One
minute, please" sound as dreadful as Margaret Thatcher finding herself with Daniel Ortega at high tea.

Besides, it wasn't one minute, it was a cramped, achy five—
and his hair wasn't setting well at all—before a man's voice
came on, a study in laconic uninterest, with, "Yeah, who's
this?"

"Schwartz, Schwartz, Schwartz! Didn't *one* of your three
employees get it? You have a staff problem."

"Be quick, I'm busy."

Always eager to oblige, Schwartz said, "Ten minutes in
person, your office, now."

"Why?"

"Bernard Sonnabend?"

"No, that's another law firm."

"Bernard Sonnabend's late client?"

"No."

"His late client Abe Zeigler, a clever man who ended
brainless?"

There was a small pause. "No. And that's in bad taste."

Schwartz sighed. "Okay, but this is absolutely my last offer: Bernard Sonnabend's late client Abe Zeigler's mistress

Mary Smith sunning at the Sheldrake on a lounge, on a trust fund?''

There was a longer pause.

''And for good measure,'' Schwartz said, ''how about Roberto Cruz?''

''I don't know that name. But, right. My office in half an hour. For ten minutes only.''

The voice rang off before Schwartz could thank Mr. Weinstock—if he was Mr. Weinstock—or if he was Mr. Trujillo, thank him and ask if he were related to the caudillo of the same name.

Schwartz set off slowly toward the big buildings; thirty minutes for a few blocks seemed a fair test of his recovery.

A painful twenty-five minutes later Schwartz stepped from the elevator into the thirty-third-floor lobby. Through the glass end wall subdued sunlight showed the building's round glass towers reflected in the mirror faces of two other skyscrapers. A cloud showed in them somewhere, reflected, lost. Schwartz crossed to a black glass desk, to the dark-haired receptionist's smile, pretty as a picture, perhaps actually a picture, another reflection detached.

He smiled back. ''Hi. I'm Mr. Schwartz, Mr. Weinstock's 2:43 to 2:53 appointment. Am I too early? Too late? Both?''

Perhaps because of her working environment not easily dazzled, the young woman maintained the peppermint smile and asked him to go right through. She meant it: a six-foot curve of glass wall swung open, and Schwartz entered a waiting room. It had two leather armchairs and a large leather sofa all in light sea green and another black glass desk behind which another young woman, with red hair, asked him to have a seat.

He did. He waited three times the length of his appointment turning vellum-thick pages of international property magazines whose texts ended with mottoes like ''A Substantial Sum

Is Required'' or ''The Title Honorary Margrave May Be Pur-
chased with the Schloss.''

Finally, a third woman came out of another glass wall and
told him Mr. Weinstock would see him now. She had ash-blond
hair, fiery red shoes, and the voice, Schwartz recognized, of
winter and its discontent.

Schwartz went in, the glass swung shut. Sixty feet in front
of him stood Sonny Weinstock at his desk in an office so glassy
and grand that Schwartz might have fallen to his knees, struck
blind, but for the countervailing gloom of an enormous collection of art so intensely bad that Schwartz might have fallen to
his knees, sick to his stomach, which didn't feel so hot anyway.

In this dizzy equilibrium, Schwartz's hands went to his
mouth to megaphone: ''Hello out there. I'm Schwartz. That's
some cheerleading section you employ. What are they: broken
homecoming queens?''

Sonny Weinstock was a tall, blubbery man. Bits of neck
hung over his pink button-down collar. He nodded. ''You have
ten minutes. Would you like to sit down, or is yours a stand-
up act, Mr. Schwartz?''

Schwartz took a walk and took a seat. ''Thank you, I'm a
bit stunned coming from the minimal glitz of your holding tanks
out there into all this rococo kitsch. That painting against the
wall, for instance: how do they get that thing that looks like a
third-hand condom to stick to those brown lumps?''

Weinstock looked at his watch.

Schwartz said, ''I see I'm not going to win your heart and
mind with laughter, Sonny. May I call you Sonny?''

''Sure,'' he said, sitting behind his desk. It was long, black-
lacquered, and crammed with photos in elaborate silver and
gold frames, and lotus trays and daffodilled ewers after Louis
Tiffany.

Schwartz looked around. Where sculpture and painting

didn't block it, the view was through three quarters a vast circle of glass, one of the four towers that cornered the skyscraper.

"This building's a version of a medieval keep, isn't it?" Schwartz asked.

"That's right," said Sonny.

"For the Castle of Avarice?"

"Ah, I hadn't heard that before. I'd heard Castle Covetous. Mr. Schwartz—"

"I know. I can't afford your fee clock and your free clock is running. Why should a man have two lawyers for his estate?"

Sonny Weinstock gave a tiredly ironic smile and put his hand out on the desk. Even without the excess flesh, his features would have been sloppy. Where his father's were large and clear, the son's were pudgy, fuzzy, hapless. He slid down the knot of his tie and unbuttoned his collar. "Many people have more than one lawyer: different functions, specialties, you know."

"So where exactly does Mary Smith's trust come from?"

Sonny cocked his head. "Where? From a trust. A trust is a trust. Mr. Zeigler set that up several years ago, since he wasn't young and felt he should provide for his companion. It's not unusual. Does anything bother you about it?"

Schwartz's stomach started to burn. He wasn't getting anywhere with Mary Smith, so he took an educated guess: "Why haven't you been to the police about this?"

"Because there's no reason why I should," Sonny said, pushing a purple egg, fake Fabergé, with his thumb. "They haven't asked to see me about Mr. Zeigler's death. If and when they do, Mr. Schwartz, I'll answer their questions. Which, you know, I don't have to do with you. The trust for Miss Smith is, of course, filed for probate. I'd ask your interest, but that would take from your"—he looked at his watch—"four minutes."

"Yes," Schwartz said. He shut his eyes. His stomach was shooting needles into his groin. "Abe Zeigler is a distant cousin, but I'm interested on behalf of another family member." Schwartz opened his eyes and leaned forward for emphasis, also for holding the pain. "You said you didn't know the name Roberto Cruz. That's funny, like saying you never heard of the Miami Dolphins because you're not a fan."

Sonny looked at the egg. "Did I say that? I meant to say I have no connection of any sort with him."

Schwartz nodded. "That's more like it. Any first-year law student down here would know that name, let alone the senior partner in a firm renowned—is that that word I want, 're-nowned'?—for defending the dukes of drugdom, among whom Cruz is a prince, though I'm not here to discuss your partner Mr. Trujillo."

Weinstock picked up a photo, looked at it, and set it down. It fell. Setting it up, he knocked down two adjacent frames.

"I hope I'm not making you nervous?" Schwartz asked.

"No," he said, "and you're not making me late. You still have two minutes."

"Two?" Schwartz wanted his stomach to let him concentrate. "Well, then, here's my big question. It either hooks you or . . . Since, from Miss Smith's eloquent facial, if not verbal, expression, I understand Abe Zeigler's trust was modest—let's say a hundred thousand, no more than two—what was he doing as *your* client?"

"I do all sorts of law, Mr. Schwartz. Anyone can—"

Schwartz was holding up his hand. He stood, folding his arm across his jacket, pulling in to rub his stomach. "You're not *anyone's* lawyer. I have it on good authority that you won't touch anyone who isn't very wealthy, stinking rich. I haven't checked probate, but I'd bet whatever you declared for Abe isn't very big. And I don't think you took him on because of his radiant personality or heart of gold.''

Weinstock pushed his chair back. ''Well, your time's up. Who did you hear this nonsense from?''

''Your father.''

The purple egg toppled at Sonny's hand and rocked on its side. He narrowed his eyes. ''Ah, yes,'' he said. ''I should have known. You've had an audience with the Great Man. The Great Man told you what a bitter disappointment I've been.''

Schwartz said yes.

Sonny continued to narrow his eyes until they were squeezed shut, as if he had stared into the sun. ''And let me guess, he somehow let you know the scale of his good works: 'They were suggesting eight figures, sir,' he said. Something like that?''

''Very much like that.''

Sonny opened his eyes. They were bloodshot now. His fingers tapped the desk, rocking much as his father's had, tapping the table. ''And of course you were impressed. Everyone is. You found him one hell of a grand old man—so cultured, so long-suffering, so *kind*.''

Schwartz felt his stomach trying to turn itself inside out. He sat down again. ''I found him awful, Sonny. A man with an ego as big as your art collection and maybe as ugly.''

Sonny passed a hand through his hair. The motion from his father, suggesting the impatience of power, had been elegant. This one merely drew attention to the limp, thinning hair of the son.

Then Sonny stood, picked up a heavy silver frame, and came around the desk toward Schwartz, who looked up hoping he wouldn't be hit with it. But Sonny was smiling, an inelegant droop-shouldered smile, not Cy's brilliant, billion-dollar grin, and his lips, full as his father's, were slack—"sloven lips," his father would say. Still, it was a smile, and Schwartz saw the way to the son's heart was through his father's—with a carving knife.

Sonny pointed. "See? My kids. And all the *chatchkes* on the desk? Silver, gold, lapus, malachite? Photos of *my* family, gifts from my kids. They're worth everything. Do you know what the great Cyrus Weinstock, *my father*, gave me?"

Schwartz said, "Two million, when you came of age."

Sonny stroked the glass and silver in his hand. "No, the real legacy: hatred, self-contempt enough for two lifetimes—" He stopped, went back, and carefully replaced the picture on the desk. "Do you love your father . . . like your father, Mr. Schwartz?" Sonny's back was turned, still bent over the desk.

"I did. He's dead," Schwartz said. "I still think of him—"

"Fuck it!" shouted Sonny, turning. "You have something to say, say it. I charge a hundred dollars a minute for my time; for that, I'll listen to anything—your bad jokes, your critique of my art collection, even your attacks on my father to win my approval." He stopped, took a breath, and continued more quietly. "But I'm listening for free, so what you say had better interest me." He pointed a finger. "Go ahead."

"I think," Schwartz said, "that your father's a monster, but I also think he knows what's going on. And what I'm going to say is conjectural; I'm trying it out." He stopped to breathe deeply and rub his stomach.

Sonny sat down on the edge of his desk; the side of his shirt came untucked from his trousers.

Schwartz said, "Despite appearances, Abe Zeigler had a lot of money, and he had something going with you. I don't know—his capital, your investment contacts, maybe. Whatever it was, it ran into big trouble and he was killed. For what he

did? To warn you? You see, I don't think you had him killed,
and not because you have cute pictures of your kids. No, I think
you're sitting on something big and nasty and you're afraid it's
going to blow your ass away any minute, Sonny, and leave
those kids without a loving dad. I don't know what you're into;
I don't know if your father was right that you're involved with
the drug trade. I know that if it *is* drugs, you're in big trouble:
those people aren't much for turning cheeks. That's it."

Sonny's eyelids were half-closed.

"Very good, Sonny," Schwartz said. "You do a great line
in boredom." He stood. "I'm going now. I'm only a visiting
fireman, policeman, not working with the locals. I'm going to
be around for a little bit longer, and I'll leave my number with
Goneril or Regan out there. So if you want to talk with someone—off the record . . ."

He headed toward what he remembered was the door part
of the dark glass wall. "Oh, I have to ask," he said, stopping
as the wall swung open, "*is* your partner related to Trujillo the
dictator?"

Sonny said, "I believe so. Distant cousins, Mr. Schwartz,
like you and the late Mr. Zeigler."

C H A P T E R 4

If she took a cab back, Florida Fruit wasn't too far. Rose walked to Washington Street because she hated the convenience stores nearby on Collins, with their puckered oranges and a same "fresh" barbecued chicken on sale four days in one of their greasy rotisseries. Besides, she liked the sensation of the produce store: a hall of bins—apples and celery, parsley next to the black-purple clubs of eggplant. There were pineapples and string beans, yellow melons, and the pale green mangoes blushing red. And the smell of limes and Spanish onions and bananas blown in the cool arcs of the corner fans.

Rose pulled the shopping cart to the corner of Tenth and stopped. Sometimes the cabs wouldn't go on such a short trip, but most times they understood. She set up the cart, leaned on her cane, and stuck her arm out.

A tall man walked up and asked, "A cab, lady?"

"Yes, but just to the Marlowe Court on Collins."

"Sure." He nodded. "Lemme get your shopping."

He picked the cart up by its handle and took Rose lightly

by the arm, around the corner to the cab. It was nice when they were considerate like this. He put the cart in front and opened the back door.

She turned, facing the sidewalk, backing in, holding the top of the door. "I'll do it," she said. "It just takes time."

He said, "Watch your head."

She sat back, brought one leg up, turned on the seat, and pulled the other leg in. But now there was a mistake. Someone else was already in the backseat. The door slammed shut.

"What?" she asked.

The man beside her pointed a gun.

She asked, "Is this a holdup?" knowing it wasn't a holdup.

The front door shut. Rose didn't feel afraid, just sensitive, like opening her mouth at the dentist's when she knew there'd be no drilling. She heard the door locks click. The taxi started. It had been yellow and there was a meter. A real taxi. Ah, where was the cabbie photo? Would it look like the big man driving?

If she kept asking herself questions and stayed still, she thought she could keep calm. Fairly calm, considering. Why didn't they blindfold and tie and gag her? Oh, that was simple: they didn't have to. She was old and didn't see well and couldn't be heard if she tried to yell. She felt she was doing well.

"Ask about the pills," the driver said.

The man beside her turned. He was big, like the driver. Cuban, she thought, or anyway Latin. He had no—what were they called? No distinguishing features. Except his size and the gun. No, no, a gun wasn't a feature. She wondered if she was in shock.

"You on pills?" he asked.

Of course she was. She was mostly on pills, with fruit and yogurt added for variety.

"Hey, old lady! You on pills? You hear me?" the man yelled.

That was it. She was calm as long as she spoke to herself, silently. Talking to—them . . . Rose opened her mouth. She coughed. Coughed and coughed. She put a hand out; the driver understood and passed back her handbag. She coughed, thinking that if he wasn't a real cabbie, it was a shame because he'd be a very good cabbie. She took out the handkerchief and coughed into it. "I need pills," she said. Her voice sounded scratched and away from her, like an old record in another room.

"You got some with you? How much, how many days?" the man asked.

Rose knew before she looked in the bag: "One, one day."

"What happens after that?"

Oh, she was being kidnapped. That was why he asked. Was this shock? His gun looked like a small power tool. A cordless drill, maybe. Flatter. It was very ordinary looking, a gun. Toy guns looked very similar. Or was it that toy guns—

"Hey, old lady!"

"Yes. Well, after the pills run out, besides the pain, my metabolism becomes unstable." There, she'd said that well, almost normally.

Rose sensed his stare. She continued. "I can become very ill after that, without the pills, so that, besides the pain, I suppose my life would be endangered." She liked "besides the pain," but perhaps "endangered" would confuse him. No, he would have heard "in danger."

She closed her eyes. Kidnapping was very quiet. When she opened her eyes, the blur outside the car was still mostly white. That and the noise told her they were still in the city. Yes, the driver and the man beside her were very quiet. She closed her eyes.

Now, why would she be kidnapped? Easy—Lenny. It would
have to be. It was easy to know that, an instant deduction. No,
it was a fast elimination of alternatives. A few days ago she
would have thought Stanley was behind it, but she'd learned
otherwise. And they weren't kidnapping her for ransom: no
money to be had there!

She wondered if she was smiling. So this had to be connected with Lenny and his limousine hit-and-run business. Oh,
no, it didn't. Suddenly Rose felt cold. If with her thyroid condition she felt cold, it must be shock. It must be connected with
Abe, with Abe's murder.

Rose opened her eyes. The blur outside had green mixed
with white and pauses in the noise. Suburbs, outskirts. Oh, it
had nothing to do with Abe. It was time she faced it: his murder
was a horrible accident. Some mad killer, some terrible mistake.
Perhaps . . . She looked to her side. The man was nodding,
half-asleep. Would it be so difficult to grab his gun? Yes, it
would. And if she had it, she wouldn't know what to do with
it.

This was a long ride. It was the right thing to stay quiet.
That was easy: she didn't wish to speak with these men. Her
kidnappers. Her abductors. Rose found the idea of abduction
faintly amusing—the stuff of cheap romantic fiction—sexual,
ridiculous, and comforting. Comforting because such writing
never held real risk, discomfort, pain. Violence, rape, bloody
murder. So if this was the real thing, why wasn't she more—
discomforted?

She thought to close her eyes again but found they opened.
She'd dozed off. The road was quieter now and green, green,
green blurred by. She wanted to look at her wristwatch. They
wouldn't want her to. She coughed, took off her glasses and
brought the handkerchief to her mouth. There. Almost an hour.

The car slowed. It turned onto gravel and a gate swung.

Rose put on her glasses and narrowed her worse eye. Her window slowly passed a sign with large letters.

Then the man next to her said, "Now you just do what you're told, old lady."

Rose decided she was fed up with "old lady." She said, "I will. My *name* is Rose."

The man laughed when he said, "Yeah, Rose, do what you're told." An hour later, doing what she was told, she'd found that the kidnapping *was* connected to Lenny, and she'd helped work out the note she was about to read. Paco dialed, got through, and handed Rose the phone.

"Stanley," she said, "this is Rose Fine. I'll say this slowly but only once, so listen carefully. I'm being held prisoner until Lenny Schwartz leaves Miami, until he can be reached at a New York number which you'll give me when I call again in twelve hours or twelve after that. Don't try to contact the police and don't try to find this place, Faulkner. I have only a day's worth of pills, so Lenny has to leave soon or I'll be in danger."

Paco took the phone from her and hung it up. He raised his hand in front of her face, ready to slap her. "What did you say after you said not to try finding this place, Rose? Fog— something?"

Rose said, "I'm sorry. I was nervous. It was something I call my cousin Stanley—*'ferkahkte.'* That's Jewish for 'darling.' "

She saw the big hand drop and decided she'd pushed her luck enough: she wouldn't remind him to rinse the fruit.

C H A P T E R 5

An hour after leaving Sonny Weinstock, Schwartz leaned against the Neptune Plaza's tiki bar, looking out over the swimming pool to the beach. The white-gold sand was ashen in the spreading overcast. The hotel pool, swamp green at its brightest, had darkened to a darn tank or dank tarn, the one that closed over the House of Usher. From the hotel, toward which he looked for Linda, electric cable hung from windows on several floors. Schwartz felt Eddie Poe wouldn't have been caught at a defunct bar like this whose thatch of brown plastic was less tiki than tacky.

Then Linda, in uniform, came in through the pool's side-street entrance. In uniform, she looked more ordinary, a good thing considering what he needed to discuss.

She kissed him lightly on the cheek and asked what was so important. The kiss seemed casually proprietory, the kiss of a wife. This reminded him he had a wife who sometimes kissed like this.

"Well," he said, "I have to ask—"

"Is this a proposal? Are you going to leave your beautiful,

clever, funny wife? Want to marry me, Lenny?'' she asked happily.

He tried to guess the attitude behind her sunglasses. ''The sun's gone,'' he said.

Linda nodded, taking the glasses off. ''Ah, you mean it's still only a little lust for Linda?'' Her eyes were bright, all surface.

''I'm onto something important in the Abe Zeigler murder. Nothing hard, some circumstantial business. You know, undertones, nuances.''

She said, ''I'll bet you're hot on nuance.''

''Yes, in New York I'm known as old nuance nose. But in New York a homicide team would at least have done the groundwork.''

Linda leaned over, looking into the empty bar well. A white-brown pigeon flapped up and flew out to a greeny-orange blotch of crotons. ''What ground is that?'' she asked.

''A lawyer named Melvin Weinstock, defender of the richest indefensibles. I'm sure Abe was mixed up with him in some business.''

Linda hitched her trousers up and tucked her white shirt tight beneath its belt. She said, ''I don't see any problem besides your refusal to abandon your wonderful family and fine career to come down here to the steamy south and start again as lusty Patrolman Schwartz.''

Schwartz stared at her; her irony was very deadpan. He said, ''That may be your problem. My problem is why your department hasn't come across Weinstock yet and whether or not I should point him out.''

Linda stepped close to Schwartz and put her hand onto his shirtfront. ''How's your battered midriff?''

''Better,'' he said. ''Bearing up.''

She dropped her hand and leaned back against the bar.

"I'll tell you something, Lenny: if *I* don't know, then you certainly don't know that the department *hasn't* found this lawyer. I think your problem's in not telling us—the investigation team, the chief, or even me, officially. And I think your other problem, an even bigger one, is that you're messing around too much with an ongoing investigation. Please stop. You can see how compromised I'll be if you don't."

Schwartz considered compromise. "Yes," he said. The wind picked up, blew Linda's hair across her eye. He lifted his hand to brush it back but stopped and scratched his own unitchy neck. "But I'd still like you to sit on this, just for a few more days. Please?"

"A few days," she repeated. "Well, why not, seeing as I'm already so compromised with you, by you."

Schwartz felt foolish. He said, "So that's why you haven't brought me home to meet Mom and Dad Gomez." Now he felt patronizing; he hoped he'd kept suspicion from his voice.

She turned to him without a smile. "I haven't even brought you *home* to meet me. If I did, you could meet the folks; they're in the condo block next door."

"And why haven't I been to your place?" he asked. "I thought we'd been through that and agreed it was no place to be ashamed of for any reason."

Linda tapped the edge of her sunglasses on the bar, a Formica stippled with dead flies. She folded the glasses and looked across to the beach. "Did you hear we're going to pick up an edge of that Melvin storm system in the next few days?"

"Oh."

"Oh? Do you really need it in words, Lenny? Right: as you've probably noticed, I'm impulsive. But I'm not self-destructive. I keep our hot relation out here. Hotel-room flings. Flings," she repeated, and laughed. "A romance of running, a beach romance, a summertime thing. It's always summer here on the beach: you've seen the brochures. If I took you home, across the bay, I'd be letting myself . . ." She turned to him. "Come off it, Lenny. I know what this is for you: a few days of fun, romantic fantasy—a little guilt, a little sunburn. That's all."

She put her hand on his shoulder, pulled close, and stroked his arm. "Look at you, so *cute* with your frizzy hair and beat-up tummy and wrinkly Brooks Brothers jacket. You're a cute cop. But you're wrong: my emotions aren't as hard as my tri-ceps or glutes."

"Your glutes are beauts," he said.

She tapped his shoulder. "That's it, keep it light. And okay, I'll sit on this for a few days, let's say three, max. Then we'll go in together and tell the investigation what you know."

"Thank you," Schwartz said. He went to kiss her cheek, but her cheek moved off.

"On duty," she called from the gate.

Schwartz walked into the hotel, attempting to forget Linda by imagining how he might pressure Sonny Weinstock into tell-ing him everything. Something. Anything. At the desk he picked up a telephone message. It was from Stanley. It said: "Emer-gency. Call immediately."

Immediately was only after twisting his way through the growing jungle of electric wires outside his room. But there was no answer, except the quiet voice of Harry Lee on answer-phone, asking for the caller's name and number, not giving Stanley's.

Schwartz set the phone down frowning. Unlisted numbers. No names. Should he try Rose? No, he'd try to keep her from suspicions about her honest Abe. His frown was about this next unpleasant business, but he could think of no one else. Linda had been the only one who . . .

The Miami phone book had pages of Gomezes. But she

said they were doctors, and they lived next door. That would be Brickell Avenue. He wished he wasn't doing this.

There—Gomez, E.M., MD. He turned back some pages and found the same address—Favela-Gomez, Dolores, MD. Well, so what? He dialed the Dade County Library and found they were open until eight. He drove right over.

As Cyrus Weinstock had said, the library was wonderfully efficient. As he hadn't said, Schwartz was able to find what he was looking for, county and state medical registers going back to the forties. But he didn't stretch his luck to look for Roman law. He stretched it to dial the home number on the card Cyrus Weinstock had given him.

And when it held and he was put through, he used the direct approach to a swollen ego: he told him the problem was huge, it was impossible, really, really presumptuous to ask if *anyone* could help, let alone one whose time was as valuable . . .

Weinstock, sounding like a born-again Bernard Baruch, said, "Yes, it's a difficult task, but very few things are impossible, young fellow, when there's a will and energy and you aren't *absolutely* the worst-connected person in the town." He asked Schwartz's number and promised to call back within fifteen minutes, if only to tell him how long it might take to obtain the information.

Schwartz paced the lobby by the phone. He wished he didn't have to do this. Maybe, even if it came out badly, there could be another interpretation.

Cyrus Weinstock called within his fifteen minutes, and Schwartz knew he'd found the information from his first words, "Detective Schwartz," the big voice almost erotic with smugness. He said that as Schwartz had thought, Ernest M. Gomez and Dolores Favela-Gomez of South Bay Towers were not doctors. But he'd found ("A few people in medical circles hereabouts seem to like me, for some strange reason") that both had retired from the medical profession—retired as *nurses*, after working twenty-five years at St. Francis Hospital. It was strange, Cyrus Weinstock said, how some people needed to appear better than they were.

Schwartz agreed promptly, thanked him profusely, and paid his only unironic compliment by lying profoundly that, no, actually, he hadn't yet met Sonny.

Schwartz drove back to the beach in a mist rolling in from the sea. How strange was it for Linda's parents to appear "better" than they were? He wished he hadn't found out, but he found that finding out made him feel a bit better. His stomach felt somewhat better, he felt a little more relaxed. He had, he felt, some tiny idea of what was going on.

C H A P T E R 6

This was Jaime's moment. Carmen had helped him practice. He'd sat quietly while Cruz had stopped an argument between two board members first by joking them into attention, then by threatening them into work. After that, Jaime had listened to the factory report (Colombia) and then to the two shipping reports (Panama, Mexico) without filing his fingernails or combing his hair. He adjusted his darkest tie, bright black, running his fingers lightly down the lapel of his new double-breasted black-and-white-check suit (Lapidus, $3750). His cuff links were small diamonds, and his report lay before him typed so neatly that it might have been a book or something, a piece of newspaper, even, without the pictures or ads.

At the other end of the boardroom table, Cruz made notes on a large pad of paper. The four other men, two on either side of the table, looked at him. The two on-duty guards sat on chairs either side of the doorway. They held small television sets on their laps, much as a pair of dowagers might hold Pe-

kingeses, with which they checked various entrances to Broadmoor, Cruz's private garage, and his own three floors.

Jaime knew it was a good business meeting, one of the best.

Cruz dropped his pen. "Any other business?" he asked,
looking up.

Jaime bit his lip back from saying "Sure" and raised his
hand, not too high, not too low, just like he'd practiced with
Carmen.

Cruz nodded. "Jaime."

Jaime coughed. "Thanks. Thank you, Mr. President, Ramon . . . uh, other board members." He coughed and looked
down at the notes. He sipped from the water glass before him.
"Approximately four hours ago Rose Fine was picked up and
that went fine. Good." Jaime looked up.

All five men were giving him their attention. Four of them
had no idea what he was talking about.

Jaime referred to his notes and continued. "She arrived
about three hours ago, more or less, at a secure place which for
reasons of security I'm not gonna say, mention, here. We had,
they did, I mean, made her . . . More or less about two hours
ago, approximately, she called a relative of hers to give
Schwartz, Detective Schwartz, I mean, the message that we,
they, that she was bein' held and had one day, Schwartz, the
detective had, before her pills ran out and her health would
maybe be in trouble, like she'd snuff it. So he'd better leave,
not this person she was talkin' to, I mean, but who'd he'd speak
to. The relative would speak to. Schwartz, Detective Schwartz,
to get him out of town out of our business without anyone get-
tin' hurt or she'd die. Rose Fine would. Not get out of town,
she'd die. When Schwartz is out, she gets put back okay. When
Detective Schwartz, I mean. Thanks, thank you." He looked up.

Only Cruz was looking at him.

"Thank you for the report, Jaime," Cruz said.

Jaime nodded and smiled and tried to sit down but hadn't stood, so rocked back and forth in his chair with the effort. But it had gone good, like he'd practiced with Carmen. And he hadn't brought up that it was his idea about Bob's redneck crew that turned out to be right, because that would only piss off Roberto.

One of the four others, the owner of a factory and an agricultural investor from Colombia, rubbed the sides of his thighs under the table, trying to warm himself in air so overconditioned he thought he saw his breath puff out.

Cruz tapped his thick black pen. "That operation was very well done, Jaime, and I know it would have got rid of Schwartz as we planned. Except I've received some new information from a reliable source that your old friend Schwartz—"

"He ain't my—"

"Jaime!"

"Yeah, sorry. Go on."

Cruz said, "Thank you."

At one side of the long table, Ramon A. Colon, a Panamanian who'd risen from humble hired killer to killer with ninety thousand producing acres and twelve houses in four countries, pushed his thumb hard into the table's lower edge to stay awake.

"I've just found out," continued Cruz, "that your old friend Schwartz is maybe onto something that could lead us to recover certain *misplaced funds* and also to settle *certain accounts*, since our trail ran out when a certain *Marielito* crew named José disappeared from Miami with a certain redneck crew we didn't even have a fockin' name for! So we gotta go back on your nice pickup job because now we do not want to drive Schwartz from the area, Jaime. And you're gonna move in two minutes and phone to get the old lady all released and back safe and in one piece to her door. And then we're gonna follow Schwartz nice and easy to go where he takes us.''

Jaime pulled at his tie. Why couldn't Roberto give him credit for tracing Bob's crew? ''You mean I done the kidnap and this whole fuckin' report for nothing?''

Cruz said, ''No, Jaime. I said thanks. Now we've gotta change our plans according to these new changes. Understand?''

Jaime stood. ''And I gotta wear these *funeral* clothes for all this shit?''

''Sit down, Jaime!'' Cruz shouted. ''You're starting to ruin the fockin' meeting again. I tell you what: when your pal Schwartz leads us wherever, you can kill him.''

Mr. Colon stopped pressing his thumb.

Jaime wanted to ask about the redneck, to ask why Roberto could say ''Schwartz'' at the meeting when he had to say ''Detective Schwartz,'' but the good news put it from his head. He said, ''Now you're talking, Mr. President,'' and smiled.

Cruz said, ''The meeting's closed. Hey! Everybody use the shredder before leaving.''

Jaime picked up the neatly typed sheet, happy that he'd used real good paper like this to shred.

Cruz watched the men lining up at the machine. It was none of their business that he wasn't going to tell his reliable source about the change in plans. That could help keep Schwartz off guard. Still, there was the risk that Schwartz might kill the source. Well, that was the breaks; besides, they'd already got what they wanted from Linda.

CHAPTER 7

Stanley put down the phone, confused. Rose wouldn't play stupid pranks. And there was a man who'd said "Wait" before Rose came on. Yet what could he do but try Rose's apartment? No answer. He sat by the phone, unable to think; his head felt thickened, congealed. He looked at the piece of paper in his hand but couldn't focus. Then Maxi came up to the chair and nuzzled him, and Stanley got up and walked out of the Florida room through the hall and into the library. Maxi walked along, head to his master's hip.

What did this mean? Stanley looked at the walls of books. What good were they if he couldn't think. He might as well be a dog.

"Sorry, Maxi," he said aloud, sitting on the desk. Maxi nuzzled the paper. Then Stanley dialed the Neptune Plaza, but Lenny wasn't in, so he left a message. Why shouldn't he call the police? Because . . . Stanley began to think again.

They could kill her. Rose was kidnapped to make Lenny leave town. *Why* didn't matter. If he called the police, they could find out and kill her. Who? That wasn't the point! What could he do?

Maxi knelt under a Regency library table, nosing the head of a sphinx.

Stanley looked at the message he'd taken down from Rose:

Rose prisoner Lenny—NY (tel. no. he can be called at) R call again 12 hrs & 12 hrs later. No police. don't find place falconer? Faulk . . . ? *1 day pills in danger* if L doesn't leave soon

What was falconer? No, Faulkner, it was definitely Faulkner. It meant something; it didn't fit. "Maxi!" Stanley said.

Maxi looked up. The sphinx was nearly noseless.

Faulkner was a clue. Stanley went to the shelf with atlases and maps and pulled out the Miami-and-vicinity street finder. There was no Faulkner in the street index, no Faulkner in the reference; no park, no school, nothing named Faulkner.

Then what? Something associated with William Faulkner. Sure, Rose the librarian passing a message to Stanley the reader. What association? The south. South Beach? South Miami? No, no, too vague.

If Lenny were in, what would he advise? Lenny, her kidnapping was connected with Lenny. So what was he up to? Finding out about Abe. But no, that . . . No. But those gangsters at the track. "Maxi!" he shouted. "Las Palmas Farms used to be Wild Palms Stables. Rose must have seen something. You see, Maxi? Faulkner: *The Wild Palms!*"

Maxi may not have seen. He went on chewing the riddle: what has a nose at three in the afternoon, half a nose at 3:10, and probably no nose at all by 3:15?

Then Stanley found the Las Palmas Farms address in the phone book and hurried to the kitchen, Maxi padding attendance, and he found himself explaining a plan to Harry that he was making up on the spot. Harry didn't like it. He said they should either wait for Mr. Schwartz or call the police. The plan couldn't work. Besides, Harry wanted to know why Mr. Stanley was so eager to risk his life for someone who, frankly, didn't like him.

"Because she likes me better now. Harry, I mean, what else can I do: mouth my fourteen-dollar El Presidentes and cheat on my diet until I drop dead of cholesterol and boredom?"

Again Harry tried to talk him out of it, succeeded in getting Stanley to call Schwartz once more, and when there was still no answer told him he'd have to go alone, and when he saw Stanley would, of course went with him, begging that Stanley at least wouldn't take the gun which was ridiculous not so much because of the carved wooden handgrip Stanley had added, palm trees and a sunburst sunset incised like on wooden yo-yos of Harry's childhood, but because Stanley had never fired it or any other gun and Harry wouldn't touch it with the phobic aversion of someone who continued to have twice-weekly night-mares of his two years in the penitentiary eighteen years before.

Stanley took the gun in the pocket of his dark green bush trousers. They took the green Jeep wagon and they took Maxi, who lay in the back like a heap of black rugs.

As they pulled out of the drive, Harry told Stanley that this rescue was impossible. Stanley agreed and told Harry the best route would be the Tamiami Trail out to 997 and then south.

And now that Stanley had decided he was going to rescue Rose, he felt no fear, felt, as a matter of fact, a great, viscous stupidity, as if his thoughts were turning to molasses, sticking to each other, losing shape. He did nothing but look out the window watching the shop signs go from English to Spanish and back to English. So this was bravery, he thought, this men-tal laryngitis.

Now there were no shops, just low stucco houses. And now the houses thinned and saw grass and palmetto appeared between the clumped developments that swept like forest fire into the Everglades. Stanley turned on the radio. There was news and weather: rain, it said, would spread from the southeast by morning.

Harry asked Stanley what he thought about all those rescued Haitians put in custody and refused political-refugee status. Stanley thought it was awful. They'd be sent back to Haiti and probably killed. He started to think of Rose and stopped, remembering the call for help he received from the Haitian lobby group. Then Stanley said they'd better concentrate on the planning they had to do.

Harry agreed and was quiet. Stanley watched the edge of the farms come up like a green ridge across the flat grassland. Then they turned south down 997.

Fifteen minutes later Harry said, "They'll kill us."

"Yes," Stanley said, "we have to be careful." They were passing palm plantations packed green, frond upon frond. They passed a thoroughbred racing farm, a nursery of bougainvillea, groves of picked avocado trees. The thought came to Stanley that he might be all wrong about this Faulkner–Wild Palms thing.

"Harry, this is silly for you. You're hired as a butler and chauffeur only."

"No, you originally hired me as a bodyguard. Ten years and this is my first chance for honest employment with you."

Stanley saw fields of hibiscus, red, white, and orange. Maxi was a gentle dog. Still, thought Stanley, if anyone was a little afraid of dogs, they'd be a lot afraid of Maxi. The acres of dark netting were an orchid farm. Then more, racehorse stables, then this steamy, ordered farming, exotic and businesslike. Stanley looked at the map and told Harry to take the next right.

They slowed, turned, and sped up, passing a truckload of
Cuban farm workers bareheaded and in straw cowboy hats.
Half a mile later they came to it, big gates closed on a ten-foot
chain-link fence, LAS PALMAS FARMS FORMERLY WILD PALMS STA-
BLES across both gates. They slowed. Feather palms dropped
gracefully along the fence and down the drive to where the
wooden horse fencing began. And way, way back were buildings.

They sped up until the fence turned in a quarter mile up
the road, where it was bounded by an old mango plantation.
They passed a dirt track going into the trees and came, a few
hundred yards on, to the buildings, where Harry turned and
drove back to the dirt track and turned in, bumping and lurch-
ing under the big leaves going purple brown beneath the green.
Stanley looked for the occasional shine of the link fence through
the heavy mango trunks. It seemed to go on and on. Empty slat
boxes and loading pallets lay stacked beside the trees. Stanley
put three Maalox in his mouth against the bite of his ulcer.
Then the fence shine stopped and there was only thick green,
like a wall of reeds or bamboo. He showed Harry and Harry
parked the Jeep just off the track.

Stanley realized that they were here now and there was no
plan, and if the fence was in back of that green, he'd try but
wouldn't be able to climb it, wouldn't, damned fat old man.

"What I'll do," he said, "is hold this gun and try to shoot
it. I think I can get Maxi to growl. I mean, those are my *capa-
bilities*, Harry."

Harry said, "What I can do is, if I get close enough, I can
use martial arts to disarm and incapacitate a guard. If I can't
get close enough . . . I hope you don't believe those kung-fu
videos you watch."

Stanley wanted to ask Harry if he, too, assumed they were
trying to get to the buildings they'd seen, but it seemed too

obvious, stupid. Harry said they should leave their wallets in the locked Jeep, just in case. Waiting for Maxi to have his fill of emptying, Stanley considered the outcomes in which their discovered wallets might be helpful. Then they were walking, Stanley holding Maxi's lead tight, at the edge of the trees. It seemed very dark for four in the afternoon. The fence had stopped where an irrigation ditch became the property line. The reeds grew thick and twelve feet high along its banks.

Maxi sniffed and strained for the water. They pushed into reeds and slid down the mud to the ditch edge. The water was eight feet across. Stanley looked at the water and the steep slope up the other side. Harry looked at Stanley.

"Maxi," Stanley whispered. "He's a Newfie; he gets to do what *he* should, too."

Harry shrugged, let himself down into the water, and swam the few strokes across, where he waited propped on the bank for Stanley.

Stanley let Maxi into the water and, holding the lead, slipped down in beside him. He threw an arm over the dog's thick neck, and to his "Go ahead" and Harry's hushed "Come, Maxi, come," the dog swam Stanley across and pulled him up to grab Harry's outstretched hands. And it was then, smiling at their success, that Stanley understood how impossible this return trip with Rose would be. He almost smiled, reasoning it wouldn't matter; they'd never get that far in their attempt.

Then they were crawling up through the reeds, Maxi content to follow in the clearing wake behind the bodies. Harry went on to the edge of the reeds and looked out. Then he slid back slowly and told Stanley that someone had passed fifty yards away from him, walking farther down along the reeds, where the fence came out again. The man had on a yellow windbreaker and seemed to be carrying a gun. So their best bet seemed for him to go up ahead again and at his signal, when this guard was far away, make for the tree across by the wooden fence, a big-leaved ficus they could hide under. It was about a hundred open yards, so Stanley should cross quickly.

Stanley began crawling to the edge of the reeds, wondering what his best attempt at quickly would be.

It was his first three steps, the running ones before he was jerked sideways by Maxi so that his left knee started to go; from then on his best effort was the brisk limp of a hunchback. But he made it under the ground-sweeping limbs into a series of dark tangled tents of branches and the foot-long rubbery green leaves. Harry was out at the tree's front edge, motioning.

Stanley crawled forward on the mat of dead leaves, Maxi up with him, sniffing at the two-inch palmetto bugs scurrying back for their disturbed cover. He looked out through the space Harry held open. Inside the wooden fence stood some horses, and back from them some others grazed, and beyond that and such a long way back were the buildings, brick stables either side of a long brick house. God, Maxi had been good, but Maxi went nuts around horses, nuts with love, but all it would take was one of his rumbling woofs and they'd all be . . . And never mind Maxi having to be so good. He himself would have to be—well, someone else, someone younger, fitter, stronger. . . . Anyway, not an overweight seventy-six-year-old munching Maalox with a knee about to play a nasty trick.

"A thousand feet?" he asked, backing to Harry's ear.

"No, maybe seven hundred, seven-fifty." Harry's finger came up across Stanley's lips. He pointed back. Stanley pulled Maxi close and stroked his neck.

"Whatsat? Who's in there?" a voice called from the other side of the tree.

Harry disappeared into a dark green tunnel. Branches parted. Maxi growled. Something yellow was crashing through toward them, then Harry's blue-jean jacket came over the branches and crashed down. Stanley held Maxi. Branches crashed, cracked, there was a heavy grunt, a short groan, and a loud crash.

Harry dragged the body backward by his arms. He told Stanley to help him strip the man. Maxi stopped growling and lay down and watched. They tied the man's legs with his trousers and gagged him with his underpants and T-shirt. Then Harry took off his jean jacket and put it back to front on the shorter man, tying his arms behind with the sleeves. He pulled the laces from the man's sneakers and tied his thumbs together. He put on the man's yellow windbreaker and asked Stanley the time. It was 4:55. Only. Stanley felt he'd been out here for days.

"Okay, Mr. Stanley. They're going to shoot us dead, for sure, but here's our best bet. In say half an hour, when it gets pretty dark, we'll walk out back to the reeds and boundary fence, you and Maxi the far side of me, and we'll walk abreast so maybe from a distance they'll think we're this guy. Half an hour. I don't think he'll keep much longer. And we'll get a lot closer to the buildings that way."

"Great plan," said Stanley. He thought it was an awful plan but he had nothing better to suggest. So they sat and kept quiet. The bound, unconscious man kept very quiet. Everything was very quiet. Stanley could hear the horses moving through the paddock. He rubbed Maxi's ear. Good, Maxi was napping.

"Mr. Stanley, this guy had a gun, some kind of an automatic. I, well . . . I put it up in the tree. You understand how I can't—"

"Of course. Anyhow, it would only get us in bigger trouble," Stanley whispered.

Then they were quiet again. The quiet seemed to sit on them. Maybe, Stanley thought, *this* was fear; a quiet where your thoughts seemed like screams. All he wanted was forty pounds and twenty years less. Make that eighty and forty.

Then Harry said he thought they shouldn't wait the other fifteen minutes in case the guard was missed and others came looking for him. So Stanley shook Maxi and they crawled to the other side of the tree, stood, and walked straight over to the edge of the reeds without anything happening. Then, Maxi outside, Stanley in the middle, and Harry in the yellow windbreaker, they walked back along the reeds until the ditch curved away and the fence came up.

Stanley whispered to Harry to have a look. Harry said he was looking; he'd say something only if he had to. Harry asked Stanley if Maxi was walking abreast. Stanley said yes, yes, wondering how abreast of two humans a full-grown male Newfoundland could walk. Still, the dog was black and the light was going. They kept going, walking along the fence.

Stanley realized he'd lost all awareness of his ulcer, probably because of his very loud heartbeat, yes, probably because the heart attack he was about to have was a way of curing an ulcer. He needed to think of something else. Rescuing Rose? No, not that! He took his gun out of his pants pocket. God, it was wet. Ruined. He tilted the barrel and watched the water drip out. But the powder would be dry inside the bullets, wasn't that right? Wasn't that where the powder was?

Harry told him to stop. He said they were going to turn and walk in a line about a hundred feet toward a tractor midway between them and the stables. Then they'd get behind it and see where they were.

They turned and began to walk. Stanley saw the tractor ahead. It looked large and very safe. He followed Harry, held Maxi's lead in his left hand and his trusty .45 in his right. He had no trust in it. Everything was so quiet. About thirty feet more. Then there was a loud bang and a whizzing by his ear.

For a second he couldn't put the sounds together. Something had fallen by the stables and an insect had gone by. . . . Then there were more shots and Harry grabbed Maxi's lead and ran to the tractor, shouting, "Run, Mr. Stanley, run!"

Stanley could manage a slightly faster walk, limping. He found the .45 coming up, seemingly on its own, straight out in front of him. He kept walking, shut his eyes, and pulled the trigger. It went off. He'd shot the gun. He opened his eyes and Harry pulled him down behind the tractor. There was a tremendous explosion of gunfire continuous as an air drill. Bullets pinged off the tractor and whacked into the ground, throwing up earth and gravel. Stanley stroked Maxi's head.

He asked Harry what they should do. Harry shrugged and said, "Smile," so Stanley told him he was a wonderful man; he was lucky and proud to know him. Maxi was growling. The shooting had stopped but Maxi was unhappy. Then a bullet hit under the tractor, spraying gravel into Maxi's chest. He started barking, and before Stanley could ask Harry to help hold him, Maxi had pulled the lead from his hand and gone loping out from behind the tractor with great deep woofs toward the stables.

Stanley looked unhappily at Harry. The idea of poor dumb Maxi being shot by gangsters was too much. Gangsters.

"Gangsters!" Stanley yelled, standing, keeping his eyes open, and firing a shot in the direction of the nearest stable. He saw Maxi disappear around a corner, barking. Harry was trying to pull him back. Some men were screaming in Spanish. Stanley shot at the building again. A man ran out, screaming, running away from Stanley, no, from Maxi, who ran out after him. A brown horse trotted out after Maxi. Stanley kept walking, but now Harry stopped pulling him back and was pushing him forward, up behind the stable end wall.

Spotlights came on in the stable yard. Harry stuck his head

forward and pulled it back. He said all the lights were on in the
house, but he couldn't see anyone. Stanley nudged him: the
brown horse clopped by with Maxi at its side. The horse looked
bored; Maxi looked up at it adoringly, and Stanley walked out
and picked up his lead. He was back with the dog behind the
wall when he realized no one had shot at him. This made him
remember there had been a great deal of shooting at him minutes before. He began to feel dizzy. Harry said, "That was very
foolish, Mr. Stanley." Stanley said what was *foolish* was calling
him "Mr. Stanley" and expecting him to take the bawling-out
seriously.

Now the lights were going out. Stanley gave the lead to
Harry and put a few Maalox in his mouth. They heard a car
start at the other side of the yard. It drove off down the drive,
stopped, started again, and faded from hearing. Maybe they'd
taken Rose away. Worse, Stanley thought, worse. They'd hurt
her: this stupid rescue plan of his had hurt her, even, my
god . . .

"Should we go back now?" asked Harry.

"No, we'd better go on. I guess I mean inside. Harry, I
don't know what the hell I mean. Let's go."

Stanley put his gun out and then his head. All the lights
were out. He walked out slowly, staying tight to the stables.
Harry followed with the dog. No one was around. They passed
the stables. They ducked beneath the dark back windows of the
house. Some light came palely through a screen door. Stanley
asked Harry how many bullets were left in the gun. Harry
wasn't sure. Three or four, he thought. Stanley took a deep
breath, opened the door, and went in.

It was a kitchen. A big plastic bottle of Coke was on a
counter, open. The light came from a door into a hallway. The
deep silence was coming into him again. Stanley motioned to
Harry with his head and went toward the doorway. If Rose was

dead, if Rose was dead, if Rose was dead . . . But despite the litany Stanley felt a peculiar excitement, as if he were a child again playing hide-and-seek at someone else's house. The hallway was full of closed doors, like in a dream, he thought.

The first door was locked. The next, across the hall, was not. It was a linen closet with such a good fresh smell it made Stanley want to put his head down on the sheets and sleep. He shut the door on his temptation. Harry pointed down along the hall. Under the last door on the left came a line of light. Stanley walked toward it, not being able to hear his footsteps or Harry's or Maxi's. It felt so unreal. He began to think that perhaps this was because he was dead, they *had* shot him, shot all of them. And what was he supposed to do with the door? Kick it open and shoot? Knock politely? And what if it were locked?

It wasn't. As Stanley stood with his hand turning down the door handle, all idea of guile or strategy or self-defense left him. He put his gun back in his pocket, opened the door, and looked in.

Rose lay on a cot, dead. His fault. He went up to her. "Rose," he said. She opened one eye. "Who is that? Could you please give me my glasses from the table?"

The glasses were shaking in his hand.

Ten minutes later Stanley stood outside the house with his arm around Rose. A light rain had started. It felt good, even the mud it washed from his face onto his lips felt good. He asked Rose if she were sure she wanted to stand. She nodded. He wasn't sure if his arm was supporting Rose or if Rose was supporting him on his arm. Rose supported herself on her cane. Her other hand lay on Maxi's head, her forefinger moving back and forth over the thick, muddy hair. She'd never liked the dog before. Stanley watched her stroke his dog until he heard the Jeep come up the drive.

Maxi flopped into the back and shut his eyes. Rose sat with

Stanley behind Harry. Harry had it figured: he told them not to hurry. Somewhere, he said, just about when all the lights went on and off, the bad guys had changed their plans, had wanted to let Mrs. Fine go. Which didn't, Rose said, make Stanley and him any less heroic.

They drove through the wide-open gates. Stanley said it didn't feel heroic; it felt more like a dream, a fairy tale.

"So what does that make me," asked Rose, "Sleeping Beauty?"

"Why not?" said Stanley. "Why not?"

BOOK IV

CHAPTER 1

The most private place at Wolfie's was the short space of two-seat tables squeezed between the counter and the Twenty-first Street windows. Schwartz sat at one of these waiting for Sonny Weinstock and trying to think of a nonquixotic reason for staying with this, hanging on, continuing to stick his nose in and neck out. Now, after nine at night, the restaurant wasn't crowded, but Schwartz was distracted by the fierce-looking woman sitting at the next table, facing him, talking to herself over a buttered bagel and cup of tea.

Of course Rose's kidnapping angered him, but since they'd changed their minds and let her go so he *wouldn't* be forced away, wasn't staying around, doing what they wanted, ridiculously, suicidally quixotic?

The woman, glaring through Schwartz, said, "How dare you think, how could you dare think . . . ? Ha, ha, ha. You're so dumb you're funny."

Schwartz looked down at his tea and untouched strudel.

No, he was staying because there had to be some connection between Roberto and Abe Zeigler's death.

But wasn't that mere hanging in for personal honor, his need to be the *mensch* of La Mancha? Certainly there was a lot of crime here, but this wasn't his patch, his concern. Why not? And then there was Linda. Ah, yes, that . . .

Sonny Weinstock was standing over the table. "Sorry I'm late," he said.

His father wouldn't have said "sorry"; his father wouldn't have worn a white cotton-silk sweater with dangling threads and duck-sauce stains.

The seventy-year-old waiter ran up as Sonny squeezed himself into the chair. "Nothing," Sonny said. "I just ate. Here." He handed the waiter a ten-dollar bill.

The waiter put up his hands as if he were being robbed. "I wouldn't take it if I didn't serve you, sir."

"Okay, a pastrami on rye and a Coke." As the waiter left, Sonny leaned forward.

Behind him, the woman twisted her face sarcastically. "Oh, sure, sure. You tell me Mother's just going to sit in that dark apartment? Ha! Zz, zz!"

"You know why I'm here?" Sonny asked.

Schwartz shrugged. "You wanted to catch more of my act."

Sonny took a pickle from the bowl, bit off half of it, and said, chewing, "Ronny, my son. For Christ's sake, they tried to take him right in front of the house today."

"What time was that?" Schwartz asked.

"Just before five. My wife called; I came right home. The kid's nine years old! He was skateboarding on the sidewalk and they pulled up and asked him directions. And the back door opened and someone was reaching out for him when, thank

God, our gardener pulled in, saw what was happening, and jumped out of his truck. So they got scared and roared off. I mean, when I think how close Ronny was to being kidnapped—''

Schwartz was shaking his head. "No, Sonny. They didn't want to grab him. They wanted to warn you, to scare you, to let you know they're on to you. Did your gardener see anyone, any detail?''

Sonny held the half pickle at his mouth like a microphone. The woman shook her gray-iron hair. Her black eyes gleamed.

"You're right," Sonny said. "No, he didn't get a close look. Yes, they want to scare me, and they succeeded, Schwartz. If my kids or wife were hurt . . .''

Sonny paused and put the pickle in his mouth. The woman at the next table tore off a hunk of bagel with her teeth, brushed hair from her eyes, and chewed fast, lifting her teacup with absurd, pinkie-out delicacy.

"Okay," said Sonny. "I'm going to tell you a story and ask your opinion. The story's all fiction, understand?''

Schwartz nodded.

"For convenience I'll use real names, but the story's fiction.''

The waiter came and set down the Coke and sandwich, told Sonny he'd like it because the pastrami was terrifically lean, and left the bill. The woman behind Sonny was saying something about Teddy. Sonny turned to look at her and turned back with a hard smile.

He said, "There once was a lawyer named me, some of whose clients put him in the way of big money-making deals. So as to spread the risk, I'd sometimes get backers who wouldn't ask questions. One of these fictional characters was called Abe Zeigler. About seven years ago he put up a million—''

"A million dollars?" Schwartz asked.

"Yes, a million into a—let's say a lucrative importing business from South and Central America and the Caribbean."

Schwartz said, "Ah, yes."

"Abe was the ideal investor: greedy and quiet. When he died, his share in the company was worth about thirty million."

"Thirty million dollars?" Schwartz asked.

"Thirty, thirty. But it was complex," Sonny said, stopping to bite into the half sandwich.

The woman's voice asked, "Teddy? What's Teddy going to do? Shh! Use French? Send her to college? Ha! Teddy's got zz, zz!"

Sonny turned to her again and turned back with the same sour smile. He said, "First I set up a simple company. Then, after I met this sea captain with a lot of interesting contacts and ideas, this company grew into three, four, five. Fictional companies, say, Bermudan, Bahamian, Grand Cayman. A set of Chinese boxes, Schwartz, and Abe Zeigler the ideogram on each one. He didn't mind fronting, you understand, as long as the profits were so good. But by about a year ago it was becoming too dangerous. As hidden a partner as I was, a few near misses convinced me to stop this particular form of import. So then this same sea captain came up with another scheme—running people with money from countries where they were out of favor, for one reason or another, and landing them here in south Florida."

Schwartz put up a finger. "Wasn't that chicken feed compared to the other?"

"If you call a million a trip chicken feed."

Schwartz didn't ask if the million were dollars. He put his finger down. The woman laughed bitterly and coughed.

Sonny finished the first half sandwich and picked up the second. He held it before his mouth and said, "We were just into our first run, but something went very wrong and Abe was shot. Either this captain took off with the money, or his crew pirated it, or some combination. In any case, the government of the country concerned got onto it, I'm sure. That's what I've worked out. That's who killed Abe: his name was on the registry records. But now, somehow, they've found me."

He brought the sandwich closer to his mouth. "Schwartz, I'm talking about the Haitian government. A boat called *Sport King*: does that ring a bell?"

Schwartz said, "No. Wait—ding, ding ding! The one in the news? The dead kids and now the States holding them all for extradition?"

Sonny nodded, chewing. A piece of pastrami, tongue shaped, fell onto the table. "In this fictional story I'm telling you," he said, "I don't want to end up a drum skin in a Tontons Macouté voodoo rite."

Schwartz thought of the flickering Neptune Plaza TV: the outline of small bodies taken away under sheets. He said, "You don't want that for your kids, either."

Sonny wiped his mouth with a paper napkin. His lower lip came away from his mouth curled in anger. Then it slackened and hung limp. He wiped his neck with the napkin. Some mustard smeared on the sweater neckband.

The woman said, "Father? You think Father cared what happened to a *daughter*? Shh. Shh. Zz. Don't make me laugh, Teddy." She stuck out her tongue at the teacup. "Naa-naa!"

Schwartz said, "Sonny, the good news is that the Haitians aren't after you. There are no Haitian agents in this fictional story. The less good news is who *did* kill Abe and who *is* onto you. Are you sure that only *people* were being run on that boat?"

Sonny tapped his fork on the side of the coleslaw bowl. "That's all I knew about. Who are these other—"

Sonny stopped, looked down at the table, and thought,

frowning, shaking his head. Schwartz thought he must be going through a list of names he'd rather not know, now.

Schwartz said, "Stop when you get to the C's—Cruz, Roberto."

Sonny looked up. "I've never had anything to do with him. That's on the record. Neither has Trujillo."

"And your clever skipper?"

First Sonny went red as lean pastrami, then pale as its trimmed fat. "I don't know," he said. "I don't know. It's possible. You know it's Cruz?"

Schwartz nodded.

"Schwartz, if I told this, not as fiction, to the police and the DA, what would I get?"

Schwartz shut his eyes and said, "Not the life sentence you deserve. You're very rich and well connected, and if you named enough names from all your business schemes, and if you let your father help you—oh, he'd help; he'd lap up that chance for magnanimity—I'd guess you could plea-bargain down to five in a nice, middle-class prison. You'd serve two and a half and come out, I'd just bet, to lots of money salted away, even after all the high-profile confiscations they'd make." Schwartz opened his eyes.

Sonny was smiling. "Two and a half. Hmm, I'd figured three. How long do you think I have?"

"I wouldn't hang around much longer than tomorrow morning if I were you. They'd give you that long: they'd figure you'd spend a sleepless night after their kidnap warning. Yes, tomorrow by lunchtime. Oh, and you'd better bring the wife and kids in with you, Sonny."

Sonny bit his bottom lip. "I see," he said. "That doesn't give me much time to straighten my desk."

Schwartz pushed back against his chair. His stomach hurt. He pointed his finger at a middle roll of Sonny's sweater. "I don't care about you or your desk. Listen to me, Weinstock; I know these people. They kill and torture. They'd torture you for information; they'd torture your wife and little Ronny, kill them before your eyes before they killed you. I don't know your son. He's probably a spoiled brat but *you're* not his fault and he shouldn't die for you."

"Stop it!" Sonny shouted, banging the table. The pickles tipped. He steadied the bowl.

"Sure," Schwartz said. "But that's who you're dealing with. Now, I'm willing to help, to tell the police how wonderful you've been, but I want two things. First, I want you to use your substantial influence to keep the Abe Zeigler part of the story as far from the press as possible."

Sonny said, "I see. He's your relative and so . . . Well, I don't know."

"He is my relative and you don't see and you do know. You know how stuck you are. You're dead or you're in some sort of prison. I can help make it one where you're not forced to play Miss Mary Smith to some big, bad stud's Abe Zeigler."

Sonny said, "I'll try."

"No," said Schwartz, "you'll *do* it. And the second thing I want is your old skipper's name and hangouts, and any other crew names you've got. Now."

Sonny ran his hand through his hair. It fell back stringy over his damp forehead. "You know," he said, "I graduated summa from Princeton and was president of *Law Review* at Columbia."

"Yeah, yeah, and I did okay at Harvard and here *I* am spending my life with garbage like you."

Sonny narrowed his eyes. "But you really don't like my father."

"No." Schwartz laughed. "You're nuts, but honest Injun, I really don't like your father."

Sonny said, "Bob Williams. The captain. Bob Williams. He was the only one I knew. And I set the meeting places. Wait, except once, last year: a little redneck place down on Card Sound, just this side of the toll bridge. Georgia something . . . Georgia Jack's Crab Shack. That's it."

Sonny stood and put ten dollars on his bill. He leaned heavily over the table. "See the woman behind me, the crazy? Like my mother but not as crazy. My father drove her crazy. He hid her away for years in a dark room. Drove her crazy then hid her away. When she died four years ago, the Great Man put up a school of psychiatric medicine in her name." Sonny straightened and took a pickle. "Charming?"

"Charming," said Schwartz to Sonny Weinstock's fat behind swaying toward the door.

"Charming, Teddy and Betty. Wovely," said the woman at the next table, now in the voice of a little girl. "Wovely as a colostomy, shh, zz!"

C H A P T E R 2

In the headlights of the cars as Schwartz left Wolfie's, the rain blown over the street looked like a series of curtains. Next door, a man in a mackintosh stood in front of the cigar store crisscrossing its windows with masking tape.

Schwartz turned up his collar and walked faster toward the Neptune Plaza. There were lots of loose ends to tie up, if he got the chance, but perhaps the storm had turned; perhaps a hurricane would hit the beach. And the beach wasn't more, after all, under its condos and hotels and restaurants, than a skinny sandbar between the bay and rolling ocean.

Inside the lobby, Schwartz shook his hair like a drenched dog. Jorge, the clerk on duty, handed him a message with a big, knowing smile. "From that policewoman," he said.

"What's so funny?" Schwartz asked.

"Nothin', nothin'. Except she's great lookin'. I wouldn't mind havin' *her* arrest me."

The note read: "See you first thing in the morning." Schwartz looked up and said, "No, you'd mind."

The young man chewed gum and smiled. "Whatever you say, sir."

"Are you working all night?"

"Till eight in the morning."

"If Officer Gomez, that policewoman, comes in, would you ring my room, anytime?" asked Schwartz, putting a ten-dollar bill on the desk.

Jorge took it, nodding. "What about this storm veering around? If it picks up any, it could be a hurricane. But you'd be okay, up on the eleventh floor, there. It's down here that would flood out."

"Good night, Jorge," Schwartz said, wondering if Jorge's enthusiasm was a plea for danger money or a simple pleasure in catastrophe.

The hall up on his floor was worse than ever, an electrical warehouse of cables, coiled wire, and jumbles of junction boxes. Schwartz picked his way through. What would all the old people do if a hurricane hit the beach? Evacuate? Resign themselves to whatever swept in from the sea and swept them out? Schwartz was sore and tired. He sat on the edge of his bed undressing, feeling like one of the old and resigned.

Resigned to what? To going out to that crab shack first thing in the morning. No, just before first thing.

Schwartz went to sleep. When he woke, he kept his eyes shut and listened to the wind, a moan over the crash of surf. A venetian blind banged over the window he'd cracked open for air. He'd close it. He opened his eyes. Then he lay very still and forced his eyes wide open to make out the figure in the dark.

Yes, now he saw it was what he'd first thought: a naked woman standing at the desk, her back to him. He would have to stay very calm.

"What the hell are you doing here?" he heard himself shout. He switched on the light.

Linda turned. His gun was in her hand. "That's no way to welcome a naked friend and colleague," she said. She looked at the gun. "I got that nice boy Jorge to let me in; I think he has a crush on me. Anyway, he said you wouldn't mind."

"No," Schwartz said, "the only thing I mind is that he owes me ten dollars." He wondered what Linda would do with the gun. "I'm sorry I shouted: I woke and saw you and was startled."

"Sorry," she said, still by the desk. "I was about to get into bed when I thought I'd take a look at this funny gun of yours. You've never shown it to me, you know."

Schwartz sat up. His stomach felt awful, about a thousand times better than yesterday. "Well, now you've seen it."

Linda lay the .38 across her hand. "But what happens when you have to use it quickly and you're fiddling with the safety?"

It wasn't much, but it was a chance. He said, "All right, let me show you," and held out his hand.

It was working: she came and handed him the gun. He said, "Here—" and stopped. "Why'd you take out the bullets?"

She shrugged. "I don't know, just looking at that safety and working it, I thought it best."

Schwartz handed her the gun and rubbed his eyes. "Well, I don't use it much. When I do, it's fast enough for me; I'm a police detective, not a cowboy."

Linda looked at the gun. Schwartz shifted and patted the bed beside him. Linda set the gun on the bedside table and got into bed.

"How's your tummy?" she asked.

"Bad and much better, thanks." He put his arm around her shoulder and stroked her hair. Where was her gun? "When did you get off work?"

"At midnight. I changed at the station, drove home, got into bed, and tried to sleep but thought of you. So after tossing for a few hours I got up, drove over here, and flirted with Jorge to let me in so I wouldn't wake you." She put her hand on his cheek. "I have today off. I thought maybe we could stay here, watch the storm together."

"Sounds nice," Schwartz said.

"You're not busy?"

"Busy? Oh. No, nothing much is happening with my little investigation," he said, pulling Linda close. Her gun must be close.

Linda pushed back from him and held his face in her hands. He tried to stay calm, sweet looking. He felt she could somehow pull his face off his skull with her bare hands. She brought her face close and kissed him.

He kissed along her cheek, small biting kisses to her ear. "You know," he whispered, "when I said I was no cowboy, it only referred to my work. I can be wild enough, otherwise."

She put her arms around him. "How?"

He was about to tell her. He didn't: if he told her now and she didn't trust him, he was lost. He'd have to wait, go about it gradually.

"Well, gently wild," he said, and kissed her breasts and thought how he must, as a good policeman, do this.

Linda said, "That's very gentle."

He kissed, slowly sliding to her stomach, beginning to forget his rationale, sliding.

Linda said, "That's very gently wild."

An hour later he lay on her shoulder, an arm across her, beneath her breasts. Her eyes were closed and she was breathing deeply and was, he knew, awake. At five, ten minutes before, she'd been waiting at the bathroom door when he came out, his loving and attentive guard. Or had this last hour stirred and *lulled* her? He couldn't go on with this game, couldn't keep it up, he winced to think, forever; that was, as long as she could.

His hand slid up the inside of her thigh. His pillowcase! The sleezy Neptune Plaza had provided a half-ripped pillowcase; he'd given Linda the good one from unconscious chivalry, and now there was this reward.

She turned toward him, eyes closed, with a deep, half-smiled sigh. Schwartz slipped the case off his pillow, slid it partly under his turned hip, and with his thumb and forefinger set to enlarging the rip.

Linda said "Oh" with her eyes still closed and reached down to direct his other hand. He'd have to risk one quick sound.

He pushed up and took his hand from her. She turned, reaching for it, then reaching up, eyes shut, to find his face. He tore the pillowcase.

"What's that?" she said, opening her eyes.

Leaning into her, he tore it again, caught the cloth by both ends and slipped it looped over her head. As he felt her go tense, Schwartz kissed Linda's mouth very gently. His arm wrapped hers, stroking it lightly back from over the edge of the mattress.

He whispered, "You excite me so much, so much. You, you, Linda, you make me want what I never . . . I want to do it, make love to you all day just the way you want." He felt her body loosen, felt her lie back.

"Darling," he said, turning, moving a knee across her, biting his lip against the stomach pain as he made fast the blindfold with another knot and softly tucked its edges away from her nose and cheeks. Now he was on his knees either side of her neck. She kissed him, opened her mouth for him. After a while he bent to her ear and whispered, "Wait, darling."

He watched her as he left the bed, turned to look at her passing it, walked nearly backward looking at her as he opened the door and she lay still. Then he took what he wanted and was afraid she'd be up, blindfold off with the gun in her hand, but when he looked, she lay still. So he closed the door and walked to the bed and told her to stand up. He guided her out from the bed and kissed her. He'd have to do this well—slowly and elaborately well so that she'd think he meant it.

Then he put an end in her hand and set it and her other hand softly to her sides and began walking around and around her. If he could just do this. He wrapped the thick blue electric cable around her waist and forearms, then over her shoulder and down her back and between her legs, then up her front and over her other shoulder. Then he did this two times more about her torso, making a halter.

He asked her if it was too tight, and when she shook her head no, he kissed her mouth then laid her on the bed and took another thick coil of electric cable, this one red, and wound each of her ankles three times, leaving slack between, and threw the cable under the bed, went to the other side, and pulled it up around and tied it to the mattress, kneeling and pulling hard to take up the soft slack.

Then Schwartz, excited himself, half forgot that he was tying her up for security, not sex, and bent over her and kissed her again and whispered what he was going to do to her, how he would do this to every tight bound piece of her, and when she nodded and said "Oh," he asked her if she wanted the bit, and when she nodded with her mouth hung open, he took the length of electric wires that were twisted green, red, black, and blue and put them across her open mouth and wrapped them that way twice around her head, then pulled them down under the halter of blue cable and up and tied them so that her head couldn't nod no from side to side but only a little up-and-down yes.

And when, through the electric wires, she said no, it wasn't too tight, he checked the bindings over her body and felt they were very tight.

Then Schwartz shut his eyes and opened them and remembered what he was doing and whispered "Wait" and put his hand under the mattress by her head and drew out her .357 Magnum handgun and took it to the bathroom, where he unloaded it before he quickly washed. Then he came back and started dressing quickly, hoping first that she still didn't understand so that he could shock her, then knowing she now understood, so that what had kept her from understanding earlier was that though she could kill him she loved him as he, who could never think he could kill her, did not at all love her. It was genetic, this, maybe maternal, learned social selves. But it didn't matter now.

He drew the chair up by the bed and loaded his .38. It was ridiculously Mitchum-macho, this, that forties film noir come to life. It didn't matter now.

He said, "It was the only thing that made sense, Linda, you working for Cruz, the only thing that explained all these *sequences*." He stopped. He didn't now like looking at her so tied and naked. He pulled the sheet and bedspread up. He started to take off the blindfold but stopped. He wouldn't want to see her eyes.

He said, "Your folks' two nurses' pensions couldn't buy those two apartments; maybe twenty nurses' pensions could. You had Cruz's money come to them. I'll bet your folks are nice, Linda. Jesus, I hope they believed whatever story you told them about it." He rubbed his stomach. The venetian blind went banging at the window.

"And the final tip-off wasn't even your fault; it was your jerk killer employer. An hour after I told you about Sonny Weinstock, Cruz began threatening his family, a little boy. Very crude stuff." He stopped, stood, put on his raincoat, and came back to the chair.

"Maybe I could have worked it out much earlier, but I didn't want to think about you like that because . . . Well, that was, of course, the whole *idea*. And I'm still not sure how you've managed to jerk around your department's investigation of Zeigler. But you're certainly tough and clever enough."

Schwartz was talking to a point on the wall over Linda, just below the framed photo reprint of a Miami street scene of the 1920's, when maybe it was simpler, less corrupt. Well, simpler.

He said, "I have to trust someone; I guess I'll call your own people on you—later on. Anyway, as you said, it's your day off; they won't miss you."

He leaned over, spoke lower: "Did you really think I didn't know from the first minute that you were here to stop me?"

Linda made a no sound through the wires.

"Then why did you let it happen?"

She made a longer, half-articulated sound. It was, without the consonants, "You know."

He looked at her from the door. He knew. He'd tied up some loose ends. He went back to the bed and undid her blindfold.

He looked, then he gagged her mouth with it and left.

CHAPTER 3

The dawn sky was an iron pot on which darker streaks of gray were edged with green, like mold forming on grease. Schwartz sat in his car, the open map beside him, the umbrella dripping, collapsed on the floor. If he left now, the chances were he'd be too early. But what was he supposed to do: go back to his room and while away the time watching Linda struggle to untie herself? Maybe Linda would untie herself. He glanced down at the map and started the car. He'd be too early.

The streets were empty. He passed a police car as he turned for the causeway. Who could he trust? The wind came in long gusts against the side of the car. He turned on the radio. Tropical storm Melvin had promoted itself to a hurricane, but it was reported turning, hitting, if anywhere, north of Palm Beach County. But hurricane evacuation routes would be available should it turn again. The report said gusts at the edge of the storm could reach ninety miles an hour. Some flooding was expected.

Light traffic appeared on the East-West Expressway; a line

of cars was turning off toward the airport. What did this exodus know that he didn't? No, they were probably airport staff going to work. The road emptied again out on the Dolphin Expressway and stayed empty as Schwartz slipped south onto the Florida Turnpike. There was nothing out here but the wide, wet, and windy road with an occasional car or truck approaching as a wall of spray or, wipers turned to high, passed in a hiss.

It was just after seven when Schwartz came to the turnpike's end, south of Homestead. Here, he had a choice for coffee of two or three hamburger outlets, vast offensively bland buildings each in its acres of parking lot. Inside one, he sat for a minute before a big Styrofoam cup of coffee, sniffing its steam. It smelled like steam. He looked up. No hurricane in here—no wind, no weather, just the molded seat and molded table, molded cup and kitchen staff. And from completely hidden speakers whined tunes from which music was completely hidden. He left the cup and wended his way through Burgermacs toward the comforts of the hurricane.

The road Schwartz took now, marked ALT. RT. N. KEY LARGO, soon turned into a swamp causeway lined with lean, tall Australian pines, packed together like a wall whose soft top bent and whipped. It was a very long, straight, narrow road with no traffic, except, way back in the rearview mirror, a dot of another car.

Schwartz hit the steering wheel with the flat of his hand. He pulled to the side and stopped. Yes, of course, there in the rearview mirror the dot of a car had stopped for him. Maybe it was the straightness of this road? Rain splintered off the windshield. No, there'd been stretches of the turnpike with nothing behind him for miles. Well, they'd had forever to fix the car with an electronic tracker. Cruz had. Cruz was crude but that sophisticated. Perhaps he could call from the crab shack.

He pulled out and drove on. Through the window's rubber

seal, the wind blew and whistled. Raindrops splattered flat over
the windshield as in the drier at a car wash. Splatter, tracks and
droplets. Wipe. Splatter, tracks and droplets.

The avenue of pines thinned out, then the road was lined
with reeds bent forty-five degrees in the gusts. Behind them
showed small and larger ponds of water, frothed, spitting at
their edges. Now slatted crab traps were piled at cuts in the
reeds; boats were beached, land-anchored to posts and scrub
trees. On both sides of the road, houseboats, floating shacks,
bobbed in cut channels. Schwartz passed a long collection of
boats and traps and pilings. He stopped the car and backed up.
On his right, nailed to a hodgepodge of red siding, was the sign:
GEORGIA JACK'S—CRABS BY THE PLATE OR THE CRATE. He parked
the car on the gravel so it pointed back toward more solid land.

The wind blew the car door out of his hand. He leaned his
hip against it to slam it shut. The door to Georgia Jack's was
padlocked. Schwartz banged with the side of his fist and then
went back to wait in the car.

A pickup truck went past. He watched it down the road
until it was a dot passing another dot, the one following him,
parked. They probably had binoculars, among other hardware.
He turned on the radio. The eight o'clock news was devoted to
Melvin: hurricane warnings, flood warnings, school canceled in
Dade County. In his childhood it had been snow; a deep deli-
cious silence followed by sirens from the Brooklyn schools and
fire stations followed by his mother's head in the door of his
small room, saying, "Lenny, terrible news: school's been called
off," and the smell of cocoa on the stove and toast.

Not this howling, hissing gray, the heavy air so fast it
left you breathless. Or was that nerves: the car down the
road and the odds against anyone bothering to open up a crab
shack in a hurricane. He noticed another sign nailed to the red
boards:

EVERY NIGHT DANCE CHEEK TO CHEEK ANY
CHEEK U LIKE * TUE & THUR WET T-SHIRT
CONTEST FREE DRINK FOR LADIES

He found a classical-music station from Miami. Would anyone show up? And who would contest free drink for ladies? And what would Cyrus Weinstock think of this Monteux recording of Bruckner's Fourth? It sounded fairly Brucknerian, all dying horns and swollen strings. If he got to call from here, he'd flip a coin on which police to trust. When would it open? Well, at least there was the company of Bruckner swooning in the storm for another hour.

A motorcycle appeared in the rearview mirror. It pulled into the graveled space before the door and stopped. It was a Harley with matching driver. Schwartz wondered if the fat, bearded honcho in the poncho was Georgia Jack.

"I'm Jack," he said, unlocking the door. "Come out checkin' 'gainst the blow. Be five minutes till I can get you a drink. Damn! Don't it stink? Been in the business thirty years and I ain't used to it. Sweat, piss, beer . . ."

"Rancid lime, cigarette ash, and . . ." Schwartz said, following Jack in and pausing to sniff again. "Maraschino, spilled maraschino and spoiled crab."

Jack got the lights. The place was still dark, a dusty room with a long bar and short stage for the Tue & Thur contests.

"You got a good nose," Jack said, pulling off his poncho.

Schwartz hung his umbrella from the bar. "I should have: I'm a detective."

Behind the bar, Jack's thick shoulders rolled as he turned to Schwartz. "What kind?"

"New York police kind."

Jack's black and orange Harley T-shirt sagged, no contest winner. "What in hell she want now? Irene's in New York?"

"Not Irene."

"Bobby-Ann? Oh, shit, I've given Bobby-Ann 'bout twice what I should've." The aging cyclist crossed his arms and looked sadly at the muscles and the tattoo "Hell's Angels, Waycross, Ga." running from the folded flesh.

Schwartz smiled. "Nothing to do with women or you or your bar, I promise."

Georgia Jack sighed. "Man, sunshine out of a storm. I'll cook up coffee. Want one?"

"Thanks. Black, no sugar." Schwartz looked at the phone across the bar.

"What's your name?" Jack called.

"Schwartz. Len Schwartz. Here's my ID."

Jack said, "No sweat, man. Long as those ball-breakin' ex-old-ladies of mine ain't sent you. You a Jewish boy, huh?"

"Yes," Schwartz said, tensed for the deep-south racism that would be offered as friendliness.

"My Atlanta granddaddy's a good ole Jewish boy. Cool dude, ridin' cycles since the twenties. He's near ninety now, but I still give him a spin round the block when I'm up Atlanta." Jack came back with two mugs. "Here you go. What you lookin' for?"

Schwartz heard a car pass in the direction of the bridge. "A boat skipper named Bob Williams. Know him?"

"Sure. Wait on," Jack said, turning behind him where boards creaked. He looked out a window and came back shaking his head. "Back part is built out on pilin's. I sure don't want that water comin' up much higher."

Schwartz sipped the coffee. It was a heavy coffee cup and real coffee.

Jack said, "Bob's sometimes in here. A real captain— licensed. He works some fancy boats, not a crab-pot puller like 'round here. But I ain't seen him now, oh, three months, maybe.''

''Know where he lives or hangs out?''

Jack drank coffee and shook his head. ''No, only knew him from here.''

''Know anyone who might know?''

''No . . . Yes I do. Ole Vince Blessing. He sometimes crewed for Bob. Other times he sometimes works out his brother's farm out back Florida City on the edge of the Glades. Rednecks, guess you'd say. Here,'' Jack said, reaching behind the bar and bringing up a phone book. ''Be listed under his brother BB. B.B. Blessing, meanest sonabitch I ever met. Man's such a mean redneck he give other rednecks a good name. Here.'' He turned the book.

Schwartz looked. ''I have a Miami area map. Will this be on it?''

''Hell, no,'' Jack said. ''I'll draw you a map.'' He took a piece of paper and a pencil from next to the phone. ''Out here on the road marked to the Everglades Park, but you go straight and then it's the second or third turn right. One of those, 'cause Vince said he seen me and some buddies out there on our bikes.''

Schwartz watched Jack draw slow straight lines. ''Jack, there might be some people in here after I leave. I don't think they'd do anything but ask—''

Jack was smiling, pointing to somewhere below the bar.

''No,'' Schwartz said. ''I know you can handle yourself, but please don't try. . . . I mean, if they come in here asking, I *want* you to tell them just what you've told me.''

''You got it,'' said Jack.

''Can I use the phone?'' asked Schwartz.

''Sure. Should I tell 'em you're calling Vince?''

"Who? Oh. No, tell them I'm calling the cops," Schwartz said, ducking under the bar, wondering which cops he would call and what help he could expect in this storm.

Five minutes later, driving back along the straight swamp road, Schwartz picked up the following spot in his rearview mirror. They'd gone past the crab shack when he'd been inside, waited out of sight, and picked him up again with the binoculars or bug. At least they hadn't hassled Jack; they couldn't fall that far behind.

Schwartz turned up the radio and lifted his accelerator foot. The car was driven by the wind too fast. Now Bruckner was up between romantic angst and orgasm. He wondered if Linda had untied herself. He didn't understand her. He understood *himself* with her: spoiled, infantile, a vanity seeking its deep massage. And she must have known from Cruz about his bribe. But what he understood changed him as little as what he didn't.

Maybe this Vince Blessing would know where Bob Williams was. As Schwartz swung right, back onto U.S. 1, he glanced at the mirror. Yes, of course, about five hundred yards behind him.

After turning left at the sign for the Everglades, Schwartz thought he'd lost them in the bit of traffic that appeared. But after the railroad tracks and produce warehouses gave out to flat farmland, he saw them again at their confident distance behind.

Now the wind was coming harder. Bits of leaves stuck to the rear window. From a scraggly line of thatch, the dead trunk of a royal palm swayed like a burned flagpole. Where the sign pointed left for the national park, Schwartz continued straight. The road got bad; water splashed up in the bumps. He passed the first right. He'd take the second. As he slowed, he saw he had to: the road he turned off ended in a canal gate a few hundred yards on.

This road was unpaved. When the car wasn't rocked by ruts, the side gusts rocked it. Brown water splashed over the hood. This road had to dead-end, too. What farm? It looked like everglades out here. Canals and canals and off them drowned grass. He came to a fence on his left and slowed. Under a metal American flag the size of a postcard was a black rural mailbox saying B BLESSING. The rain fell harder.

He looked into the mirror before he turned. No, nothing; they wouldn't have to come down the dead end. He drove the car into the orange-mud water covering the drive and headed for the group of junk cars from behind which the patched roof of a house rose. Schwartz parked by the rusted, windowless shell of a Nash Ambassador. He took a breath and patted the .38 under his coat. No, he'd be polite and direct and just ask about Williams. Maybe his tail would get bored, like he was.

He pushed up the umbrella and ran toward the house in the downpour. Water dripped through the porch roof. He peered through a screen door. Darkness. He knocked hard on the frame with the umbrella handle. "Anyone at home?" he shouted.

"Sure. C'mon in out of the rain," a voice called.

Schwartz stepped into a dim, dirty kitchen. Before him at a table sat two mean-looking men. The meaner one, he decided, was the one pointing the shotgun at his stomach.

CHAPTER 4

When Schwartz had put his gun and bullets and his open ID wallet on the table, BB Blessing motioned him to the floor, where Schwartz sat beside a large olive-drab duffel bag.

Vince Blessing said, "See, I told you it wasn't but time before the police would be onto us."

BB stared at his brother. Schwartz looked at BB, a long scrawny man, shoulder bones and hipbones poking from his workshirt and gray overalls. His eyes were close and narrow over a nose whose end turned up so suddenly its nostrils seemed pig vertical. A rag was on his head.

After a long pause BB said, "Shut up, Vincent."

Vince said, "Only authority you got now, you peckerhead, is that twelve-gauge." Vince, in grease-covered T-shirt and blue jeans, didn't look much like his brother; he had bright black eyes under a thatch of brown hair, and his nose didn't flip up. And Vince's mouth was fuller, set in a small pink smile in the beard stubble and grease streaks of his face.

BB looked hard at Schwartz and said, "Shut up, Vincent."

Schwartz said, "Look, I only came to ask about Bob Williams."

"Shut up the both of yew!" BB yelled. Then he said, "Damn!" and grabbed the rag from his head and threw it to the floor next to Schwartz.

It was a dish towel with a recipe in pictures for key-lime pie. Schwartz saw the picture of the can of condensed milk stained red with blood. He became frightened.

Vince said, "Bob Williams? He's dead, shot in the back dead at the wheel of the boat."

"Vincent here killed him, mister," BB said, smiling, two black gaps showing in his brown front teeth.

"No sir, that ain't true. I was there, Mister—"

"Schwartz, Schwartz."

"Mr. Schwartz, but it was Hozay shot him after he shot Frank and Hozay made me help throw both them overboard."

"Sure," said BB, sighting down the barrels at Schwartz's head, "then you bring that murderin' nigger here—"

"Hozay wasn't no nigger, was a Cuban, BB," said Vince. "Hey, and Mister, don't you let BB scare you with that gun none."

BB said, "Haw! Yew say, Vincent."

Schwartz saw absolutely no reason why he shouldn't let BB scare him. He heard strange whimpering noises from under the rain upstairs.

Vince laughed. "Know what them are, is BB's famous fierce hounds supposed to be warnin' him anyone comes around here a mile off. They're all up pissin' under BB's bed. But, what the hell, place stinks so up there you never gonna tell the difference, BB."

BB scratched his long chin. "Dogs is jest scared of the storm."

"Hurricane," Schwartz said.

Vince said, "Hurricane? *Now* what's your great plan, peckerhead? Mister, BB here shot Hozay with that gun. Just let both barrels go *blam, blam* right into Hozay's stomach. Then he made me put ole Hozay in a sack and drop him with some stones into the big irrigation canal out there half-mile back."

BB was nodding. "So there, Vincent. Who's a peckerhead now? You tellin' Mr. Swat here I wouldn't shoot him when you know damn well I would, and you too, you go on burnin' me."

Schwartz saw even less reason not to be afraid: both brothers were crazy. Perhaps if he talked . . . perhaps their madness would allow him to use up time until . . .

"We gonna get out of here, Mr. Po-liceman Swat," said BB. "And you gonna drive us in that good new car."

Schwartz pushed back against the duffel bag. The wind was screaming at the door; a dog began to howl upstairs. He put his head down, arms around his knees, and spoke at the dish towel. "Listen, BB, Vince: the police know where I am. They'll be here soon." Schwartz half nodded; half of this was true.

BB said, "That don't bother me none. That's good reason to get quit of here right now."

"BB," Vincent said, "you're so stupid you make me shamed to be kin. You think the police gonna come here, find nothin' but a pack of scared shit hounds and figure, 'Oh shoot, guess we'll come back another day when maybe ole BB's to home.' "

"Vince is right," Schwartz said, his head still down, trying to control the pain in his stomach by looking at the picture of the bottle of key-lime juice. "And there's something else, BB. I didn't come here alone. My car was followed by some very bad guys also looking for Bob Williams. Drug dealers. They're more armed than the National Guard. They—"

Schwartz looked up to the laughter, a high wheezy "Hee-haw" coming from BB as he rocked the chair back with his heels.

"Vincent, tell the po-liceman what we got in that oilskin there."

"Ain't what *we* got, now; it's what *you* got. Mister, BB's got him a couple them little Uzi machine guns plus lots of ammunition plus two pistols and bullets for them, too, most of what were Hozay's. Yes, sir, my big brother's got him some real *weapons* to play with. Why, it's like givin' one them idiot childs who gotta play with fire a Christmas present of five gallons of gas and a brand-new Zippo lighter. Yes, sir."

Schwartz said, "You don't have a chance, BB."

BB rubbed the top of his close-cropped head then looked at his palm. "Anyway," he said, "I'm ready, 'cause this here's stopped bleedin'. Offsa Swat, this here's from where my baby brother near to bust my head open and kill me, an hour back. I always tried so with him but he always been so *wayward*! An' I don't believe that bull-dickey story you say 'bout some car full of drug dealers. Ain't no other car out there."

Vincent was laughing, shaking his head and laughing. "You know what I'm lookin' at now, BB? One dead Florida rednecked fool! Don't you get it yet? All that extra money—"

"Shut up! Shut up!" BB screamed, turning the shotgun on Vince.

Vince shut up.

BB stood and put the shotgun to the top of Schwartz's

head. "Now, you listen. You and Vincent gonna put the oilskin in the backseat of your white car. Then you two gonna put that there army bag in the trunk. An' then you gonna drive with Vincent sittin' up there with you and I'm gonna sit in back an' use the shotgun or maybe one them machine guns to keep you doin' what you should. Yew hear?"

"Yes, I'm here," Schwartz said. "Are you?"

BB said, "Vincent!"

Vince had stood and was walking to the other side of the table with his hands up. "Just want to get that last peanut-butter jelly sandwich here. Hell, BB, just 'cause you gonna get my ass killed in five, ten minutes don't mean I gotta go out workin' for you on an empty stomach. I mean, unless you want that sandwich. Be glad to split it." Vince picked up the white bread in his dirt-black hand.

BB shook his head and motioned Schwartz up with the shotgun. Schwartz decided that Vince wasn't as mad as BB, had at least some peanut-butter-jelly style. Vince folded the white-bread sandwich with black fingermarks into his mouth and bent to the other side of the oilskin from Schwartz. They lifted it and pushed through the screen door into rain now split and driven sideways. Schwartz decided BB wasn't entirely stupid: the oilskin of weapons could have been carried by one man, but this way both were occupied, incapacitated. Schwartz looked out. No other car was in the few hundred yards visible under the tumbling gray-black sky. After they set the oilskin on the floor of the backseat, they walked back to the house, where BB had each get at an end handle of the duffel bag.

This was heavy: Schwartz's half was eighty, maybe a hundred pounds. He felt the crinkle of thick plastic inside the canvas. Outside the house, bits of leaves and grass wisps hit at his face. BB backed off Vince and Schwartz and locked the trunk.

Then the two of them got in front and BB sat behind, and when the doors were shut, he handed Schwartz the keys.

In the wind roar, Schwartz had been pumping and pumping the accelerator. If he flooded it, maybe they'd open the hood and the angled rain would . . . He turned the key and the car started perfectly. He turned the car and slowly bumped down the track.

Vince half turned his head. "BB, I'll tell you one thing I truly *appreciate* about this goddamn peckerhead suicide run you got me in: it's leavin' this shit mud farm of yours for good. Leavin' all this mean crawlin' mud, bent over, bent so mud-fuckin' much over those slow lines of avocados, bent liftin' those crates with your mud-snake voice goin' 'Hurry up, damn you, Vincent, you worse than the worse nigger hand here, Vincent!' Hell, yes, truly! Good-bye to all that low mud-gator life!"

The shotgun tapped Schwartz's head. "Yew just turn right out this gate here and left down to the end of the road and then straight on out steady."

Schwartz turned the wipers to high and asked if he should put on the headlights. BB told him not to until they were in Florida City, where there'd be other cars with headlights on. Not so stupid, Schwartz thought. Where were the Miami Beach police? Of course, when it came to it, he had to call them; no other force knew who he was or about Abe or, indeed, of Linda. Well, now it was all Chief Pearlman's show. But how would he get people out here? Damn, he hoped he was right about Chief Pearlman. In the rearview, BB had taken out an Uzi with a full clip. Schwartz shook his head: the great Israeli export.

"And Vincent," BB said suddenly, "that's no gratitude you got there for that farm that's fed you an' me who brung you up like you was my own son."

"Oh, fuck you, BB," said Vincent. "Way you kicked my

ass all those years up there Okeechobee, up in the cane. If you
was a father, you was like one them fuckin' *battrin'* ones like as
not to kill his kid.''

BB said, ''Still might, Vincent. You so wayward might just
try out this machine gun on you, you keep rilin' me.''

Schwartz turned left onto the paved road. Maybe he could
drive them into a ditch. He leaned forward to look through the
shrinking wedge of cleared screen. Nothing. No, there was
something up at the crossroad.

He stopped the car. ''BB, isn't that a car up there, just
after the other road goes right?''

''Where you see that?'' BB asked.

''No,'' said Vince. ''Ain't one, it's two stopped cars. One's
pointed to us, other side of the road, and the other's facing same
way as us this side.''

Schwartz peered through the wipers. ''Where do you see
that?''

BB brought the shotgun to the side of Schwartz's jaw.
''Don't bother lookin', but you better believe him. Vincent, he
got him the eyes of a dang turkey buzzard. Now, supposin'
they's what you say, drug dealers—''

''You know why they're here, BB.''

''Shut up, Vincent. I gotta think. I don't wanna go back
to that farm not much more than you do. Damn, payin' out
good money to lazy nigger hands never do shit but watch
me break my ass showin'm how the damn work *should* be
done!''

The wind was a steady roar with gusts that screeched.
Schwartz looked out the side window. Across a drainage ditch
three thatch palms waved hallelujah hands and when it gusted
bent full out, bowing to some wrong-way Mecca. Maybe BB
would sit here thinking all day. And now there were two cars
waiting up there.

Vince leaned to Schwartz: "You know up Okeechobee?"

"No."

Vince nodded and spoke quietly. "No. Why should you? Well, take child-labor laws. Ain't none. Ain't no ordinary laws there. Ain't really America there. There was this time, once, I was maybe nine years old workin' the cane fields, throwin' it up onto the truck beds in that heat and nothin' you could see but cane forever, cut and bein' cut, 'cept maybe way off under a palm some them light humpy-back cows, and two Yankees stopped for directions someplace and one says Brazil. That's right. One says to the other, 'cause I was right there givin' directions, one says, Jesus it's not even America, look at that, one says, could be *Brazil* or maybe *Africa*. And the other one says yes, sure, and a hundred years ago. Too fuckin' true, Mr. Swat. And mister, when I saw all that extra money back at the farm, I washed my hands of the—"

"Shut up, Vincent," said BB. "Okay, I got us a plan. We go up near to the junction real easy, then we gun the car in close to the one facin' us with me shootin' out the back window as they won't be expectin' that, and *wham, bam*, we gonna shoot straight through them suckers."

Schwartz's mouth opened but no sound came out.

Vince said, "BB, if I thought that plan could work, you could go on an' shoot me in the head right now 'cause there wouldn't be anythin' in there for you to hit. Shit, I always known you were mean but never knew you was *re-tarded*."

A shotgun barrel tapped Schwartz's jaw. BB said, "Get goin'."

Schwartz got going, which was obviously more than the Miami Beach police had done. Had Linda bluffed them? Linda in the buff bluffed well and Schwartz had . . . He saw the two cars now, as Vince described. And Schwartz, bluffed, had muffed it, played into Cruz's heavy hands. He'd had enough of other people's plans for his death.

Schwartz said, "Roll down your window now, BB, and hold on, and Vince, get down. Here we go."

Schwartz pressed on the accelerator. At forty, the wipers couldn't clear the screen. They came into the junction at fifty. BB started firing the machine gun. Schwartz pulled the wheel hard down to the right.

Water sprayed high and higher and the car was sliding, slipping, floating sideways and BB stopped shooting and screamed, "Jammed! Jammed! Come on you black bitch gun fire. Fire!" and Schwartz ducked as he thought the car would hit sideways into the back of the black limo and grabbed the wheel steady and the bullets came into the side of the car first with thuds like panel beating and then through the back window in two hard cracks. He inched his eyes up to see nothing but water and guessed the shinier lake they skidded the edge of was the road. Then he brought his head up and saw BB's scrag skull rise in the rearview and BB throw the Uzi out the window. Schwartz let the water slow the car so that maybe he could hold it.

BB yelled, "Should've used the shotgun. Would you believe that jammin' on me like that. Piece of Cuban shit, that Uzi."

"Israeli," Schwartz said, "and all too good." He saw both the limos coming down the road behind him.

Vince sat up. "Sure you just didn't sort of freeze up all chicken shit, BB?"

"Yeah," said BB, "then how come you stayed all crunched under like some damn turtle, Vincent?"

Vincent turned. "Shit, them cars ain't that far off yet."

Schwartz was driving too fast, but he saw he'd opened up

another hundred yards between the lead limo. The shotgun patted his shoulder.

"Mr. Po-liceman, you drive real good," BB said, forgetting that Schwartz had decided to take a road of his own. "Shoot, I don't even see how you can see. Look here, I figure them boys followin' us ain't nothin' more'n a bunch of Cuban pimps what's used to Miamah whoorehouses not way out here, so maybe we can get us into the park an' just hide out from them, seein' as Vincent and me's two country boys."

In the rearview mirror Schwartz thought he saw BB nod to himself.

Vince said, "Oh, sure, BB, if we was in the country. But we ain't. Ain't no cane field, no orange grove we're used to. Shit, you really crazy, BB. You got us on a one-way road into the fuckin' glades that no one know but some ole Seminole Indian. Shit, BB, this ain't the country, this the *jungle*!"

Schwartz let the accelerator up to turn into a near-right-angle bend, slowed, but then skidded past sluice gates on an irrigation canal and swung back onto the road, just missing a ranger's truck going the other way. The right front tire moved off the road in a bang of stone and gravel. Behind them the limo was coming slowly out of the bend.

Schwartz remembered that BB hadn't known how he could see. That was easy: he couldn't. Everything before him was slightly different shades of wet. They were picking up speed as they passed the entrance to Everglades National Park. The sign said PARK CLOSED. The car came onto a long straight doing seventy-five. They passed two more signboards saying PARK CLOSED. The limo was passing the entrance maybe a quarter of a mile back.

Schwartz saw the steel gate across the road marked CLOSED. He swerved left, skidded half off the road then back on, so he let out his breath, then skidded off to the right, skidded left and right, and held back on the road doing sixty.

BB was having a good time. "Mister, you're a hot driver. Damn!"

"I'm a scared driver, damn!" Schwartz said. He thought he might be shouting. "Can I at least know what we're all going to die in the coming car crash *for*?"

Vince laughed. "Tell the man, BB."

"Shut up, Vincent."

Vince said, "There's three million dollars back there in that bag in the trunk."

"Ain't so, Mr. Swat," said BB. "It's three million and one hundred and forty-eight thousand dollars, U.S."

Vince said, "Maybe you remember BB's farm back there; you understand he's a man would sweat an' cheat an' lie to save himself a dollar forty-nine. Well, three million's just about two million more than there should have been, which is why I figured Bob was runnin' more'n a bunch of Haitians on ole *Sport King*. And when I finally figured out where that money was hid, which is what Hozay made me do, and saw how much it was, I said *no way*, Hozay, but then 'cause we were hidin' out up BB's, BB sniffed it out and, well, shit."

Now Schwartz understood. Now, finally, peering at a spill-way of a road in a hurricane, chased by two limofuls of hard-ened killers and driving at least one killer not hard but soft-in-the-head-as-dangerous who had a shotgun stuck into his back, Schwartz understood.

"BB," Schwartz said, "with your trusty twelve-gauge, or even if the other Uzi works, you're going to be no match for those sweethearts back there. I sort of know them. Especially with your brother and me not doing more than pointing our fingers into the wind and yelling *bang, bang*."

Schwartz saw the stream pouring across the road and braked in reflex. The car floated, spun twice, hit the sand shoulder, and half spun onto the road facing back. Schwartz turned it and went on. He figured he was doing his best to get them killed like this, humanely. If he lived, would he tell Karen about Linda?

"Well," said BB, "I got that figured."

Vince said, " 'Bout as well as that dash through them cars back there, peckerhead?"

"No. Shut up. Here's what. I'm gonna give you two them pistols here but keep the bullets till you ain't got any choice but shoot at them others. I mean, if it comes to that."

Then BB pointed and said, "There! In there!"

Schwartz skidded to a stop, backed, and turned left down a road marked ROYAL PALM: ANHINGA TRAIL, GUMBO LIMBO TRAIL. What was an anhinga? An Indian tribe or a bird? "BB, there's no way out of here but this road."

"That's why they won't think we been dumb enough to go down here," BB said.

Vince said, "No, maybe not, if they don't know you." He turned around. "BB, I thought there for a moment you almost had a real *human's* idea, 'cept as we can still see them two limo cars up on the main road back there, they can still see *us*, you goddamned jackass!"

"Maybe not, Vincent, maybe not."

Schwartz decided not to volunteer his thoughts on binoculars or electronic homing devices. He shook his head. He was living out some demented fantasy of BB's that the cash would somehow protect them. Him.

Vince said, "Not much rain now. Look at all that grass there bendin' and blowin' looks for a thousand mile."

"Rivers of grass, they call it."

"Who calls it that, Offsa Swat?"

"The guidebooks, BB. Well, this section of the guided tour is over. Here's the end of the road," Schwartz said. "Yes, maybe those limos won't follow us. Maybe they're just ornithologists out to spot roseate spoonbills in a hurricane."

BB said, "Stop jabberin'. They shot up this car. I had one them bullets whiz into the seat here just over my head. Spoonbills, my ass!"

Vince laughed.

"How much time you think we got on them, Offsa Swat?"

"Maybe three minutes, BB."

"Let's go, then."

Then Schwartz and Vince strained in a jog down the path marked ANHINGA TRAIL with empty .38 and .45 in outside hands, the heavy duffel bag between them. BB followed with his shotgun and the second Uzi. The path turned into a boardwalk going out over the swamp. There the wind was higher: when the gusts came, they fell forward to keep upright. Rain needled their faces. Six inches below their feet the water was brown and foamed. And then, at a curve out over a churning lake, they saw back to the parking lot where two black cars flanked the white one.

"Well, you're the po-lice, Mr. Swat. What you guess they'll do?" BB asked into Schwartz's ear.

"They'll split up, I guess, half down that Gumbo Limbo Trail back there, half down this. And I guess this trail has to dead-end or loop back on itself, after it splits, up there. I guess then they'll kill us and take that bag away and have a good time, I guess."

BB spat and said, "Shee-yit. Sheeyit and more sheeyit!"

Vince said, "Now you talkin' sense, brother."

BB kept them moving. Now the water splashed through and broke over the boards. They came to a roofed observation deck around which the trail looped back, and where they turned away from the wind which sucked out their breaths and huddled over the shotgun BB pushed into Schwartz's sore stomach.

"What you think now, Offsa?"

Schwartz was coping with the pain. He had to pee. "I think you should give yourself up to the nearest policeman—me. You too, Vince."

"I surrender, Mr. Schwartz," Vince said, chuckling.

"Okay, BB, now I've done the right thing but see you're not seriously considering that option. Well, to get away from those guys, I'd consider jumping into this pond and swimming out to that hammock, there."

"What hammock?" BB asked, his eyes narrowing and crossing slightly. "How you know Hozay was in a hammock?"

Vince kept chuckling, shaking his head.

Schwartz said, "That island; they call them hammocks. See, it's very improbable that we'd do it, BB. And they couldn't see us if we made it over there."

Vince nudged Schwartz. "You gone dumb as BB? We jump in there they won't see us 'cause we gonna drown or be sucked into quicksand or get our asses chomped by 'gators."

"Shut up, Vincent. Okay, You, mister, you get in first and Vincent gives you the bag and then gets in and the two of you float back there and hold the bag crost your bellies like I seed them things—otters, it was—do on 'The Wonderful World of Disney.' 'Cause that bag's all watertight inside. Then I go in."

"And what, BB? Paddle your dumb ass with them two guns?"

BB looked at the Uzi, made a face, and tossed it into the water. He stepped back and pointed the shotgun and said, in a high, strangled voice, "Go on an' do it now or I'm gonna kill both you."

That voice convinced Schwartz to kick his loafers off. He let himself down over the wooden railing slowly, holding on, and went in. The water felt much warmer than the air and not much wetter. He held on to a piling post. He figured BB's head had densities and spaces but they weren't fixed. You might laugh at BB and have him laughing with you as he killed you because of some rearrangement of molecule and mood inside his head faster than anyone, BB especially, could gauge. Schwartz let the .38 go in the water.

He took the bag Vince handed down and wedged it to the post. Then Vince smiled and lowered himself into the water, hanging on to the boards with one hand and taking hold of the bag's end handle with the other, letting go of his empty .45. Then he and Schwartz looped the end handles over their inside arms, fell back onto the water with the bag across their middles, otters to a three-million-dollar abalone, and pushed off against the pilings.

Schwartz looked up to see BB about to jump in, hugely grinning, like a scarecrow doing a deep knee bend, calling out, "Hoo-ee! Hoo-ee! It's gonna work!" and then a current caught Schwartz up so fast and hard it knocked his breath, so he thought he'd been picked up by a speedboat. It turned him over. He felt Vince's legs kick under his then separate away. A mud taste filled his mouth.

Schwartz surfaced, opened his eyes, ducked, and hit his head against the pilings. He tried to hold the bag, tried holding a plank edge with his other hand, but the current swung his legs and then the bag under the planks. He thought he saw someone crouching, way down on the curve of the boardwalk. He let go, was sucked underwater, came up, bumped his head, was sucked into a rush of branches as he struggled to hold the bag, kicking hard to keep his head above the water. He heard,

"I'm killin' you for this," and then, "No, you never won't, you wet peckerhead."

Schwartz let go of the duffel bag, rose up, and let himself be swept along with the tangle of branches and logs. One of the logs, three feet from him, was five or six feet long. It turned toward him and opened an eye the color of sliced lime.

CHAPTER 5

Schwartz was splashing water at the alligator, yelling "Go away! Just go away!" when it did, or the current slipped Schwartz back from it and pulled him underwater. He tried to cross the current; his forehead scraped across a branch, his knees stuck in mud. He lifted his head out, spat water, and opened his eyes to branches. He reached one, pulling slowly until his hand grasped the thin trunk, and then pulled harder, crawling and hoisting himself up, but not onto land. He dragged into a large clump of bushes and spindly, spotty trees flooded or growing submerged.

Schwartz pushed himself up and turned, backing in, to keep the tangle from his face. He saw the end of the duffel bag showing at the edge of a wreckage of branches six feet before him, and he kneeled and then flopped forward, got a hand to it, and then with two hands began to pull back, sitting in water to his shoulders, pushing back with his feet against the underwater roots. When he'd pulled the bag half out, he wedged it in a V of two blotch-gray branches and again pushed backward into the thicket of brush.

The wind howled and Schwartz shivered. He saw he was within the big loop of the boardwalk, an inner lake clumped with submerged islands. Through the whipped leaves he saw down the boardwalk to where a man moved bent over something like a machine gun. A machine gun would be something like a machine gun. Inches from his eye, a snake moved its head. It flapped long wings and flew away. Schwartz felt hysterical, laughter wetting his wet pants. Then he realized it was a bird; an anhinga was a bird. This was, after all, their trail. The wind was making him very cold. He'd tell: if he got out of this, he'd tell Karen about Linda, beg forgiveness, see a therapist.

The drops of rain seemed plopping on his head in pats, running down. His fingers came white off his face. He shielded his eyes and looked up: it was a thicket of birds, branch after branchful—white, gray, and black, egret and heron and snaky anhinga—animals, like him, sheltering from the storm.

He brought his head down. Fifteen feet before him the current slid through the water like a blacksnake. Out of the snake's back popped Vince's head. "Hey! Hey, help!" it said.

Schwartz lunged, tripping over roots into the waist-high water, and waded to the edge of the mud bar toward Vince's outstretched hand. He caught it around the wrist and pulled back small step by step. Vince came slowly; he seemed to heavily pull back. Then Schwartz saw why: Vince was pulling BB with his other hand. Then they both pulled BB and put him on his knees, bent across the duffel bag, taking the shotgun he'd somehow held on to from his hands.

Vince stood and bent and stuck his fingers in his mouth and vomited. Schwartz turned, set the shotgun against a tree, and felt sick. When Vince stood up again, Schwartz pulled him back into the brush.

Vince shook his head. "Don't know why I didn't let him drown. Wouldn't have been murder; more like cleanin' up pol-

lution." He coughed, spat. "Thanks for your help. I meant
that before—about bein' your prisoner."

Out at the water, BB's head began to roll back and forth
across the bag. His eyes opened, his hands stroked the canvas.
He looked around, smiling. "Well, this beats it. This sure's a
sign we was meant to have this money, Vincent."

"C'mon get your ass back in here, you damned drowned
rat," said Vince. "I can see three guys, two back there, one
back this walkway out here, and they ain't carryin' boo-kays of
flowers."

BB stood shakily, found the shotgun, and used it to lean
on. He smiled a mean grin. "Yew two all dripped in birdshit
in there!"

Vince said, "Shoot, what I bother savin' you for? You
don't get in here fast, you gonna be out there all dripped in
blood!"

Schwartz thought why not? He said, "BB, I want you to
know that you're my prisoner. I know the shotgun's useless,
but I'll take it, please."

BB leaned back against white splattered leaves and raised
the shotgun to Schwartz's face. Schwartz now understood why
not.

BB said, "I figure she'll shoot. You wanna see, Mr. Po-
liceman?"

Schwartz shook his head.

"Yew, Vincent?"

"Nope. But I tell you, BB, I'm in this here man's custody,
so you ain't dealin' with no willin' *accomplice* type here."

Schwartz asked, "All right, BB. What are you going to
do?" His throat was sore; they must have all been screaming
since they left the car.

The shotgun aimed at Schwartz, BB stepped onto a low
tree fork, crouched, and leaned into the branches. He said,

"Maybe I can pick off that one on his own, him with them bright clothes on."

Schwartz looked. The man was closer. He wore cherry shoes, avocado trousers, and a lemon shirt. The man was Jaime, and his only sedateness was a machine gun, a neat little number in basic black.

BB was frowning, either in thought or to keep the droppings from his eyes. "Then, Vincent, you can get that machine gun off him and we can go for the others."

But for the birds above, Schwartz would have rolled up his eyes.

Vince said, "Time you get anywhere near enough him, that other bunch don't find us up that gumbo limbo way gonna show up here with more of them guns. You goddamned peckerhead. If I hadn'ta just puked up everythin' I had, I'd do it again, you make me so sick!"

Schwartz turned into the thicket and pushed down some branches. Beyond was water, a few islets, and two hundred yards off, the other boardwalk. On it was a dark figure—Cruz, no doubt, in dark suit and tie and matching automatic—and the big man with him would be one of the guards who'd beaten him. Schwartz let go of the branches. Great: they were hiding in the world's thinnest thicket.

"BB, we better all squat down as low as we can," Schwartz said, setting a very squat example.

Vince squatted. BB came off the tree fork and squatted. The wind blew, the rain fell, the birds shat.

"Now," Schwartz said, and paused. Perhaps this was all he had to say: "Now"—an insistence on the existential present. "Now, BB, to get close to that boardwalk you're going to have to swim a very long way to avoid the current. And they're bound to see you. Besides, there really are alligators in there. I came close to a big one—nine or ten feet." Maybe this was

working. He might have been a scoutmaster talking to a week-
end woodcraft group. A demented woodcraft group. "I'll tell
you, BB, maybe you're used to alligators but I'm not. I was
scared. It looked to me like . . . like a leather submarine with
teeth.''

BB raised the shotgun back to Schwartz's face. "Yew don't
shut up that bullshit, mister, I'm gonna shoot your mouth off.''

Schwartz decided not to point out BB's pun.

Vince said, "Mr. Schwartz, you wasn't kiddin' back there
at the farm about those police comin', was you?''

Schwartz shook his head. He'd been hoping, not kidding.
Drowning, not waving.

BB's white-lined face was moving: its mouth opened, ends
turned up. It was a smile. "So where they at, all these po-lice?
They comin' down here in speedboats?''

Schwartz was wondering what he *had* thought: not boats.
Helicopters. Helicopters in a hurricane? If he got out of this,
he'd tell Karen everything. He was so shivering cold. His hands
ran birdshit. As a kid in Brooklyn it was good luck; when pigeon
shit landed on you playing under the elms on Eastern Parkway,
that was luck. And here he was all grown, under the—what?
cottonwood? buttonwood? ironwood?—and quite covered in
luck.

Someone was shouting, but how could anyone be heard in
the wind? It was Cruz.

"Schwartz! You and the others. Schwartz! Come on, we
know you're out there. Stop fockin' with me. I want those
fockin' rednecks you're with. That's all. Schwartz! Let's do a
deal. Fock! You dealt with us before. Schwartz! Schwa—''

The voice stopped, must have turned so the wind didn't
carry it. "The wind must carry it," Schwartz said. "Look at
that.''

He pointed to Jaime, hands to his mouth, yelling straight at them in dumbshow.

BB said, "You ain't makin' no deals lose me my money. An' this one here ain't nothin' but a spick nigger clown. I'm gonna get him!"

BB went forward and Schwartz yelled "No!" but BB aimed and pulled the trigger. *Click.* The shotgun went click. He pulled the other trigger; it didn't fire. Good. Now, if BB hadn't been seen . . .

Vince said, "Well, we was lucky, BB. Need luck, with you, 'cause you got a brain like somethin' I wouldn't put in pig slops."

BB said, "Shut up, Vincent."

Jaime started shooting at them.

Schwartz grabbed BB and pulled him down. Vince went off squirming on his side into a bush. The bullets whizzed through the wind like hornets. Some birds flew off. Two feet to Schwartz's left, water splashed up with three little pops. He let go of BB and backed into the brush. Firing came louder from behind him. Schwartz pushed his shoulders through a tangle of branches and let himself fall down onto a heavy bush. There was a white unfolding shaking in his face. A great white heron lifted, then a second, their long necks stretched spearlike behind the blade of their beaks.

But it wasn't too uncomfortable.

Vince said, "That you, Mr. Schwartz?"

He was lying on Vince. He rolled off into the water, onto the stiff broken stalks. "You okay, Vince?"

A racket of firing shook into the brush. Dark bark ripped open white and splintered.

Vince said, "So far. But I know we ain't got a chance, so I gotta tell you somethin' that's been botherin' me. I mean

I gotta tell someone. Those Haitians, Mr. Schwartz. I really thought Bob was gonna land them Stateside. But when he said he had to put them off on that island to get new plans and then come back for them, I started listenin' to Hozay tellin' me Bob and Frank was always plannin' to ditch them and kill us.''

The firing continued; bullets thwacked through leaves and wood to the right.

"You hearin' me?''

Schwartz shut his eyes against the gunfire. "Yes."

"But I still sort of believed Bob would pick them up. Them Haitians were nice folk. Real neat and polite an' all dressed up wadin' out to the boat like they was comin' to church. But then, I mean after we left them on that little island, Hozay knifed Frank and shot Bob at the wheel. . . . No, I mean hidin' out there in Miami at this Cuban place with Hozay after we ditched the boat an' took the safe, I saw it on TV, you know, in Spanish, but I knew them kids had died. Nice little kids. Shoot, I don't have religion but I just wanted to tell you, not die without sayin' I feel real bad 'bout those folk an' their kids dyin' like that. What's gonna happen? True they gonna send them all back to Haiti to be killed and tortured?''

Schwartz opened his eyes. He kept the side of his head down in the water. "I don't know, Vince. Last night I heard the Sandinistas had offered them political asylum, a place they can live.''

He turned his head. Vince's chin was on his fist in the water. He looked sad. Not afraid but sad in this clattering machine-gun noise and screaming wind and birdshit, poor simple frightened animals. His little fears about telling Karen! Jesus, Vince Blessing had more honesty. Schwartz had to. Had to endure such clattering?

Schwartz looked up at birdless branches flattened in the

wind from a helicopter overhead. A helicopter! A police helicopter! Good ole Dave Pearlman had come through. He tapped
Vince and pointed as the copter veered off toward Jaime's
boardwalk, out of sight. Then there was a huge chopping roar
and a crash and then, unbelievably, nothing but the wind and
lighter banging from machine guns on the other side. Had he
imagined the helicopter?

Vince said, "Look at that! That sucker crashed!"

Schwartz twisted around, lifted branches, and stuck his
head underneath. The police helicopter had crashed into the
deck, smoking fuselage showed up only LICE. Jaime didn't show
up at all, and past the wreckage a police officer was in the water,
holding the edge of the dock.

Vince pointed back and told Schwartz he saw two more
helicopters in the empty sky. Schwartz took Vince's eye for it
and pointed forward the few yards to where BB lay pressed
along the duffel bag, arm and legs wrapped like a lover hugging
in the water at the beach.

They crawled out and Vince said, "BB, you okay?"

BB spoke into the bag. "I'm okay. I know how happy that
make you, Vincent, knowin' your big brother's okay. This bag
saved me, Vincent. And this where I'm stayin, right safe here
with my money."

Schwartz listened to the wind. The firing had stopped. He
started pushing backward into the thicket to check the other
boardwalk.

With his back and butt and shoulders, he felt the last
branches give way, then his chin was jerked back hard and a
knife blade pressed across his throat.

"Stay very still, you fock."

"I'm still," he whispered, feeling the motion of his speech
press his throat into the blade.

"Tell me what's out there, Schwartz."

"Two brothers. The crazier is wrapped around a bag of money."

"Much?"

"Three million and one hundred and forty-eight thousand dollars."

"Listen, you're still not worth killing, but you make a sound and I'll change my mind."

Schwartz felt the blade drawn very lightly, cutting the skin across his throat.

Roberto went off to the right, twisting through branches. Schwartz's hand came off his neck red from the tip of his index finger to halfway up his thumb. Schwartz pushed left and moved into the branches. Roberto was really spoiling his day out in the Everglades.

Schwartz picked up the shotgun, lifted the branches, and looked out. A thousand yards away a helicopter hovered, pouring its light onto empty water. Ten yards away Roberto hovered with his knife over BB.

He said, "Get the fock up off my money, redneck."

Schwartz considered his own very red neck. Between him and BB, Vince crouched with his hands up.

BB held to the bag and turned his head. "This here's mine, Chief. Guess I earned it 'bout as hard as yew did."

"You stupid fock, you're not worth talking to. You don't get off the bag, I'm gonna cut off your fockin' neck." The blade Roberto held was thin and long and had two shining edges.

BB turned his head into the bag again and pushed out into the water.

Schwartz saw that the helicopter had moved to only nine hundred and seventy-five yards away, illuminating nothing.

Roberto said, "If you're not off my money when I count

three, I'm gonna kill you. And this scared *conjo* with his hands up won't help.''

Schwartz squatted and pushed the gun out, barrel first, toward Vince.

"One," said Roberto.

BB and his bag pushed out. Schwartz stretched flat and extended his arm.

"Two," said Roberto.

Schwartz pushed the stock with his fingers so the barrel hit Vince's heel. He turned, saw Schwartz, and shook his head.

"Three," Roberto said, paused a second, and lunged over the water. BB rolled under, pulling the duffel bag on top, but the knife had sliced his wrist. Roberto lifted it to stab under the water, and Vincent roared and sprang out, toppling him on the turning duffel bag, hands at Roberto's thick neck.

Schwartz got to his knees, picked up the shotgun, and fell forward into the water. He stood, wading, lifting the shotgun stock up to hit Roberto, but he couldn't see. The bag was turning arms and legs and heads. BB came up hugging the bag one-armed, the other flung back, his wrist flapped loose, cut red to the white bone. Schwartz shook his head to clear his vision. The bag was turning slowly; Roberto rolled up on top, pulling the knife out of BB's back.

Schwartz stood fixed in the wind, only the shotgun wavering. The movement slowed before him. BB disappeared under the water as Roberto's head came up behind his slow slow stabbing hand, rolling up slowly, swollen, his cheeks bulged and purple, his eyes popping like plums from their sockets, and Vince's hands slowly turning up appearing locked around the throat. Roberto's throat, but by the time Schwartz felt his hand bear down on the gun barrel it wasn't Roberto's but Vince's head turning up and Schwartz screamed, dropping the rifle,

and waded out to the bag. He grabbed Vince by the hair and
pulled, but Vince wouldn't let go of Roberto, who wouldn't let
go of BB, who wouldn't let go of the bag, so that Schwartz felt
himself being slowly swallowed into the turning, and he punched
Vince hard in the side of the head so that Vince fell back and
fell off with Schwartz and both stood, Vince not so much breathing as roaring in and out, and watched the current catch at the
rolling bag of two men, then let them go, then catch deep hold
and spin them twice, men and bag, before it pulled them under.

The current curled and slid and slithered off. Nothing surfaced.

Schwartz waited for Roberto to come up. What was three
million to Roberto? Then he knew. Roberto couldn't let go; his
cojones wouldn't let him go. Nothing surfaced. Roberto said *cojones* didn't mean you'd live forever.

Vince stopped roaring. "Where they go?" he asked.

Schwartz shook his head and watched the current. BB
wasn't letting go. No, BB was consummating his life's one love.
An end-of-the-line romantic, like Bruckner, if he knew it, *liebes-
tod* by water. And nothing surfaced.

Schwartz pulled Vince back. "No, Vince. Nothing we can
do. The helicopter would see them down there if the current
lets them up."

They crawled in the water and the mud up to the tangled
branches and turned and fell back against them. The branches
scraped Schwartz's skin. They felt comfortable. And the cut on
his neck wasn't bad.

"Vince, why'd you risk your life for BB?"

"Bad blood. We had nothin' but bad blood between us,
but it was ours." Vince dropped his head between his folded
arms. "Damn! If anyone was gonna kill that mean bastard, it
wan't gonna be some stranger come crawlin' out of the swamp.
Was gonna be me. I tell you somethin': I hated BB,

Mr. Schwartz, but if he's dead out there, I'm gonna be sad. Why is that? Damn! Why is that?''

Schwartz shrugged, wiped birdshit from his face, and waited for the helicopter.

CHAPTER 6

From the parking lot, Schwartz looked out at a sky of faintest blue, as if the storm of two days past had drained it to such pure transparency that only now the color seeped back in, the standard stain.

Stain: How was it possible to keep Rose clean from Sonny Weinstock's dirty song to the police with its several verses about Abe? Should he bluff it out? Was that what Rose would want? Schwartz studied his fingernails. His own six-hour aria the day before was so successful that he feared, despite the depositions, he'd be called back for encores at the trials of Sonny and Linda and Jaime and Vince, not to consider the possibility of inquests on BB and Roberto's deaths. Jaime's survival from under the crashed helicopter and squashed dock was the triumph of bad taste. And there was bad taste in his mouth: Last night on the phone, Cyrus Weinstock had veered from tearful to imperious.

"Lenny, please. My son is refusing to speak to me. He won't speak to my lawyers. Could you speak to him? I'm an old man, Lenny. This is, you understand, my only son."

Schwartz thought, Good for Sonny, said, "No, I don't think so."

"You don't seem to understand, Inspector Schwartz. I could see that Sonny get a sympathetic judge. Sonny is a slob, a pathetically weak character, but it's *my* name he'll be dragging into prison with him. So it's not that he deserves it, but I can do a great deal for him."

Schwartz had said, "I believe you've already done too much." But he was angry at himself. He didn't want to side in any way with Sonny, a greedy killer who'd end up doing a few dozen months at a prison infamous for good living and business contacts better than at the Boca Raton Polo Club. Meanwhile, simple Vince would be lucky to evade the state's electric chair. Cruel and unusual punishments. And there was no satisfaction in mocking Cyrus Weinstock, blind ego at the end of its short tether.

Cruel and unusual. Schwartz left the car and walked onto the beach. He scooped some sand. It ran through his fingers coarser than it looked. He brought his eyes close to his hand. Now the sand was hard yellow angles, blocks of red, fragments of seashells like broken columns. Tricks of perspective. A woman jogged past. Yesterday at the police station, he'd walked out to the lobby with Dave Pearlman and almost bumped into Linda, leaving in custody of her lawyer. She'd said, "Sorry, Chief." Her lawyer tapped her shoulder. Pearlman, arm in a sling from his helicopter buffeting, looked away in anger.

Schwartz hadn't been able to. "Why did you let Cruz buy you?" he asked.

Her lawyer, a tall woman in a dark suit, touched Linda's arm and shook her head.

"You know," said Linda.

He couldn't pull his eyes from her. "Why did you let me leave the hotel?"

The lawyer said, "Don't answer."

"You know," said Linda.

Then they walked away. He knew. He knew.

Schwartz scuffed his foot in the sand, back and forth into a little furrow, a trench. That's what they called them in the First World War—trench confessions, trench conversions. In Vince's order of things, Schwartz the cop had stood father confessor; in Schwartz's there was only the try to tell himself the truth. And had he? What the hell did all that mean, that swearing to tell Karen about Linda?

He looked at his watch and decided to go up the beach side to meet the others. An old man was walking toward him swinging a putter like a walking stick, a white, old-fashioned golf cap jaunty on his head.

He smiled. "Wonderful day," he said to Schwartz. "Like the beginning of the world."

Schwartz tried a smile, mumbled, "Yes." He turned his head: In the beginning was the Eden Roc? That was, damn it, like the slogan of the sixties: "Today is the beginning of the rest of your life." He hated that, hated how behind its laid-back surface lay the can-do Babbittry of money ethic, and at a farther layer back the fab news that history—even your own—was bunk. So you were responsible to nothing and no one else, for today was forever until tomorrow became fab and wiped today from the tape cassette of life. . . .

Then *what* did he want of that old man: Hello there. My gallstones could pave the beach? The man had smiled, had only wanted to share some happiness, for heaven's sake. Or life's.

He walked up the ramp before the Fontainebleau and looked at the free-form pool which wasn't free-form, which suggested half-a-dozen kidneys, while over it, from a heap of plastic resin rocks, fell a steady stream of chlorinated water. And this was the garden, the most natural part. Miami Beach: Should

Collins have cleared the coastal jungle to farm? Should he have gone in with Flagler the developer? Should Flagler have sold it to rubber-rich Firestone, and should Firestone have sold it, finally, to this glitz grotesquerie? Or, Schwartz thought, was all this just some transferred anger, something he couldn't face?

Inside, he looked out over the lobby bar and saw Stanley with Rose by the window.

"I'm sorry I can't stay long," he said, bending to kiss Rose's cheek.

"But time for a little champagne," said Stanley, pouring a glass.

Schwartz hoped there'd be no awkward toasts to Abe's memory.

Rose said, "Enough small talk: tell us all you can."

Schwartz drew his chair in and looked at Stanley. Stanley wore a Vanderbilt-blue blazer and Zeigler-striped-green-and-purple jersey underneath. He smiled at Schwartz.

Schwartz took a breath, took a sip of champagne, and said, "This lawyer Sonny Weinstock ran a terrible drug business; his captain worked for another group on the side, an even worse lot. It seems the captain double-crossed these people and to get even they struck out at whoever they could find. They found Abe without knowing that Weinstock was hiding behind Abe's name." Schwartz looked at Stanley and wiped the sweat from his brow.

It was up to Rose now. If she asked—

Rose screwed her eyes up, took off her glasses and wiped them, put them on, and squinted milkily at Schwartz. Stanley was rocking his champagne glass, watching the bubbles.

"So," she said, "the important thing is what's going to happen to those poor Haitians."

Schwartz said, "You're right. I suppose you haven't heard, then. The Sandinistan offer of sanctuary seems to have shamed

our government to make the same offer. About a third of them
are going to Nicaragua, the rest will be settled here. There's
talk of pressure for the three million dollars taken off that boat
to be divided among the Haitians, but Stanley can tell you more
about that than I can.''

Rose looked at Stanley. "Are you up to good again behind
our backs?''

"Harry does most of the real work,'' Stanley said, shrug-
ging. "The letter writing, you know.''

Rose said, "I don't, but Stanley, I wouldn't mind learning.''

Stanley reached across for Rose's hand. She gave it.

Schwartz looked out the win-
dow as the plane banked, turning north. Rose was no fool and
Rose was right; she didn't need to hear the worst about Abe
Zeigler. He was dead and she, thyroid and cataracts and limp,
was totally alive and had responsibilities to the living. And if
she had to cope with what she well might guess of Abe, she'd
cope. So why shouldn't he—younger, healthier?

There below him was the stretch of Biscayne Bay: splendid,
sparkling, overbuilt, where manatees—those mustached mer-
maids and their frumpy mates—kept swimming placidly among
the speedboats that sliced them. He shut his eyes and watched
them dropping, dying, falling way down to the last crab waiting
sideways at the end of its eyes for the last flaked bit to fall . . .

He opened his eyes. No, no, the thing wasn't to mourn
but to act. Facts weren't truth or untruth; truth or untruth was
what he did with facts. Like Linda. Fact was, she fell for him
like he did for her, like an older brother. He was the bent role

model, the cop who'd taken the easy way down, she'd thought, and made it to the top.

The plane was over the beach now. South Beach was the flatter end, before the condos and big hotels walled off the sea. Linda was his vanity, his need to be ethnically hip. And she was the sister cop he could relax with, unwind and wind with, too. His infantile greed. Like Abe's with money? Of course he wouldn't tell Karen. He thought of his deposition on Linda and began to laugh. There it was, the very naked truth he mightn't be able to keep from his wife. But he would certainly try.

And he'd faced Cruz. Yes. Now Cruz was gone. No, Cruz was only dead.

The plane swung out over streaked aquamarine and turquoise into the darker purple-blue—the open, empty sea. The flight attendant was asking if he wanted lunch. Schwartz said he didn't know and took the tray.

ABOUT THE AUTHOR

Irving Weinman was born in Boston. He was educated there and at Trinity College, Dublin, and Cambridge University, England. He has been a university lecturer in English and divides his time between London and Key West, Florida. He is the author of *Tailor's Dummy, Hampton Heat*, and *Virgil's Ghost*, all available from Fawcett Books.